"I have read in my earlier years about prisoners in the revolutionary war, and other wars. It sounded noble and heroic to be a prisoner of war, and accounts of their adventures were quite romantic; but the romance has been knocked out of the prisoner of war business, higher than a kite. It's a fraud..."

—John Ransom

"One of the truly significant books to come during the period ... as significant as it is chilling."

—*LOUISVILLE COURIER JOURNAL*

"Outstanding in its dramatic picturization ... tremendous impact."

—*TULSA WORLD*

"Extraordinarily vivid, extremely readable."

—*WILMINGTON NEWS*

"Fine ... an assertion that life is good, that the pain life imposes endows the survivor with dignity and knowledge."

—*OAKLAND TRIBUNE*

JOHN L. RANSOM, *soldier*.

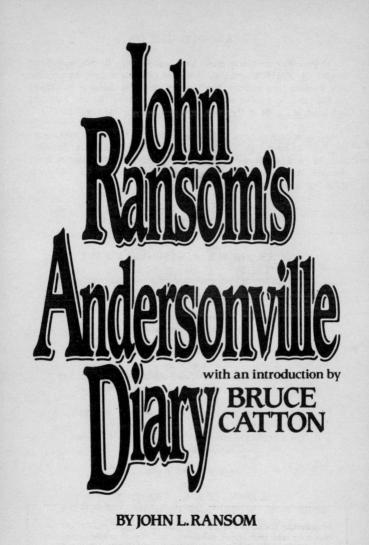

John Ransom's Andersonville Diary

with an introduction by BRUCE CATTON

BY JOHN L. RANSOM

BERKLEY BOOKS, NEW YORK

ACKNOWLEDGMENTS

The Publisher wishes to thank Josef and Dorothy Berger, authors of DIARY OF AMERICA, for their help in bringing to light the original John Ransom diary and for their insistent recommendation of it. Thanks are due, also, to the Brooklyn Public Library for the courtesy extended in lending us a copy of the original edition, now so extremely rare.

First issued privately by the author in Auburn, New York, 1881, under the title "Andersonville" and in 1883 by Douglass Brothers, Philadelphia, Pa., and in Cincinnati, Ohio, by Douglass Brothers & Payne, under the title "Andersonville Dairy." The first Eriksson edition, 1963, was published under the title *"John Ransom's Diary."*

PRINTING HISTORY
Paul S. Eriksson edition published 1986
Berkley edition / January 1988

This book is respectfully dedicated by the author to the mothers, wives and sisters of those whose names are herein recorded as having died. . . .

PREFACE

THE book to which these lines form an introduction is a peculiar one in many respects. It is a story, but it is a true story, and written years ago with little idea that it would ever come into this form. The writer has been induced, only recently, by the advice of friends and by his own feeling that such a production would be appreciated, to present what, at the time it was being made up, was merely a means of occupying a mind which had to contemplate, besides, only the horrors of a situation from which death would have been, and was to thousands, a happy relief.

The original diary in which these writings were made from day to day was destroyed by fire some years after the war, but its contents had been printed in a series of letters to the Jackson, (Mich.) *Citizen*, and to the editor and publisher of that journal thanks are now extended for the privilege of using his files for the preparation of this work. There has been little change in the entries in the diary, before presenting them here. In such cases the words which suggest themselves at the time are best—they cannot be improved upon by substitution at a later day.

This book is essentially different from any other that has been published concerning the "late war" or any of its incidents. Those who have had any such experience as the author will see its truthfulness at once, and to all other readers it is commended as a statement of actual things by one who experienced them to the fullest.

John L. Ransom

TABLE OF CONTENTS

4.

Arrival at the Worst of all Prisons · Beginning of a
Summer that Killed Thirteen Thousand Men · Bad
Water, Bad Food, and Most Inhuman Treatment · In
the Clutches of Wirtz and His Picked Out Rebel
Aids · The Truth and Nothing but the Truth ·
A Season of Intense Suffering.

5.

The Astor House Mess Still Holds Together, Although
Depleted · All More or Less Diseased · As the
Weather gets Warmer the Death Rate Increases ·
Dying Off Like Sheep · The End is Not Yet.

6.

Andersonville on Its Metal · Leading Raiders
Arrested, Tried and Hung · Great Excitement for a
Few Days, Followed by Good Order · Death Rate
Increases, However · The Astor House Mess as Policemen

7.

Removed from Andersonville to the Marine Hospital,
Savannah · Getting Through the Gate · Battese has
Saved Us · Very Sick, But by no Means Dead
Yet · Better and Humane Treatment

8.

9.

10.

11.

12.

13.

14.

ILLUSTRATIONS

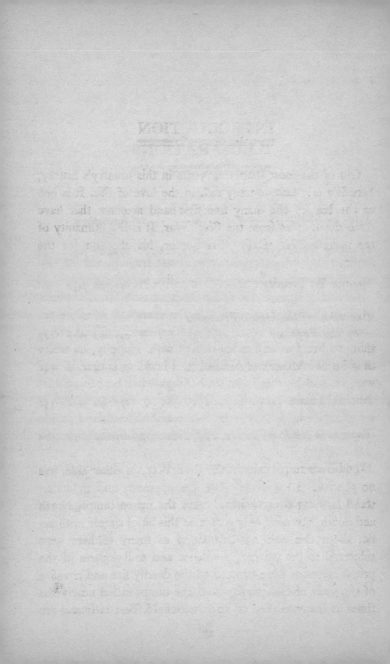

INTRODUCTION

Out of the most shattering years in this country's history, here is a tale uncommonly rich in the love of life. It is one of the best of the many fine first-hand accounts that have come down to us from the Civil War. It is the humanity of the narrator, his vitality, his humor, his affection for the living, that underscore the whole vast tragedy around him and, a century later, make it come alive before our eyes.

John L. Ransom, brigade quartermaster of the Ninth Michigan Cavalry, was only twenty years old when he became a prisoner of war in eastern Tennessee. He had everything to live for, and much to live with. Happily, he wrote as if he didn't think of himself as a budding author. A war was on, and he was in it, and things were happening that seemed worth putting down from day to day. The result is a straightforward diary, free of the embroideries and purple passages of many an author of the time, professional as well as would-be.

To become a prisoner in the Civil War, on either side, was no shortcut to survival. Quite the opposite; and to understand how appallingly lethal were the prison camps, North and South, one need only reflect on this bit of simple arithmetic: about two and one-half times as many soldiers were subjected to the hunger, pestilence and soul-sickness of the prison camps as were exposed to the deadly fire and crossfire of the guns of Gettysburg—and the camps killed nearly ten times as many as died on that battlefield. Best estimates are that the Confederacy imprisoned, over-all, some 194,000 Union soldiers, of whom 36,400 died, and the Union held captive about 220,000 Confederates, of whom 30,150 died.

If we are looking for culprits, there is not much room for choice between them. But we do better, I believe, to forget the villains, personal or collective. They obscure a bigger and more useful truth: the horrors endured by John Ransom and his contemporary POW's were not created willfully and malevolently in order to kill them—as many good people on both sides believed at the time—but by the combination of human blundering in the face of vast, bewildering problems, by hasty action, fear, blinding passions, and the climate of horror that make up war itself.

Ransom was captured in the autumn of 1863. The timing was unlucky. For more than a year the two governments had been acting on a sort of gentlemen's agreement to trade off prisoners at frequent intervals. But now, under the heightened fury of the conflict, trades were few and far between. When Grant became general in chief of the Union armies, he believed any active exchange of prisoners from that point on would help the South, in its desperate want of manpower, more than it would the North. While he admitted it was going to be rough on the prisoners, he did very little to restore the exchange. Hence the bitter disappointment that followed each new spate of hopeful rumors among the Union men in their grim fight to keep alive at Andersonville and the many other hellholes that were as bad if not as big.

Ransom's diary gives us a vivid and valuable picture of life in Confederate prisons, and it brings out two important aspects of that picture which most personal, eye-witness accounts fail to reveal. For this book shows that much of the suffering undergone by Union men in Confederate camps was of their own making. Lack of discipline, low morale, and on the part of a small but hell-raising minority low morals, seems to have added heavily to the burdens imposed on these northerners by their southern captors.

Moreover, though Ransom is held in Andersonville until he is near the point of death, he does get out at last, he does get into a decent hospital, he does get the care and food that enable him to recover; and all this, not in the North, but behind Southern lines. In other words, the book gives two sides of the picture—one of them widely neglected in the war literature.

It is sometimes said, by way of recommendation, that a book of non-fiction "reads like a novel." This is not praise enough for a tale of adventure, of suspense from beginning to end, of fierce hate and great love, of the incredible callousness of man and the incredible warmth of men—with the added knowledge that "it really happened." For the match of young John Ransom's diary, one must look long among the novels of our time.

Bruce Catton

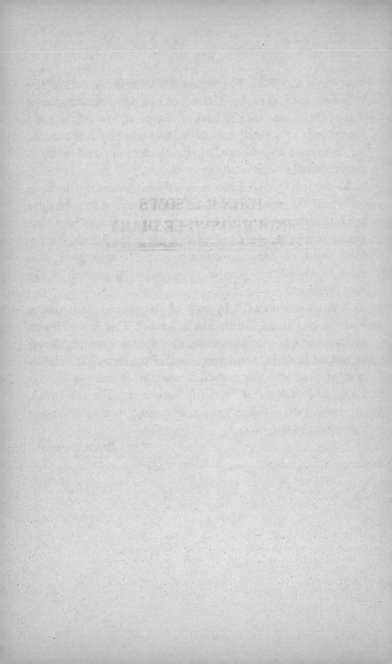

JOHN RANSOM'S
ANDERSONVILLE DIARY

CHAPTER ONE

The Capture

**A Rebel Ruse to Gobble Up
Union Troops ✷ A Complete Surprise ✷
Careless Officers ✷ Heroic Defence ✷
Beginning of a Long Imprisonment**

BELLE ISLAND, Richmond, Va., *Nov. 22, 1863.*—I was captured near Rogersville, East Tennessee, on the 6th of this month, while acting as Brigade Quarter-Master Sergt. The Brigade was divided, two regiments twenty miles away, while Brigade Head-Quarters with 7th Ohio and 1st Tennessee Mounted Infantry were at Rogersville. The brigade quarter-master had a large quantity of clothing on hand, which we were about to issue to the brigade as soon as possible. The rebel citizens got up a dance at one of the public houses in the village, and invited all the union officers. This was the evening of Nov. 5th. Nearly all the officers attended and were away from the command nearly all night and many were away all night. We were encamped in a bend of the Holston River. It was a dark rainy night and the river rose rapidly before morning. The dance was a ruse to get our officers away from their command. At break of day the pickets were drove in by rebel cavalry, and orders were immediately received from commanding officer to get wagon train out on the road in ten minutes. The quarter-master had been to the dance and had not returned, consequently it devolved upon me to see to wagon train, which I did, and in probably ten minutes the whole seventy six mule army wagons were in line out on the main road, while the companies were forming into line and getting ready for a fight. Rebels had us completely surrounded and soon began to fire volley after volley into our disorganized ranks. Not one officer in five was present; Gen. commanding and staff as soon as they realized our danger, started for the river, swam

3

across and got away. We had a small company of artillery with us commanded by a lieutenant. The lieutenant in the absence of other officers, assumed command of the two regiments, and right gallantly did he do service. Kept forming his men for the better protection of his wagon train, while the rebels were shifting around from one point to another, and all the time sending volley after volley into our ranks. Our men did well, and had there been plenty of officers and ammunition, we might have gained the day. After ten hours fighting we were obliged to surrender after having lost in killed over a hundred, and three or four times that number in wounded. After surrendering we were drawn up into line, counted off and hurriedly marched away south. By eight o'clock at night had probably marched ten miles, and encamped until morning. We expected that our troops would intercept and release us, but they did not. An hour before daylight we were up and on the march toward Bristol, Va., that being the nearest railroad station. We were cavalrymen, and marching on foot made us very lame, and we could hardly hobble along. Were very well fed on corn bread and bacon. Reached Bristol, Va., Nov. 8th and were soon aboard of cattle cars en-route for the rebel capital. I must here tell how I came into possession of a very nice and large bed spread which is doing good service even now these cold nights. After we were captured everything was taken away from us, blankets, overcoats, and in many cases our boots and shoes. I had on a new pair of boots, which by muddying them over had escaped the rebel eyes thus far, as being a good pair. As our blankets had been taken away from us we suffered considerably from cold. I saw that if

4

I was going to remain a prisoner of war it behooved me to get hold of a blanket. After a few hours march I became so lame walking with my new boots on that the rebels were compelled to put me on an old horse that was being lead along by one of the guard. This guard had the bed spread before spoken of. Told him I was going into prison at the beginning of a long winter, and should need a blanket, and couldn't he give me his. We had considerable talk, and were very good friends. Said he rather liked me but wouldn't part with his bed spread. Didn't love me that much, treated me however with apple jack out of his canteen. I kept getting my wits together to arrange some plan to get the article in question. Finally told him I had a large sum of money on my person which I expected would be taken away from me anyway, and as he was a good fellow would rather he would have it than any one else. He was delighted and all attention, wanted me to be careful and not let any of the other rebels see the transfer. I had a lot of Michigan broken down wild cat money, and pulled it out of an inside pocket and handed him the roll. It was green paper and of course he supposed it greenbacks. Was very glad of the gift and wanted to know what he could do for me. My first proposition to him was to let me escape, but he couldn't do that, then I told him to give me the bed spread, as it might save my life. After some further parley, he consented and handed over the spread. He was afraid to look at his money for fear some one would see him, and so did not discover that it was worthless until we had become separated. Guards were changed that night and never saw him any more.

The cars ran very slow, and being crowded for room the journey to Richmond was very tedious. Arrived on the morning of Nov. 13th, seven days after capture, at the south end of the "long bridge," ordered out of the cars and into line, counted off and started for Belle Isle. Said island is in the James River, probably covers ten or twelve acres, and is right across from Richmond. The river between Richmond and the island is probably a third or half a mile. The "long bridge" is near the lower part of the island. It is a cold, bleak piece of ground and the winter winds have free sweep from up the river. Before noon we were turned into the pen which is merely enclosed by a ditch and the dirt taken from the ditch thrown up on the outside, making a sort of breastwork. The ditch serves as a dead line, and no prisoners must go near the ditch. The prison is in command of a Lieut. Bossieux, a rather young and gallant looking sort of fellow. Is a born Southerner, talking so much like a negro that you would think he was one, if you could hear him talk and not see him. He has two rebel sergeants to act as his assistants, Sergt. Hight and Sergt. Marks. These two men are very cruel, as is also the Lieut. when angered. Outside the prison pen is a bake house, made of boards, the rebel tents for the accommodation of the officers and guard, and a hospital also of tent cloth. Running from the pen is a lane enclosed by high boards going to the water's edge. At night this is closed up by a gate at the pen, and thrown open in the morning. About half of the six thousand prisoners here have tents while the rest sleep and live out of doors. After I had been on this island two or three days, I was standing near the gate eating some rice soup out of an old broken bottle, thoroughly disgusted with the Southern Confederacy, and this prison in particular. A young man came up to me whom I immediately recognized as George W. Hendryx, a member of my own company "A" 9th Mich. Cavalry, who had been captured some time before myself. Was feeling so blue, cross and cold that I didn't care whether it was him or not. He was on his way to the river to get some water. Found I wasn't going to notice him in any way, and so proceeded on his errand. When I say that George Hendryx was one of the most valued friends I had in the regiment, this action on my part will seem strange as indeed it is. Did not want to see him or any one else I had ever seen before. Well, George came back a few moments after, looked at me a short time and says: "I believe you are John L. Ransom, Q. M. Sergt. of the same Co. with me, although you don't seem to recognize me." Told him I was that same person, recognized him and there could be no mistake about it. Wanted to know why in the Old Harry I didn't speak to him then. After telling him just how it was, freezing to death, half-starved and gray backs crawling all over me, &c., we settled down into being glad to see one another.

Nov. 23.—Having a few dollars of good Yankee money which I have hoarded since my capture, have purchased a large blank book and intend as long as I am a prisoner of war in this Confederacy, to note down from day to day as occasion may occur, events as they happen, treatment, ups and downs generally. It will serve to pass away the time and may be interesting at some future time to read over.

Nov. 24.—Very cold weather. Four or five men chilled to death last night. A large portion of the prisoners who have been in confinement any length of time are reduced to almost skeletons from continued hunger, exposure and filth. Having some money just indulged in an extra ration of corn bread for which I paid twenty cents in Yankee script, equal to two dollars Confederate money, and should say by the crowd collected around that such a sight was an unusual occurrence, and put me in mind of gatherings I have seen at the North around some curiosity. We received for to-day's food half a pint of rice soup and one-quarter of a pound loaf of corn bread. The bread is made from the very poorest meal, coarse, sour and musty; would make poor feed for swine at home. The rice is nothing more than boiled in river water with no seasoning whatever, not even salt, but for all that it tasted nice. The greatest difficulty is the small allowance given us. The prisoners are blue, downcast and talk continually of home and something good to eat. They nearly all think there will be an exchange of prisoners before long and the trick of it is to live until the time approaches. We are divided off into hundreds with a sergeant to each squad who draws the food and divides it up among his men, and woe unto him if a man is wronged out of his share—his life is not worth the snap of the finger if caught cheating. No wood tonight and it is very cold. The nights are long and are made hideous by the moans of suffering wretches.

Nov. 25.—Hendryx is in a very good tent with some nine or ten others and is now trying to get me into the already crowded shelter. They say I can have the first vacancy and as it is impossible for a dozen to remain together long without losing some by sickness, my chances will be good in a few days at fartherest. Food again at four o'clock. In place of soup received about four ounces of salt horse, as we call it.

Nov. 26.—Hendryx sacrificed his own comfort and lay out doors with me last night and I got along much better than the night before. Are getting food twice to-day; old prisoners say it is fully a third more than they have been getting. Hardly understand how we could live on much less. A Michigan man (could not learn his name) while at work a few moments ago on the outside with a squad of detailed yankees repairing a part of the embankment which recent rains had washed away, stepped upon the wall to give orders to his men when one of the guards shot him through the head, killing him instantly. Lieut. Bossieux, commander of the prison, having heard the shot, came to learn the cause. He told the guard he ought to be more careful and not shoot those who were on parole and doing fatigue duty, and ordered the body carried to the dead house. Seems tough to me but others don't seem to mind it much. I am mad.

Nov. 27.—Stormy and disagreeable weather. From fifteen to twenty and twenty-five die every day and are buried just outside the prison with no coffins—nothing but canvas wrapped around them. Eight sticks of four foot wood given every squad of one hundred men to-day, and when split up and divided it amounted to nothing towards warming a person. Two or three can put their wood together and boil a little coffee made from bread crusts. The sick are taken out every morning and either sent over to the city or kept in the hospital just outside the prison and on the island. None admitted unless carried out in blankets and so far gone there is not much chance of recovery. Medical attendance is scarce.

Nov. 28.—Very cold and men suffer terribly with hardly any clothing on some of them. A man taken outside to-day, bucked and gagged for talking with a guard; a severe punishment this very cold weather.

Nov. 30.—Came across E. P. Sanders, from Lansing, Michigan, and a jolly old soul is he. Can't get discouraged where he is. Talk a great deal about making our escape but there is not much prospect. We are very strongly guarded with artillery bearing on every part of the prison. The long bridge I have heard so much about crosses the river just below the island. It is very long and has been condemned for years —trains move very slow across it. There was a big fire over in Richmond last night about 2 o'clock; could hear all the fire bells and see the house tops covered with people looking at it. Great excitement among the Johnny Rebs.

Dec. 1.—With no news concerning the great subject—exchange of prisoners. Very hungry and am not having a good time of it. Take it all around I begin to wish I had stayed at home and was at the *Jackson Citizen* office pulling the old press. Dream continually nights about something good to eat; seems rather hard such plenty at the North and starving here. Have just seen a big fight among the prisoners; just like so many snarly dogs, cross and peevish. A great deal of fighting going on. Rebels collect around on the outside in crowds to see the Yankees bruise themselves and it is quite sport for them. Have succeeded in getting into the tent with Hendryx. One of the mess has been sent over to Richmond Hospital leaving a vacancy which I am to fill. There are nine others, myself making ten. The names are as follows: W. C. Robinson, orderly sergeant, 34th Illinois; W. H.

Mustard, hospital steward 100th Pennsylvania; Joe Myers, 34th Illinois; H. Freeman, hospital steward 30th Ohio; C. G. Strong, 4th Ohio cavalry; Corporal John McCarten, 6th Kentucky; U. Kindred, 1st East Tennessee infantry; E. P. Sanders, 20th Michigan infantry; George Hendryx and myself of the 9th Michigan cavalry. A very good crowd of boys, and all try to make their places as pleasant as possible. Gen. Neil Dow to-day came over from Libby Prison on parole of honor to help issue some clothing that has arrived for Belle Isle prisoners from the Sanitary Commission at the North. Sergeant Robinson taken outside to help Gen. Dow in issuing clothing and thinks through his influence to get more out for the same purpose. A man froze to death last night where I slept. The body lay until nearly dark before it was removed. My blanket comes in good play, and it made the boys laugh when I told how I got it. We tell stories, dance around, keep as clean as we can without soap and make the best of a very bad situation.

Dec. 2.—Pleasant weather and favorable for prisoners. At about nine in the morning the work of hunting for vermin commences, and all over camp sit the poor starved wretches, nearly stripped, engaged in picking off and killing the big gray backs. The ground is fairly alive with them, and it requires continual labor to keep from being eaten up alive by them. I just saw a man shot. He was called down to the bank by the guard, and as he leaned over to do some trading another guard close by shot him through the side and it is said mortally wounded him. It was made up between the guards to shoot the man, and when the lieutenant came round to make inquiries concerning the affair, one of them remarked

11

that the —————— passed a counterfeit bill on him the night before, and he thought he would put him where he could not do the like again. The wounded man was taken to the hospital and has since died. His name was Gilbert. He was from New Jersey. Food twice to-day; buggy bean soup and a very small allowance of corn bread. Hungry all the time.

Dec. 3.—Rumors of exchange to be effected soon. Rebels say we will all be exchanged before many days. It cannot be possible our government will allow us to remain here all winter. Gen. Dow is still issuing clothing, but the rebels get more than our men do of it. Guards nearly all dressed in Yankee uniforms. In our mess we have established regulations, and any one not conforming with the rules is to be turned out of the tent. Must take plenty of exercise, keep clean, free as circumstances will permit of vermin, drink no water until it has been boiled, which process purifies and makes it more healthy, are not to allow ourselves to get despondent, and must talk, laugh and make as light of our affairs as possible. Sure death for a person to give up and lose all ambition. Received a spoonful of salt to-day for the first time since I came here.

Dec. 4.—Exchange news below par to-day. Rather colder than yesterday; a great many sick and dying off rapidly. Rebel guards are more strict than usual, and one risks his life by speaking to them at all. Wrote a letter home to-day, also one to a friend in Washington. Doubtful whether I ever hear from them. Robinson comes inside every night and always brings something good. We look forward to the time of his coming with pleasure. Occasionally he brings a stick of wood which we split up fine and build a cheerful fire in our little sod fireplace, sit up close together and talk of home and friends so far away. We call our establishment the "Astor House of Belle Isle." There are so many worse off than we are that we are very well contented and enjoy ourselves after a fashion.

Dec. 5.—Cold and raw weather with no wood. Men are too weak to walk nights to keep warm, sink down and chill to death. At least a dozen were carried out this morning feet foremost. Through Robinson's influence Hendryx and myself will go out tomorrow to issue clothing, and will come in nights to sleep. We are to receive extra rations for our services. In good spirits tonight with a good fire and very comfortable for this place.

Dec. 6.—One month a prisoner to-day—longer than any year of my life before. Hope I am not to see another month in the Confederacy. A great deal of stealing going on among the men. There are organized bands of raiders who do pretty much as they please. A ration of bread is often of more consequence than a man's life. Have received food but once to-day; very cold; at least one hundred men limping around with frozen feet, and some of them crying like little children. Am at work on the outside to-day; go out at nine in the morning and return at four in the afternoon, and by right smart figuring carry in much extra food for tent mates, enough to give all hands a good square meal.

Dec. 7.—No news of importance. The rebels say a flag of truce boat has arrived at City Point and Commissioner Olds telegraphed for and undoubtedly will agree upon terms for an exchange of prisoners. Men receiving boxes from their friends at the north and am writing for one myself without much hope of ever getting it.

Dec. 8.—The men all turned out of the enclosure and are being squadded over. A very stormy and cold day; called out before breakfast and nearly dark before again sent inside. Very muddy and the men have suffered terribly, stand up all day in the cold drizzling rain, with no chance for exercise and many barefooted. I counted nine or ten who went out in the morning not able to get back at night; three of the number being dead.

Dec. 9.—Rumors that one thousand go off to-day to our lines and the same number every day until all are removed. It was not believed until a few moments ago the Lieutenant stepped upon the bank and said that in less than a week we would all be home again, and such a cheering among us; every man who could yell had his mouth stretched. Persons who fifteen minutes ago could not rise to their feet are jumping around in excitement, shaking hands with one another and crying, "A general exchange! a general exchange!" All in good spirits and we talk of the good dinners we will get on the road home. Food twice to-day and a little salt.

Dec. 10.—Instead of prisoners going away five hundred more have come, which makes it very crowded. Some are still confident we will go away soon, but I place no reliance on rebel reports. Rather warmer than usual, and the men busying themselves hunting vermin. A priest in the camp distributing tracts. Men told him to bring bread; they want no tracts. Exchange news has died away, and more despondent than ever. I to-day got hold of a Richmond *Enquirer*

HUNTING FOR GRAYBACKS

which spoke of bread riots in the city, women running around the streets and yelling, "Peace or bread!"

Dec. 11.—Was on guard last night over the clothing outside. Lieut. Bossieux asked Corp. McCarten and myself to eat supper with him last night, which we were very glad to do. Henry, the negro servant, said to the lieutenant after we had got through eating: "I golly, masser, don't nebber ask dem boys to eat with us again, dey eat us out clean gone;" and so we did eat everything on the table and looked for more.

Dec. 12.—At just daylight I got up and was walking around the prison to see if any Michigan men had died through the night, and was just in time to see a young fellow come out of his tent nearly naked and deliberately walk up the steps that lead over the bank. Just as he got on the top the guard fired; sending a ball through his brain, and the poor fellow fell dead in the ditch. I went and got permission to help pull him out. He had been sick for a number of days and was burning up with fever, and no doubt deranged at the time, else he would have known better than to have risked his life in such a manner. His name was Perry McMichael, and he was from Minnesota. Perhaps he is better off, and a much easier death than to die of disease as he undoubtedly would in a few days longer. The work of issuing clothing slowly goes on. In place of Gen. Dow. Col. Sanderson comes over on parole of honor; and is not liked at all. Is of New York and a perfect tyrant; treats us as bad or worse than the rebels themselves. Col. Boyd also comes occasionally and is a perfect gentleman. Talked to me to-day concerning Sanderson's movements, and said if he got through to our lines should complain of him to the authorities at Washington. He took down notes in his diary against him.

Dec. 13.—Nothing of any importance to note down. The officers come over from Richmond every day or two, and make a showing of issuing clothing. The work goes on slowly, and it would seem that if clothing was ever needed and ought to be issued, it is now; yet the officers seem to want to nurse the job and make it last as long as possible. Many cruelties are practiced, principally by the rebel sergeants. The lieutenant does not countenance much cruelty, still he is very quick tempered, and when provoked is apt to do some very severe things. The Yankees are a hard crowd to manage; will steal anything, no matter what, regardless of consequences. Still I don't know as it is any wonder, cooped up as they are in such a place, and called upon to endure such privations. The death rate gradually increases from day to day. A little Cincinnati soldier died to-day. Was captured same time as myself, and we had messed together a number of times before I became identified with the "Astor House Mess." Was in very poor health when captured, but could never quite find out what ailed him. I have many talks with the rebels, and am quite a priveleged character. By so doing am able to do much for the boys inside, and there are good boys in there, whom I would do as much for as myself.

Dec. 17.—I have plenty to eat. Go outside every day whether clothing is issued or not. To explain the manner of issuing clothing: The men are called outside by squads, that is, one squad of a hundred men at a time; all stand in a row in front of the boxes of clothing. The officer in charge, Col. Sanderson, begins with the first at the head of the column, looks him over, and says to us paroled men: "Here, give this man a pair of pants," or coat, or such clothing as he may stand in need of. In this way he gets through with a hundred men in about half an hour. Us boys often manage to give three or four articles where only one has been ordered. There seems to be plenty of clothing here, and we can see no reason why it should not be given away. Have to be very careful, though, for if we are caught at these tricks are sent inside to stay. Officers stay on the island only two or three hours, and clothe four or five hundred men, when they could just as well do three or four times as much. It is comical the notes that come in some of the good warm woolen stockings. These have evidently been knit by the good mothers, wives and sisters at the North, and some of the romantic sort have written letters and placed inside, asking the receiver to let them know about himself, his name, etc, etc. Most of them come from the New England states, and they cheer the boys up a great deal.

Dec. 18.—To-day as a squad was drawn up in front of us, waiting for clothing, I saw an Irishman in the ranks who looked familiar. Looked at him for some time and finally thought I recognized in him an old neighbor of mine in Jackson Michigan; one Jimmy Devers, a whole souled and comical genius as ever it was my fortune to meet. Went up to him and asked what regiment he belonged to; said he belonged to the 23d Indiana, at which I could not believe it was my old acquaintance. Went back to my work. Pretty soon he said to me: "Ain't you Johnny Ransom?" And then I knew I was right. He had lived in Jackson, but had enlisted in an Indiana regiment. Well, we were glad to see one another and you may just bet that Jimmy got as good a suit of clothes as ever he had in our own lines. Jimmy is a case; was captured on the 1st day of July at the Gettysburg battle, and is consequently an old prisoner. Is very tough and hardy. Says the Johnny Rebs have a big contract on their hands to kill him. But I tell him to take good care of himself anyway, as there is no knowing what he will be called upon to pass through yet.

Dec. 20.—James River frozen nearly over, and rebels say it has not been so cold for years as at the present time. There are hundreds with frozen feet, ears, hands &c., and laying all over the prison; and the suffering is terrible. Hendryx and myself are intent on some plan for escape. The lieutenant has spies who are on the watch. The authorities know all about any conspiracy almost as soon as it is known among ourselves. Last night just after dark two or three Yankees agreed to give the guard $10 if he would let them get over the bank, to which he promised; and as soon as they got nearly over fired and immediately gave the alarm. One of them received a shot in one of his legs and the others scrambled back over the bank; the three minus their $10 bill and a sound leg. They cannot be trusted at all and will promise anything for greenbacks. Sergt. Bullock of our regiment is here and very sick with fever; cannot possibly live many weeks in such a place as this. Col. Sanderson still issuing clothing, but very unfair, and the men who need it most get none at all. All the outsiders received a suit throughout to-day, myself among the rest. Got a letter from home, everybody is well. They say keep up good heart and we will be exchanged before many weeks.

Dec. 21.—Still cold. Have enough to eat myself, but am

one of a thousand. The scurvy is appearing among some of the men, and is an awful disease—caused by want of vegetable diet, acids, &c. Two small pox cases taken to the hospital to-day. A sutler has been established on the island and sells at the following rates: poor brown sugar, $8 per pound; butter, $11; cheese, $10; sour milk $3 per quart and the only article I buy; eggs, $10 per dozen; oysters, $6 per quart and the cheapest food in market.

Dec. 22.—A large mail came this morning, but nothing for me. A man who gets a letter is besieged with questions, and a crowd gathers around to learn the news, if any, regarding our future. Rations smaller than usual, and Lieut. Bossieux says that it is either exchange or starve with us prisoners sure, as they have not the food to give us. To-day saw a copy of the Richmond *Enquirer* in which was a long article treating on exchange of prisoners, saying our government would not exchange owing to an excess held by us, and unless their terms were agreed to, as they could not afford to keep us, the coming summer would reduce our ranks so that they would not have many to feed another winter. Rather poor prospects ahead for us poor imprisoned yanks. Lots of Sanitary stores sent on to the island for us, but as yet none have been issued, the rebels (officers in particular), getting fat on what rightfully belongs to us.

Dec. 23.—Almost Christmas and we are planning for a Christmas dinner. Very cold. The rebels are testing their big guns on the opposite shore of the river and fairly shake the ground we stand on. We can see the shells as they leave the guns until they explode, affording quite a pastime for us watching their war machines. Militia in sight drilling over in

Richmond. A woman found among us—a prisoner of war. Some one who knew the secret informed Lieutenant Bossieux and he immediately had her taken outside, when she told him the whole story—how she had "followed her lovyer a soldiering" in disguise, and being of a romantic turn, enjoyed it hugely until the funny part was done away with, and Madame Collier, from East Tennessee, found herself in durance vile; nothing to do but make the best of it and conceal her sex if possible, hoping for a release, which, however, did not come in the shape she wished. The lieutenant has sent her over to Richmond to be cared for and she is to be sent north by the first flag of truce boat. She tells of another female being among us, but as yet she has not been found out.

Dec. 24.—Must hang up my stocking to-night for habit's sake if nothing else. I am enjoying splendid health, and prison life agrees with we. Wrote home to-day.

Dec. 25.—and Christmas.—One year ago to-day first went into camp at Coldwater, little dreaming what changes a year would bring around, but there are exchange rumors afloat and hope to see white folks again before many months. All ordered out to be squadded over again, which was quite a disappointment to our mess as we were making preparations for a grand dinner, gotten up by outside hands, Mustard, Myers, Hendryx and myself. However, we had our good things for supper instead of dinner, and it was a big thing, consisting of corn bread and butter, oysters, coffee, beef, crackers, cheese &c.; all we could possibly eat or do away with, and costing the snug little sum of $200 Confederate money, or $20 in greenbacks. Lay awake long before daylight listening to the bells. As they rang out Christmas good morning I imagined they were in Jackson, Michigan, my old home, and from the spires of the old Presbyterian and Episcopal churches. Little do they think as they are saying their Merry Christmases and enjoying themselves so much, of the hunger and starving here. But there are better days coming.

Dec. 26.—News of exchange and no officers over from Libby to issue clothing. Extra quantity of wood. Rebels all drunk and very domineering. Punish for the smallest kind of excuse. Some men tunneled out of the pen but were retaken and were made to crawl back through the same hole they went out of and the lieutenant kept hitting them with a board as they went down and then ran back and forward from one hole to the other and as they stuck up their heads would hit them with a club, keeping them at it for nearly an hour. A large crowd of both rebels and Yankees collected around to see the fun.

Dec. 27.—Col. Sanderson and Col. Boyd came over this morning in a great hurry and began to issue clothing very fast saying an exchange had been agreed upon and they wanted to get rid of it before we all went away. Pretty soon the news got inside and the greatest cheering, yelling, shaking of hands and congratulating one another took place. Just before dinner five hundred were taken out, counted and sent away. Everybody anxious to go away first which of course they cannot do. Sergts. Hight and Marks stand at the gate with big clubs keeping order, letting them out two at a time, occasionally knocking a man down and it is seldom he gets up again very soon. Some of the outside went and the rest go tomorrow. It is a sure thing—a general exchange and all will be sent away immediately. Everybody in good spirits. Guess northern folks will be surprised to see such looking objects come among them. They are the worst looking crowd I ever saw. Extra ration of food and wood to-night and am anxiously waiting for the morrow.

Dec. 28.—For some reason or other no more being taken away and more despondent than ever. Very cold.

Dec. 29.—Nearly as cold weather as I ever saw at the North. All the supplies brought by hand over the long bridge, owing to the river being frozen over and not strong enough to hold up. Rebel officers all drunk during the holidays. Snow an inch deep.

Dec. 30.—No rations issued yesterday to any of the prisoners and a third of all here are on the very point of starvation. Lieut. Bossieux sympathizes with us in word but says it is impossible to help it as they have not the food for us. This is perhaps true as regards edibles but there is no excuse for our receiving such small supplies of wood. They could give us plenty of shelter, plenty of wood and conveniences we do not now get if they felt so disposed.

Dec. 31.—Still very cold and no news encouraging. Rebels very strict. One prisoner found a brother among the guards who had been living in the south for a good many years and lately conscripted into the Confederate army. New Year's eve. Man wounded by the guard shooting, and ball broke his leg. Might better have shot him dead for he will surely die. Raw rice and corn bread issued to-day in small quantities. Richmond *Enquirer* spoke of the five hundred who left here day before yesterday and they have reached Washington.

CHAPTER TWO

New Year's Day

And the Place it Finds Us * Apples to Eat and an Old Comrade Joins Us * Matters Getting Worse, with Occasional Rumors of Exchange

JAN. *1, 1864.*—A great time this morning wishing one another a Happy New Year. Robinson bought on the outside a dozen apples and gave us all a treat. Nothing but corn bread to eat and very poor quality. Dr. F. L. Lewis, Vet. Surg. 9th Mich. cavalry, came in to-day; was captured at Dandridge, East Tennessee, where our regiment had a severe engagement. Tells me all the news. Col. Acker wounded, etc., etc. Thinks it a queer New Year trip, but also thinks we will be exchanged before many weeks.

Jan. 2.—Rebel congress about to meet, and the people of Richmond demand through the papers that the prisoners confined here be removed immediately, as there is hardly enough for themselves to eat, aside from feeding us "Northern Hirelings." Hear of bread riots and lots of trouble across the river. A big fire last night in the vicinity of Libby Prison.

Jan. 3.—Received a letter from Michigan. Not quite so cold, but disagreeable weather. Nine men bucked and gagged at one time on the outside, two of them for stealing sour beans from a swill-barrel. They would get permission to pass through the gate to see the lieutenant, and instead, would walk around the cookhouse to some barrels containing swill, scoop up their hats full and then run inside; but they were caught, and are suffering a hard punishment for it.

Jan. 4.—Some ladies visited the island to see us blue coats, and laughed very much at our condition; thought it so comical and ludicrous the way the prisoners crowded the bank next the cook house, looking over at the piles of bread, and compared us to wild men, and hungry dogs. A chicken belonging to the lieutenant flew up on the bank and was snatched off in short order, and to pay for it we are not to receive a mouthful of food to-day, making five or six thousand suffer for one man catching a little chicken.

Jan. 5.—Succeeded in getting Dr. Lewis into our tent; is rather under the weather, owing to exposure and hardship. Jimmy Devers spends the evenings with us and we have funny times talking over better days—and are nearly talked out. I have said all I can think, and am just beginning to talk it all over again. All our stories have been told from two, to three or four times, and are getting stale. We offer a reward for a good new story.

Jan. 6.—Still prisoners of war, without the remotest idea as to how long we are to remain so. Some of the paroled Yankees on the outside curse and treat the inside prisoners more cruel (when they have a chance,) than the rebels themselves. Blass, a Spaniard, who has been a prisoner over a year and refuses to be exchanged, is the lieutenant's right hand man. He tied up a man a few days ago for some misdemeanor and whipped him. He is afraid to come inside, knowing he would lose his life in a jiffy. He also raises the rebel flag at the island mornings, and lowers it at night. It is a dirty rag, and the appearance of it ought to disgust any sensible person.

Jan. 7.—Rainy, cold and disagreeable weather. Henry Stilson, a fellow who was captured with me, was carried out dead this morning. He was diseased when taken, and fell an easy prey to their cruelties. A good deal of raiding is going on among the men. One Captain Moseby commands a band of cut-throats who do nearly as they please, cheating, robbing and knocking down—operating principally upon new prisoners who are unacquainted with prison life. Moseby is named after the rebel guerrilla, his real name being something else. He is from New York City, and is a regular bummer.

Jan. 8.—All taken outside to-day to be squadded over—an all day job and nothing to eat. The men being in hundreds and some dying off every day, leave vacancies in the squads of as many as die out of them, and in order to keep them filled up have to be squadded over every few days, thereby saving rations. Richmond papers are much alarmed for fear of a break among the prisoners confined within the city. It is said there are six hundred muskets secreted among the Belle Islanders. The citizens are frightened almost to death, double guards are placed over us, and very strict orders issued to them.

Jan. 9.—A signal light suspended over the island all last night for some reason unknown to the men confined here. We are cautioned against approaching within eight or ten feet from the bank. One of the raiders went through a man who lay near the bank and started to run after robbing him. A guard who saw the whole affair shot the villain dead and was applauded by all who knew of the affair. Fifteen or twenty carried out this morning dead and thirty or forty nearly so in blankets.

Jan. 10.—A brass band over to-day giving us a tune. Looks more like a wandering tribe of vagabonds than musicians. Discoursed sweet music, such as "Bonnie Blue Flag," "The Girl I Left Behind Me," and for their pains got three groans from their enemies in limbo. Dying off very fast on the island.

Jan. 11.—A steady rain for twenty-four hours, and have not been dry during the time. However it is a warm rain and get along very well. We are still issuing clothing but very slow. About one hundred per day get partly clothed up. No news of exchange. Abe Lincoln reported dead. Papers very bitter on Beast Butler, as they call him. Manage by a good deal of skirmishing to get the papers almost every day in which we read their rebel lies. A plan afoot for escape, but am afraid to say anything of the particulars for fear of my diary being taken away from me. As I came inside to-night with some bread in my haversack some fellows who were on the watch pitched into me and gobbled my saved up rations. I don't care for myself for I have been to supper, but the boys in the tent will have to go without anything to eat for this night. It don't matter much—they are all hungry and it did them as much good as it would our mess.

Jan. 12.—James River very high. A continual roar in our ears caused by the water falling over the cataract just above the island. Rebels fired a large shell over the prison to scare us.

Jan. 15.—Everything runs along about the same. Little excitements from day to day. The weather is fair, and taken all together thus far this winter has been very favorable to us as prisoners. Lieut. Bossieux lost his dog. Some Yanks snatched him into a tent and ate him up. Bossieux very mad and is anxious to know who the guilty ones are. All he can do is to keep all our rations from us one day, and he does it. Seems pretty rough when a man will eat a dog, but such is the case.

Jan. 18.—Too much exertion to even write in my diary. Talk of getting away by escaping, but find no feasible plan. Rebs very watchful. Some mail to-day but nothing for me. Saw some papers, and a new prisoner brought with him a New York paper, but not a word in it about "exchange." Am still outside most every day. Geo. Hendryx at work in the cook house cooking rations for the prisoners. Comes down where I am every day and hands me something to take inside for the boys. He tells the Lieut. he has a brother inside that he is feeding. Although it is against orders, Lieut. Bossieux pays no attention to it.

Jan. 20.—Rebel officers over to-day inspecting us Yanks. Some of the worst looking Arabs in shape of officers I ever saw. Jimmy Devers comes to our tent every night and sits with us until bed time. Is a jolly chap and keeps us all in good spirits with his sayings. Sergt. Robinson, I learned to-day, instead of being a sergeant is a lieutenant. His whole company being captured, he preferred to go with them and share their trials, than go with the officers. The men are very much attached to him and no wonder, as he is a fine fellow. His home is in Sterling, Whiteside Co., Illinois. Corp. Mc-Carten is, as his name would indicate, an Irishman, and his home is Louisville, Ky. Is a shoemaker by trade. He is also a Mason, and I am going to write down wherein the fact of his being a Mason has brought good into the camp to-day. The boys feeling rather more hungry than usual were rather despondent, when the corporal gets up and says: "Boys, I'll go and get something to eat." Went out of the tent and in twenty minutes came back with three or four pounds of bacon and two loaves of corn bread. We were surprised and asked how he had performed the miracle. Told us then that he was a Mason, as also was the lieutenant in charge, from whom the food came. We decided then and there that the first opportunity that presented itself we would join the Masons. Can see the rebels drilling across the river.

31

Jan. 22.—Cold and clear weather. Nothing to write to-day. It's a task.

Jan. 24.—We are all troubled with heart-burn, sour stomach, &c. Drink weak lye made from ashes for it. Every day some new ones come inside, but they know nothing as to the prospects of our being exchanged. All are considerably surprised to find themselves in quite so bad a place, and the subject of prison life begins to interest them. Good deal of gambling going on among prisoners. Chuck-a-luck is the favorite game. You lay your ration of bread down on a figure on a board, and a fellow with a dice-box shakes it up a little, throws out the dice, and your bread is gone. Don't understand the game myself. That's all I ever saw of the game. Lay down the bread and it's gone. Rather a one sided affair. Some men are very filthy, which makes it disagreeable for those of more cleanly habits. I believe that many, very many, who now die, would live if they adopted the rules that our mess has, and lived up to them. It is the only way to get along.

Jan. 25.—Being in this place brings out a man for just what he is worth. Those whom we expect the most from in the way of braving hardships and dangers, prove to be nobody at all. And very often those whom we expect the least from prove to be heroes every inch of them. Notably one of these is George Hendryx, who is nothing but a good looking, effeminate boy, fit, you would say, to be going to school with a mother to look after him, and for not much else. But instead, he is brave, cheerful, smart, watching every chance to get the best of the Johnny Rebs. His position in the cook-house has given him a chance to feed, I presume, hundreds of men. Near the cook-house is a store-house, and in it are several hogsheads of hams.

These hams were sent from the Sanitary Commission at the North for Union prisoners, but they for whom they were intended do not get them, and they are being eaten up by the rebels. Hendryx has managed to get up a board in the cookhouse floor, where he can crawl fifteen or twenty feet under the store-house and up through that floor. By this Yankee trick he has stolen, I presume, one hundred hams and gotten them inside where they belong. This is very risky on his part, for should he be discovered it would go very hard with him. He is about as unselfish a fellow as you can well find. This is only one of his plans to outwit the rebels for our benefit. His head is all the time, too, planning some way of escape. Well, we all hope he won't get caught. All shake in our boots for him. Was on guard last night, outside, over the clothing. There is so much clothing stole by the rebels that Bossieux put a guard of two over the boxes through the night, and if any of the Rebs come around to steal we are instructed to wake up the lieutenant, who sleeps near by in a tent. I was on duty last night with Joe Myers, and Hendryx came where we were and unfolded a plan for escape which he has been working up. It is a risky affair, and had best be thought over pretty thorough before put into execution. Robinson has been found out as a lieutenant, and taken over to Richmond to be placed with the officers in Libby Prison. We are sorry that we must lose him.

Jan. 26.—Ninety-two squads of prisoners confined on less than six acres of ground—one hundred in a squad, making nine thousand and two hundred altogether. The lice are getting the upper hand of us. The ground is literally covered with them. Bean soup to-day and is made from the following recipe, (don't know from what cook book, some new edition):

Beans are very wormy and musty. Hard work finding a bean without from one to three bugs in it. They are put into a large caldron kettle of river water and boiled for a couple of hours. No seasoning, not even salt put into them. It is then taken out and brought inside. Six pails full for each squad—about a pint per man, and not over a pint of beans in each bucket. The water is hardly colored and I could see clear through to the bottom and count every bean in the pail. The men drink it because it is warm. There is not enough strength or substance in it to do any good. We sometimes have very good bean soup when they have meat to boil with it.

Jan. 27.—More prisoners came to-day and say there is to be no general exchange during the war, and we are to be sent off into Georgia immediately. Stormy and disagreeable weather and everybody down-hearted. Very still among the men, owing to the bad news—hardly a word spoken by anybody. The least bit of anything encouraging would change the stillness into a perfect bedlam. I this morning looked into a tent where there were seventeen men and started back frightened at the view inside. What a tableau for a New York theatre! They were all old prisoners nearly naked, very dirty and poor, some of them sick lying on the cold ground with nothing under or over them, and no fire; had just been talking over the prospect ahead and all looked the very picture of dispair, with their hollow eyes, sunken cheeks and haggard expression. I have before imagined such scenes but never before realized what they were until now. And such is but a fair sample of hundreds of men fully as bad.

Jan. 28.—No officers over from Libby for a few days past. Nearly all the clothing issued. A few days more will close up the clothing business, and then probably all the outsiders will be sent inside; and for fear such will be the case we have decided upon to-morrow night for the escape (which I have not said much about in my diary). The nights are dark and cloudy. Messrs. Mustard and Hendryx both sleep outside now, and I must manage to, both to-night and to-morrow night. I have been two weeks trying to get a map of Virginia, and have at last succeeded. A negro brought it to me from the city. It has cost over thirty dollars Confederate money—at the North would have cost twenty five cents. I would not take for it, unless I could get another one, one thousand dollars in gold. We are well rigged, have some food saved up to take along; in good health and determined to get away. Lieut. Bossieux suspects, and to-day took the pains to say in our hearing that he knew an escape among the outsiders was in view, and as sure as there was a God in heaven if we tried it and got caught, and we surely would be, he would first shoot all he could before catching us, and the balance would be tied up and whipped every day until he got tired, as long as we lived. We must expect trouble. It does not change us in the least; if anything, makes us the more determined to get away. To-night we are to start, and I will write down the plans we have, running the risk of the rebels getting hold of it. At a few moments past eleven and before midnight the guard will let us cross his beat and go to the water's edge. We all have rebel clothing which we are to wear, furnished partly by a negro, and partly by the guard who helps us off. We take the quarter-master's boat which we unlock, and having been furnished the countersign give it to the picket who will pretend that he thinks we are rebel guards going over to the city, in case we are caught, which will screen him in a measure. Having passed him, we get into the boat and row across the river, give the countersign to the guards on the other side of the river, and talk with them a little, being ourselves posted on general information regarding the place. To quiet their suspicions if they have any, we then start up into the town and when out of sight of the guards take a turn to the left, and go straight to the Richmond jail; taking care to avoid patrols &c. We will then meet with a negro who will guide us ten miles up the river, and then leave us in charge of friendly blacks who will keep us through the next day and at night pilot us farther along toward our lives. If possible, I shall steal the rebel flag, which is kept nights in the lieutenant's tent, and a few other relics, to take along with me. The big bell in Richmond strikes six, and we close our diary, hoping never to look upon it again until we return to free our fellow prisoners, with the glorious army of the North. Now we leave our diary to finish preparations for the flight for freedom. May God aid us in this land of tyranny, where we have met nothing but suffering. Good bye, Belle Isle and Prison. Hail! Freedom, Home, Friends, and the Grand Army of the Old Flag! What is in store for us in the future?

Feb. 5.—Have been reading over the last few pages on my diary. It sounds well, but the rebel flag still floats over Belle Isle. Our escapade was a grand fizzle, and all hands have been punished in more ways than one in the last few days. Bossieux suspected something going on among us and had us secretly watched, and long before we had made a move toward fulfilling our projected plans we were thrown into a guard house on the island; next morning taken out of it, and underwent a severe cross-questioning. He found our rebel clothing, food we had packed, found the lock to the boat broke, and numerous other signs of an abandonment. Well, the result has been that we were bucked and gagged twice a day for an hour each time, and for four hours each of us carried a big stick of wood up and down in front of the gate, a guard to prick us with his bayonet if we walked too slow to suit him. Then Hendryx has been strung up by the thumbs. Nights we have been thrown into a damp, cold guard house to shiver all night. Every day now for six days we have walked with our sticks of wood so many hours per day, and last night were turned inside with all the prisoners to stay, Bossieux says, till we *rot*, he can place no dependence in us.

Feb. 6.—We have to laugh over our trials and tribulations. Where we had plenty a week ago, plenty of exercise, and many favors, we are now right where we were at first, fareing just as the rest, with no favors shown us. It's all right, we can stand it just as well as the rest. We have never belittled ourselves in the least in our dealings with the rebels. Bossieux told us himself, as we came inside, that he didn't blame us in the least for trying to get away, but he was obliged to punish us for the attempt. Hendryx says that he will be out again in three days.

Feb. 8.—Butler reported as commissioner on exchange and the rebels declare that they would never recognize him and would rather that we should all die here than negotiate with the Beast. Congress still in session over in the city and we watch the papers eagerly for something relative to us. The Holy Sabbath day and the church bells ringing for morning service. Don't think I shall attend this morning; it is such a long walk and then I look so bad; have nothing fit to wear. A man stabbed a few minutes ago by his tent mate, killing him instantly. They had all along been the best friends until a dispute arose, and one of them drew a knife and killed his comrade. Strong talk of lynching the murderer. Have not heard the particulars. Corp. McCarten is missing from the island and am confident from what I have seen that he has escaped and by the help of Lieut. Bossieux. No endeavors are being made to look him up, still he offers a reward for his apprehension. They are both members of the secret craft.

Feb. 9.—Great news this morning. A raid is being made on Richmond by Kilpatrick, Rebels manning their forts in sight of us. All are at work, women, children, in fact everybody who can shovel. No cars running over the big bridge. Double guards placed over us and the greatest activity prevails among them. It is really amusing to see them flying around and many are the jokes at their expense. All business is suspended in Richmond; no papers issued, and everybody with their guns or working utensils. Brass bands are playing their best to encourage the broken down Confederacy. A portion of the congress came over this afternoon to take a look at us, among whom were Davis, Benjamin and Howell Cobb. They are a substantial looking set of men and of the regular southern cut. The broad brim hats, gold headed canes and aristocratic toss of the head, alone would tell who they were. They are a proud, stern set of men and look as if they would like to brush us out of existence. Still we are not going to be brushed out so easy and they found men among us who were not afraid to stare, or hold our heads as high as their lordships. A band accompanied them and played the Bonnie Blue Flag, which was hissed and groaned at by the Yankees, and in return a thousand voices sang Yankee Doodle, very much to their discomfiture.

Feb. 10.—The hospital signal lights suspended over the island all night in order to direct the batteries where to aim their pieces in case of an outbreak which is greatly feared. Rockets sent up at intervals during the night over Richmond. Reported that there are six hundred muskets secreted among the prisoners and citizens very much alarmed and afraid of us. I hope there is but cannot believe it. It is impossible for me to sleep and I lay awake thinking how we are situated and wondering how long the play is to last.

Feb. 11.—Cold and pleasant. A good deal of fighting going on among us—a discontented set of beings; just like so many hungry wolves penned up together. Rebels still at work fortifying all around Richmond. A number of Yankees have been taken out on parole of honor to work building breastworks etc., but a very few will go and it is considered a great crime among us to work for them. Have they forgotten our existence at the North? It seems as if we were neglected by our government but will not judge them hastily until we know more. There are perhaps sufficient reasons for our remaining here. Very strongly guarded, nevertheless we talk of escape and are all the while building air castles.

Feb. 12.—Lieut. Bossieux has sent a squad of men from the island composed of runaways over to Castle Thunder to remain during the war as hostages, among whom were our friends Myers and Mustard. I never expect to see them again.

Feb. 13.—Very cold. The rebels are again settling down and getting over their scare. Not much to eat now and the men more disheartened than ever. A rebel preacher delivered us a sermon of two hours length from a dry goods box. He was listened to attentively and made the remark before closing that he didn't know as he was doing any good talking to us. It was like casting pearls before swine and he would close his remarks, to which a Yankee told him he might have stopped long ago if he had wanted to; no one would have made any objections. Was told that six hundred are to start for Georgia to-day and subsequently six hundred every day until all are removed from Richmond. Lieut. Bossieux says it is so but there is going to be an exchange of sick in a few days and all outside hands shall be sent north with them.

Feb. 14.—Had quite an adventure last night with the raiders. One of Capt. Moseby's robbers was trying to steal a blanket from our tent by reaching through the tent opening when Dad (E. P. Sanders), who is always awake, threw a brick hitting him on the arm, breaking the brick, and as he jumped, hallooed to us, "Come boys, let's catch the rascal," and out of the door he went. Dr. and myself nobly rushed to the rescue and reached the door just in time to see Dad turn a short corner way up the street and close on to the heels of Mr. Robber, but he slipped and fell and the thief got away. Were soon snugly ensconced in bed once more congratulating ourselves on losing nothing as we thought. But on getting up this morning I found my shoes gone and am barefoot in the middle of winter. However I can get more and have no fear on that score. Six hundred sent away to-day, some say to our lines while others think to Georgia. Rebels say to our lines, and that a general exchange has been agreed upon. Great excitement among the men. Evening.—Lieut. Bossieux called me outside just before night and told me he was called upon to furnish some hostages to be sent to Charleston to be kept during the war, and had decided to send Hendryx and myself, with some others. Said it was better to send those who were always trying to get away. Have succeeded in buying a pair of shoes, which, although about four sizes too large, are much better than none. Thanks to the Sanitary Commission I have good woolen stockings, under clothing complete, and am otherwise well dressed. Six hundred sent away this afternoon under a very strong guard, which does not look like an exchange.

Feb. 17.—Still on the island. Another squad taken out yesterday. It will not be our turn to go for some days, even if six hundred are taken out every day. Have not been sent for as hostages yet. Hendryx and myself have decided to flank out and go with the next that go, no matter where their destination may be. If we don't get away, with a ghost of a chance, then it will be funny.

Feb. 20.—All sorts of rumors afloat, but still we stay here. Strange officers come over and look at us. Bossieux away considerable, and something evidently up. Anything for a change. My health is good, and tough as a bear.

Feb. 23.—None have been taken away from the island for a number of days. Have heard that a box came for me, and is over in Richmond. Hope the rebel that eats the contents of that box will get choked to death. I wrote to the Governor of Michigan, Austin Blair, who is in Washington, D.C., some weeks ago. He has known me from boyhood. Always lived in the neighborhood at Jackson, Mich. Asked him to notify my father and brothers of my whereabouts. To-day I received a letter from him saying that he had done as requested, also that the Sanitary Commission had sent me some eatables. This is undoubtedly the box which I have heard from and is over in Richmond. Rebels are trying to get recruits from among us for their one-horse Confederacy. Believe that one or two have deserted our ranks and gone over. Bad luck to them.

CHAPTER THREE

Pemberton Building

A Good-bye to Belle Isle * Good Place to be Moved From * Astor House Mess on its Travels * New Scenes * The Raid on Richmond and Consequent Scare * All's Well, if it Ends Well * Men Shot

PEMBERTON BUILDING, Richmond, Va. *Feb. 24.*— We are confined on the third floor of the building, which is a large tobacco warehouse. Was removed from the island yesterday. Was a warm day and it was a long walk. Came across the "long bridge," and it is a long bridge. Was not sorry to bid adieu to Belle Isle. Were searched last night but our mess has lost nothing, owing to the following process we have of fooling them: One of the four manages to be in the front part of the crowd and is searched first, and is then put on the floor underneath and we let our traps down through a crack in the floor to him, and when our turn comes we have nothing about us worth taking away. The men so ravenous when the rations were brought in, that the boxes of bread and tubs of poor meat were raided upon before dividing, and consequently some had nothing to eat at all, while others had plenty. Our mess did not get a mouthful and have had nothing to eat since yesterday afternoon, and it is now nearly dark. The lice are very thick. You can see them all over the floors, walls, &c., in fact everything literally covered with them; they seem much larger than the stock on Belle Isle and a different species. We talk of escape night and day—and are nearly crazy on the subject. No more news about exchange. Papers state that Richmond is threatened, and that Kilpatrick's cavalry is making a raid on the place for the purpose of releasing us and burning the town. Unusual bustle among them.

Feb. 25.—We divide the night up into four watches and take turns standing guard while the other three sleep, to protect ourselves from Captain Moseby's gang of robbers. We are all armed with iron slats pulled off the window casings. They are afraid to pitch in to us, as we are a stout crowd and would fight well for our worldly goods. We expect to take it before long. They are eyeing us rather sharp, and I guess will make an attack to-night. Very long days and more lonesome than when on the island. Got rations to-day, and the allowance did not half satisfy our hunger.

Feb. 26.—Rather cold, almost spring. Guards unusually strict. Hendryx was standing near the window, and I close by him, looking at the high, ten story tobacco building, when the guard fired at us. The ball just grazed Hendryx's head and lodged in the ceiling above; all we could do to prevent Hendryx throwing a brick at the guard.

Feb. 27.—Organizing the militia; hauling artillery past the prison. Have a good view of all that is going on. Bought a compass from one of the guards for seven dollars, greenbacks; worth half a dollar at home. It is already rumored among the men that we have a compass, a map of Virginia, a preparation to put on our feet to prevent dogs from tracking us, and we are looked up to as if we were sons of Irish lords in disguise, and are quite noted personages. Cold last night, and we suffer much in not having blankets enough to keep us warm. The walls are cold and damp, making it disagreeable, and the stench nearly makes us sick. It is impossible for a person to imagine prison life until he has seen and realized it. No news of importance. Time passes much more drearily than when on Belle Isle. Were all searched again to-day but still keep my diary, although expecting to lose it every day; would be quite a loss, as the longer I write and remain a prisoner the more attached am I to my record of passing events. A man shot for putting his head out of the window. Men all say it served him right, for he had no business to thus expose himself against strict orders to the contrary. We are nearly opposite and not more than twenty rods from Libby Prison, which is a large tobacco warehouse. Can see plenty of Union officers, which it is a treat to look at. Hendryx had a fight with the raiders—got licked. He ain't so pretty as he was before, but knows more. I am very wise about such matters, consequently retain my beauty.

Feb. 28.—Had the honor (?) of seeing Jefferson Davis again and part of his congress to-day. They visited Libby and we were allowed to look out of the windows to see them as they passed in and out of the building. Strut around like chickens with frozen feet. David Benjamin walked with the President and is a much better looking man. Prisoners were notified that if they made any insulting remarks they would be fired at. Have no more exalted opinion of them than before.

Feb. 29.—Excitement among the Johnnies—flying around as if the Yankee army were threatening Richmond. Cannot learn what the commotion is, but hope it is something that will benefit us. LATER: The occasion of the excitement among the rebels is that Dahlgreen is making a raid on Richmond, acting in conjunction with Kilpatrick, for the purpose of liberating prisoners. We are heavily guarded and not allowed to look out of the windows, nevertheless we manage to see about all there is going on.

Feb. 30.—Rebels in hot water all night and considerably agitated. Imagined we could hear firing during the night. This morning small squads of tired out Union soldiers marched by our prison under guard, evidently captured through the night. Look as if they was completely played out. Go straggling by sometimes not more than half a dozen at a time. Would give something to hear the news. We are all excitement here. Negroes also go by in squads sometimes of hundreds in charge of overseers, and singing their quaint negro melodies. It is supposed by us that the negroes work on the fortifications, and are moved from one part of the city to another, for that purpose. Our troops have evidently been repulsed with considerable loss. We hear that Dahlgreen has been shot and killed. At the very first intimation that our troops were anywhere near, the prisoners would have made a break.

March 1.—Working along towards Spring slowly. A dead calm after the raid scare. We much prefer the open air imprisonment to confinement. Have considerable trouble with the thieves which disgrace the name of Union soldier. Are the most contemptible rascals in existence. Often walk up to a man and coolly take his food and proceed to eat it before the owner. If the victim resists then a fight is the consequence, and the poor man not only loses his food but gets licked as well.

March 2.—The food we get here is poor, water very good, weather outside admirable, vermin still under control and the Astor House Mess flourishing. We are all in good health with the exception of Dr. Lewis, who is ailing. I was never tougher—seems as if your humble servant was proof against the hardest rebel treatment. No exchange news. Trade and dicker with the guards and work ourselves into many luxuries, or rather work the luxuries into ourselves.

Have become quite interested in a young soldier boy from Ohio named Bill Havens. Is sick with some kind of fever and is thoroughly bad off. Was tenderly brought up and well educated I should judge. Says he ran away from home to become a drummer. Has been wounded twice, in numerous engagements, now a prisoner of war and sick. Will try and keep track of him. Every nationality is here represented and from every branch of the service, and from all parts of the world. There are smart men here and those that are not so smart, in fact a conglomeration of humanity—hash, as it were.

March 3.—The ham given us to-day was rotten, with those nameless little white things crawling around through it. Promptly threw it out of the window and was scolded for it by a fellow prisoner who wanted it himself. Shall never become hungry enough to eat poor meat. Guards careless with their guns. An old man shot in the arm. Hendryx tried to pull a brick out of the casing to throw at the shooter. Barbarians these rebs.

March 4.—And now we are getting ready to move somewhere, the Lord only knows where. One good thing about their old prisons, we are always ready for a change. Have made many new acquaintances while here in Pemberton, and some agreeable ones; my boy Havens has fever and chills. Is rather better to-day. It is said we move to-night. Minnesota Indians confined here, and a number of sailors and marines. I am quite a hand to look at men, sometimes for hours, and study them over, then get to talking with them and see how near I was right in my conjectures. Its almost as good as reading books. The Astor House Mess is now composed of but four members, E. P. Sanders, F. L. Lewis, Geo. W. Hendryx and myself; we still adhere to our sanitary regulations and as a consequence are in better health than a majority of those here. Sanders may be said to be at the head of the mess, (we call him Dad,) while Lewis is a sort of moderator and advisor, with Hendryx and myself as the rank and file. Are quite attached to one another, and don't believe that either one would steal from the other. I certainly wouldn't take anything short of pumpkin pie or something of that sort. Of course a man would steal pie, at least we all say so, and Lewis even declares he would steal dough cakes and pancakes such as his wife used to make. We are all well dressed, thanks to the Sanitary Commission and our own ingenuity in getting what was intended for us to have. False alarm of fire.

ROUTED AT MIDNIGHT

ON THE CARS, *March 7, 1864.*—We were roused from our gentle slumbers during the night, counted off and marched to the cars, loaded into them, which had evidently just had some cattle as occupants. Started southward to some portion of Georgia, as a guard told us. Passed through Petersburg, and other towns which I could not learn the names of. Cars run very slow, and being crowded, we are very uncomfortable—and hungry. Before leaving Richmond hard-tack was issued to us in good quantity for the Confederacy. Have not much chance to write. Bought some boiled sweet potatoes of the guard, which are boss. The country we pass through is a miserable one. Guards watch us close to see that none escape, and occasionally a Yank is shot, but not in our car. Seems as if we did not run over thirty or forty miles per day. Stop for hours on side tracks, waiting for other trains to pass us.

March 8.—Were unloaded last night and given a chance to straighten our limbs. Stayed all night in the woods, side of the track, under a heavy guard. Don't know where we are, as guards are very reticent.

March 10.—Still traveling, and unloaded nights to sleep by the track. Rebel citizens and women improve every opportunity to see live Yankees. Are fed passably well. Lewis feeling poorly. Watch a chance to escape but find none.

March 13.—Ran very slow through the night, and are in the vicinity of Macon, Ga. Will reach our prison to-night. Received a pone of corn bread apiece weighing about two pounds, which is liberal on their part. Two more days such riding as this would kill me. The lice are fairly eating us up alive, having had no chance to rid ourselves of them since leaving Richmond. One of the guards struck Hendryx during the night. We were talking on the all important subject, and the guard hearing us chatting away to ourselves struck over into the crowd where the noise came from and hit George in the back part of the head. He didn't speak for a minute or two and I was afraid it had killed him, which happily proved to the contrary. As soon as it came daylight he showed the brute where he had struck him, and took the occasion to dress him down a little, whereupon the rebel threatened that if he said another word to him he would blow his head off. A drizzling rain has set in.

CHAPTER FOUR

Andersonville

**Arrival at the Worst of all Prisons ✻
Beginning of a Summer that Killed
Thirteen Thousand Men ✻ Bad Water, Bad
Food, and Most Inhuman Treatment ✻
In the Clutches of Wirtz and His Picked Out
Rebel Aids ✻ The Truth and Nothing but
the Truth ✻ A Season of Intense Suffering**

CAMP SUMTER, Andersonville, Ga., *March 14.*—Arrived at our destination at last and a dismal hole it is, too. We got off the cars at two o'clock this morning in a cold rain, and were marched into our pen between a strong guard carrying lighted pitch pine knots to prevent our crawling off in the dark. I could hardly walk have been cramped up so long, and feel as if I was a hundred years old. Have stood up ever since we came from the cars, and shivering with the cold. The rain has wet us to the skin and we are worn out and miserable. Nothing to eat to-day, and another dismal night just setting in.

March 15.—At about midnight I could stand up no longer, and lay down in the mud and water. Could hardly get up. Shall get food this morning, and after eating shall feel better. There is a good deal to write about here, but I must postpone it until some future time, for I can hardly hold a pencil now. LATER: Have drawn some rations which consisted of nearly a quart of corn meal, half a pound of beef, and some salt. This is splendid. I have just partaken of a delicious repast and feel like a different person. Dr. Lewis is discouraged and thinks he cannot live long in such a place as this.

March 16.—The prison is not yet entirely completed. One side is yet open, and through the opening two pieces of artillery are pointed. About 1800 Yankees are here now. Col. Piersons commands the prison, and rides in and talks with the men. Is quite sociable, and says we are all to be exchanged in a few weeks. He was informed that such talk would not go down any longer. We had been fooled enough, and paid

53

no attention to what they told us. Our mess is gradually settling down. Have picked out our ground, rolled some big logs together, and are trying to make ourselves comfortable. I am in the best of spirits, and will live with them for some time to come if they will only give me one quarter enough to eat, and they are doing it now, and am in my glory. Weather cleared up, and very cold nights. We put on all our clothes nights and take them off day-times. The men do most of their sleeping through the day, and shiver through the long nights.

March 17.—Get almost enough to eat, such as it is, but don't get it regularly; sometimes in the morning, and sometimes in the afternoon. Six hundred more prisoners came last night, and from Belle Isle, Va., our old home. Andersonville is situated on two hillsides, with a small stream of swampy water running through the center, and on both sides of the stream is a piece of swamp with two or three acres in it. We have plenty of wood now, but it will not last long. They will undoubtedly furnish us with wood from the outside, when it is burned up on the inside. A very unhealthy climate. A good many are being poisoned by poisonous roots, and there is a thick green scum on the water. All who drink freely are made sick, and their faces swell up so they cannot see.

March 18.—There are about fifteen acres of ground enclosed in the stockade and we have the freedom of the whole ground. Plenty of room, but they are filling it up. Six hundred new men coming each day from Richmond. Guards are perched upon top of the stockade; are very strict, and to-day one man was shot for approaching too near the wall. A little warm to-day. Found W. B. Rowe, from Jackson, Mich.; he

is well and talks encouraging. We have no shelter of any
kind whatever. Eighteen or twenty die per day. Cold and
damp nights. The dews wet things through completely, and
by morning all nearly chilled. Wood getting scarce. On the
outside it is a regular wilderness of pines. Railroad a mile off
and can just see the cars as they go by, which is the only sign
of civilization in sight. Rebels all the while at work making
the prison stronger. Very poor meal, and not so much to-day
as formerly. My young friend Billy Havens was sent to the
hospital about the time we left Richmond. Shall be glad to
hear of his recovery. Prevailing conversation is food and
exchange.

March 19.—A good deal of fighting going on among us. A
large number of sailors and marines are confined with us,
and they are a quarrelsome set. I have a very sore hand, caused
by cutting a hole through the car trying to get out. I have
to write with my left hand. It is going to be an awful place
during the summer months here, and thousands will die no
doubt.

March 21.—Prison gradually filling up with forlorn looking creatures. Wood is being burned up gradually. Have taken
in my old acquaintance and a member of my own company
"A" 9th Mich. Cavalry, Wm. B. Rowe. Sergt. Rowe is a tall,
straight, dark complexioned man, about thirty-five years old.
He was captured while carrying dispatches from Knoxville to
Gen. Burnside. Has been a prisoner two or three months, and
was in Pemberton Building until sent here. He is a tough,
abled-bodied man. Every day I find new Michigan men, some
of them old acquaintances.

March 23.—Stockade all up, and we are penned in. Our

mess is out of filthy lucre—otherwise, busted. Sold my over-coat to a guard, and for luxuries we are eating that up. My blanket keeps us all warm. There are two more in our mess. Daytimes the large spread is stretched three or four feet high on four sticks, and keeps off the sun, and at night taken down for a cover.

March 24.—Digging a tunnel to get out of this place. Prison getting filthy. Prisoners somewhat to blame for it. Good many dying, and they are those who take no care of themselves, drink poor water, etc.

March 25.—Lieut. Piersons is no longer in command of the prison, but instead a Capt. Wirtz. Came inside to-day and looked us over. Is not a very prepossessing looking chap. Is about thirty-five or forty years old, rather tall, and a little stoop shouldered; skin has a pale, white livered look, with thin lips. Has a sneering sort of cast of countenance. Makes a fellow feel as if he would like to go up and boot him. Should judge he was a Swede, or some such countryman. Hendryx thinks he could make it warm for him in short order if he only had a chance. Wirtz wears considerable jewelry on his person—long watch chain, something that looks like a diamond for a pin in his shirt, and wears patent leather boots or shoes. I asked him if he didn't think we would be ex-changed soon. He said: Oh, yes, we would be exchanged soon. Somehow or other this assurance don't elate us much; perhaps it was his manner when saying it. Andersonville is getting to be a rather bad place as it grows warmer. Several sick with fevers and sores.

March 26.—Well, well, my birthday came six days ago, and how old do you think I am? Let me see. Appearances would seem to indicate that I am thirty or thereabouts, but as I was born on the 20th day of March, 1843, I must now be just twenty-one years of age, this being the year 1864. Of age and six days over. I thought that when a man became of age, he generally became free and his own master as well. If this ain't a burlesque on that old time-honored custom, then carry me out—but not feet foremost.

March 27.—We have issued to us once each day about a pint of beans, or more properly peas, (full of bugs), and three-quarters of a pint of meal, and nearly every day a piece of bacon the size of your two fingers, probably about three or four ounces. This is very good rations taken in comparison to what I have received before. The pine which we use in cooking is pitch pine, and a black smoke arises from it; consequently we are black as negroes. Prison gradually filling from day to day, and situation rather more unhealthy. Occasionally a squad comes in who have been lately captured, and they tell of our battles, sometimes victorious and sometimes otherwise. Sometimes we are hopeful and sometimes the reverse. Take all the exercise we can, drink no water, and try to get along. It is a sad sight to see the men die so fast. New prisoners die the quickest and are buried in the near vicinity, we are told in trenches without coffins. Sometimes we have visitors of citizens and women who come to look at us. There is sympathy in some of their faces and in some a lack of it. A dead line composed of slats of boards runs around on the inside of the wall, about twelve or fourteen feet from the wall, and we are not allowed to go near it on pain of being shot by the guard.

March 28.—We are squadded over to-day, and rations

about to come in. It's a sickly dirty place. Seems as if the sun was not over a mile high, and has a particular grudge against us. Wirtz comes inside and has began to be very insolent. Is constantly watching for tunnels. He is a brute. We call him the "Flying Dutchman." Came across Sergt. Bullock, of my regiment, whom I last saw on Belle Isle. From a fat, chubby young fellow, he is a perfect wreck. Lost his voice and can hardly speak aloud; nothing but skin and bone, and black and ragged. Never saw such a change in a human being. Cannot possibly live, I don't think; still he is plucky and hates to die. Goes all around enquiring for news, and the least thing encouraging cheers him up. Capt. Moseby, of the raiders, is in the same squad with me. He is quite an intelligent fellow and often talks with us. We lend him our boiling cup which he returns with thanks. Better to keep on the right side of him, if we can without countenancing his murderous operations.

March 29.—Raiders getting more bold as the situation grows worse. Often rob a man now of all he has, in public, making no attempt at concealment. In sticking up for the weaker party, our mess gets into trouble nearly every day, and particularly Hendryx, who will fight any time.

March 30.—The gate opens every little while letting some poor victims into this terrible place, which is already much worse than Belle Isle. Seems as if our government is at fault in not providing some way to get us out of here. The hot weather months must kill us all outright. Feel myself at times sick and feverish with no strength seemingly. Dr. Lewis worries, worries, all the day long, and it's all we can do to keep him from giving up entirely. Sergt. Rowe takes things as they come in dogged silence. Looks like a caged lion. Hendryx sputters around, scolding away, &c.

April 1.—This is an April Fool sure. Saw a fellow to-day from our regiment, named Casey. Says I was reported dead at the regiment, which is cheerful. Perhaps it is just as well though, for them to anticipate the event a few months. It is said that Wirtz shot some one this morning. Often hear the guards shoot and hear of men being killed. Am not ambitious to go near them. Have completely lost my desire to be on the outside working for extra rations. Prefer to stick it out where I am than to have anything to do with them. They are an ungodly crew, and should have the warmest corner in that place we sometimes hear mentioned.

April 2.—James Robins, an Indiana soldier, is in our close proximity. Was wounded and taken prisoner not long since. Wound, which is in the thigh, is in a terrible condition, and gangrene setting in. Although he was carried to the gate to-day, was refused admission to the hospital or medical attendance. Rebels say they have no medicine for us. Robins has been telling me about himself and family at home, and his case is only one of a great many good substantial men of families who must die in Southern prisons, as victims to mismanagement. The poorer the Confederacy, and the meaner they are, the more need that our government should get us away from here, and not put objectionable men at the head of exchange to prevent our being sent home or back to our commands.

April 3.—We have stopped wondering at suffering or being surprised at anything. Can't do the subject justice and so don't try. Walk around camp every morning looking for acquaintances, the sick, &c. Can see a dozen most any morning laying around dead. A great many are terribly afflicted with diarrhea, and scurvy begins to take hold of some. Scurvy is a bad disease, and taken in connection with the former is sure death. Some have dropsy as well as scurvy, and the swollen limbs and body are sad to see. To think that these victims have people at home, mothers, wives and sisters, who are thinking of them and would do much for them if they had the chance, little dreaming of their condition.

April 4.—Same old story—coming in and being carried out; all have a feeling of lassitude which prevents much exertion. Have been digging in a tunnel for a day or two with a dozen others who are in the secret. It's hard work. A number of tunnels have been discovered. The water now is very warm and sickening.

April 5.—Dr. Lewis talks about nothing except his family. Is the bluest mortal here, and worries himself sick, let alone causes sufficient for that purpose. Is poorly adapted for hardships. For reading we have the "Pilgrim's Progress," donated to me by some one when on Belle Isle. Guess I can repeat nearly all the book by heart. Make new acquaintances every day. "Scotty," a marine, just now is edifying our mess with his salt water yarns, and they are tough ones. I tell him he may die here; still he declares they are true.

April 6.—John Smith is here and numerous of his family. So many go by nick-names, that seldom any go by their real names. Its "Minnesota," "Big Charlie," "Little Jim," "Marine Jack," "Indiana Feller," "Mopey," "Skinny," "Smarty," &c. Hendryx is known by the latter name, Sanders is called "Dad," Rowe is called the "Michigan Sergeant," Lewis is called plain "Doc," while I am called, for some unknown reason, "Bugler." I have heard it said that I looked just like a Dutch bugler, and perhaps that is the reason of my cognomen. Probably thirty die per day. The slightest news about exchange is told from one to the other, and gains every time repeated, until finally its grand good news and sure exchange immediately. The weak ones feed upon these reports and struggle along from day to day. One hour they are all hope and expectation and the next hour as bad the other way. The worst looking scallawags perched upon the stockade as guards, from boys just large enough to handle a gun, to old men who ought to have been dead years ago for the good of their country. Some prisoners nearly naked, the majority in rags and daily becoming more destitute. My clothes are good and kept clean, health fair although very poor in flesh. Man killed at the dead line.

April 7.—Capt. Wirtz prowls around the stockade with a rebel escort of guards, looking for tunnels. Is very suspicious of amateur wells which some have dug for water. It is useless to speak to him about our condition, as he will give us no satisfaction whatever. Says it is good enough for us——— Yankees. I am deputized by half a dozen or so to speak to him as to the probabilities of a change, and whether we may not reasonably expect to be exchanged without passing the summer here. In his position he must know something in relation to our future. At the first favorable moment shall approach his highness. Prison is all the time being made stronger, more guards coming and artillery looking at us rather unpleasantly from many directions. Think it impossible for any to get away here, so far from our lines. The men too are not able to withstand the hardships attendant upon an escape, still fully one-half of all here are constantly on the alert for chances to get away. Foremost in all schemes for freedom is Hendryx, and we are engaging in a new tunnel enterprise. The Yankee is a curious animal, never quiet until dead. There are some here who pray and try to preach. Very many too who have heretofore been religiously inclined, throw off all restraint and are about the worst. Tried and found wanting it seems to me. Those who find the least fault, make the best of things as they come and grin and bear it, get along the best. Weather getting warmer, water warmer and nastier, food worse and less in quantities, and more prisoners coming nearly every day.

April 8.—We are digging with an old fire shovel at our tunnel. The shovel is a prize; we also use half of canteens, pieces of boards, &c. It's laborious work. A dozen are engaged in it. Like going into a grave to go into a tunnel. Soil light and liable to cave in. Take turns in digging. Waste dirt carried to the stream in small quantities and thrown in. Not much faith in the enterprise, but work with the rest as a sort of duty. Raiders acting fearful. Was boiling my cup of meal to-day and one of the raiders ran against it and over it went. Give him a whack side of the head that made him see stars I should judge, and in return he made me see the whole heavens. Battese, a big Indian, rather helped me out of the scrape. All of our mess came to my rescue. Came near being a big fight with dozens engaged. Battese is a large full-blooded six-foot Minnesota Indian, has quarters near us, and is a noble fellow. He and other Indians have been in our hundred for some weeks. They are quiet, attend to their own business, and

won't stand much nonsense. Great deal of fighting. One
Duffy, a New York rough, claims the light-weight champion-
ship of Andersonville. Regular battles quite often. Remarkable how men will stand up and be pummeled. Dr. Lewis
daily getting worse off. Is troubled with scurvy and dropsy.
If he was at home would be considered dangerously ill and
in bed, but he walks around slowly inquiring for news in a
pitiful way. I have probably fifty acquaintances here that visit
us each day to talk the situation over. Jimmy Devers, my
Michigan friend whom I found on Bell Isle, Sergt. Bullock,
of my regiment; Tom McGill, also of Michigan; Michael
Hoare, a schoolmate of mine from earliest recollection, Dorr
Blakeman, also a resident of Jackson, Michigan, a little fellow
named Swan, who lived in Ypsilanti, Mich.; Burckhardt from
near Lansing; Hub Dakin, from Dansville, Mich., and
many others, meet often to compare notes, and we have
many a hearty laugh in the midst of misery. I dicker and
trade and often make an extra ration. We sometimes draw
small cow peas for rations, and being a printer by trade, I
spread the peas out on a blanket and quickly pick them up
one at a time, after the manner of picking up type. One drawback is the practice of unconsciously putting the beans into
my mouth. In this way I often eat up the whole printing
office. I have trials of skill with a fellow named Land, who is
also a printer. There are no other typos here that I know of.

April 9.—See here Mr. Confederacy, this is going a little
too far. You have no business to kill us off at this rate. About
thirty or forty die daily. They have rigged up an excuse for
a hospital on the outside, where the sick are taken. Admit
none though who can walk or help themselves in any way.

Some of our men are detailed to help as nurses, but in a majority of cases those who go out on parole of honor are cut-throats and robbers, who abuse a sick prisoner. Still, there are exceptions to this rule. We hear stories of Capt. Wirtz's cruelty in punishing the men, but I hardly credit all the stories. More prisoners to-day. Some captured near Petersburg. Don't know anything about exchange. Scurvy and dropsy taking hold of the men. Many are blind as soon as it becomes night, and it is called moon blind. Caused, I suppose, by sleeping with the moon shining in the face. Talked with Michael Hoare, an old school fellow of mine. Mike was captured while we were in Pemerton Building, and was one of Dahlgreen's men. Was taken right in the suburbs of Richmond. Has told me all the news of their failure on account of Kilpatrick failing to make a junction at some point. Mike is a great tall, slim fellow, and a good one. Said he heard my name called out in Richmond as having a box of eatables from the North. He also saw a man named Shaw claim the box with a written order from me. Shaw was one of our mess on Belle Isle. He was sent to Richmond while sick, from the island, knew of my expecting the box, and forged an order to get it. Well, that was rough, still I probably wouldn't have got it any way. Better him than some rebel. Mike gave me a lot of black pepper which we put into our soup, which is a luxury. He has no end of talk at his tongue's end, and it is good to hear. Recounts how once when I was about eight or ten years old and he some older. I threw a base ball club and hit him on the shins. Then ran and he couldn't catch me. It was when we were both going to school to A. A. Henderson, in Jackson, Mich. Think I remember the incident, and am strongly under the impression that he caught me. It is thus that old friends meet after many years. John McGuire is also here, another Jackson man. He has a family at home and is worried. Says he used to frequently see my brother George at Hilton Head, before being captured.

April 10.—Getting warmer and warmer. Can see the trees swaying back and forth on the outside, but inside not a breath of fresh air. Our wood is all gone, and we are now digging up stumps and roots for fuel to cook with. Some of the first prisoners here have passable huts made of logs, sticks, pieces of blankets, &c. Room about all taken up in here now. Rations not so large. Talk that they intend to make the meal into bread before sending it inside, which will be an improvement. Rations have settled down to less than a pint of meal per day, with occasionally a few peas, or an apology for a piece of bacon, for each man. Should judge that they have hounds on the outside to catch run-aways, from the noise. Wirtz don't come in as much as formerly. The men make it uncomfortable for him. As Jimmy Devers says, "He is a terror." I have omitted to mention Jimmy's name of late, although he is with us all the time—not in our mess, but close by. He has an old pack of cards with which we play to pass away the time. Many of the men have testaments, and "house-wives" which they have brought with them from home, and it is pitiful to see them look at these things while thinking of their loved ones at home.

April 11.—Dr. Lewis is very bad off with the scurvy and diarrhea. We don't think he can stand it much longer, but make out to him that he will stick it through. Our government must hear of our condition here and get us away before long. If they don't, it's a poor government to tie to. Hendryx and myself are poor, as also are all the mess. Still in good health compared with the generality of the prisoners. Jimmy Devers has evidently sort of dried up, and it don't seem to make any difference whether he gets anything to eat or not. He has now been a prisoner of war nearly a year, and is in good health and very hopeful of getting away in time. Sticks up for our government and says there is some good reason for our continued imprisonment. I can see none. As many as 12,000 men here now, and crowded for room. Death rate is in the neighborhood of eighty per day. Hendryx prowls around all over the prison, bringing us what good news he can, which is not much. A very heavy dew nights, which is almost a rain. Rebels very domineering. Many are tunneling to get out. Our tunnel has been abandoned, as the location was not practicable. Yank shot to-day near our quarters. Approached too near the dead line. Many of the men have dug down through the sand and reached water, but it is poor; no better than out of the creek.

April 12.—Another beautiful but warm day with no news. Insects of all descriptions making their appearance, such as lizards, a worm four or five inches long, fleas, maggots, &c. There is so much filth about the camp that it is terrible trying to live here. New prisoners are made sick the first hours of their arrival by the stench which pervades the prison. Old prisoners do not mind it so much, having become used to it. No visitors come near us any more. Everybody sick, almost, with scurvy—an awful disease. New cases every day. I am afraid some contagious disease will get among us, and if so every man will die. My blanket a perfect Godsend. Is large and furnishes shelter from the burning sun. Hendryx has a very sore arm which troubles him much. Even he begins to look and feel bad. James Gordan, or Gordenian, (I don't know which) was killed to-day by the guard. In crossing the creek on a small board crossway men are often shot. It runs very near the dead line, and guards take the occasion to shoot parties who put their hands on the dead line in going across. Some also reach up under the dead line to get purer water, and are shot. Men seemingly reckless of their lives. New prisoners coming in and are shocked at the sights.

April 13.—Jack Shannon, from Ann Arbor, died this morning. The raiders are the stronger party now, and do as they please; and we are in nearly as much danger now from our own men as from the rebels. Capt. Moseby, of my own hundred, figures conspicuously among the robberies, and is a terrible villain. During the night some one stole my jacket. Have traded off all superfluous clothes, and with the loss of jacket have only pants, shirt, shoes, (no stockings,) and hat; yet I am well dressed in comparison with some others, many have nothing but an old pair of pants which reach, perhaps, to the knees, and perhaps not. Hendryx has two shirts, and should be mobbed. I do quite a business trading rations, making soup for the sick ones, taking in payment their raw food which they cannot eat. Get many a little snack by so doing.

April 14.—At least twenty fights among our own men this forenoon. It beats all what a snarling crowd we are getting to be. The men are perfectly reckless, and had just as soon have their necks broken by fighting as anything else. New onions in camp. Very small, and sell for $2 a bunch of four or five. Van Tassel, a Pennsylvanian, is about to die. Many give me parting injunctions relative to their families, in case I should live through. Have half a dozen photographs of dead men's wives, with addresses on the back of them. Seems to be pretty generally conceded that if any get through, I will. Not a man here now is in good health. An utter impossibility to remain well. Signs of scurvy about my person. Still adhere to our sanitary rules. Lewis anxious to get to the hospital. Will die any way shortly, whether there or here. Jimmy Devers, the old prisoner, coming down. Those who have stood it bravely begin to weaken.

April 15.—The hospital is a tough place to be in, from all accounts, the detailed Yankees as soon as they get a little authority are certain to use it for all it is worth. In some cases before a man is fairly dead, he is stripped of everything, coat, pants, shirt, finger rings (if he has any), and everything of value taken away. These the nurses trade to the guards. Does not seem possible but such is the case, sad to relate. Not very pleasant for a man just breathing his last, and perhaps thinking of loved ones at home who are all so unconscious of the condition of their soldier father or brother, to be suddenly jerked about and fought over, with the cursing and blaspheming he is apt to hear. The sick now, or a portion of them, are huddled up in one corner of the prison, to get as bad as they can before being admitted to the outside hospital. Every day I visit it, and come away sick at heart that human beings should be thus treated.

April 26.—Ten days since I wrote in my diary, and in those ten days was too much occupied in trying to dig a tunnel to escape out of, to write any. On the 21st the tunnel was opened and two fellows belonging to a Massachusetts regiment es-

caped to the outside. Hendryx and myself next went out. The
night was very dark. Came up out of the ground away on the
outside of the guard. We crawled along to gain the woods,
and get by some pickets, and when forty or fifty rods from the
stockade, a shot was fired at some one coming out of the
hole. We immediately jumped up and ran for dear life,
seemingly making more noise than a troop of cavalry. It was
almost daylight and away we went. Found I could not run
far and we slowed up, knowing we would be caught, but
hoping to get to some house and get something to eat first.
Found I was all broke up for any exertion. In an hour we had
traveled perhaps three miles, were all covered with mud, and
scratched up. I had fell, too, in getting over some logs, and it
seemed to me broken all the ribs in my body. Just as it was
coming light in the east we heard dogs after us. We expected
it, and so armed ourselves with clubs and sat down on a log.
In a few moments the hounds came up with us and began
smelling of us. Pretty soon five mounted rebels arrived on
the scene of action. They laughed to think we expected to
get away. Started us back towards our charnel pen. Dogs did
not offer to bite us, but guards told us that if we had offered
resistance or started to run they would have torn us. Arrived
at the prison and after waiting an hour Capt. Wirtz interviewed us. After cussing us a few minutes we were put in
the chain gang, where we remained two days. This was not
very fine, but contrary to expectation not so bad after all.
We had more to eat than when inside, and we had shade to
lay in, and although my ankles were made very sore, do not
regret my escapade. Am not permanently hurt any. We had
quite an allowance of bacon while out, and some spring water

to drink. Also from the surgeon I got some elderberries to steep into a tea to drink for scurvy, which is beginning to take hold of me. Lewis is sick and can hardly walk around. His days are few. Have taken another into our mess, named Swan, from Ypsilanti, Michigan. Is a fresh looking boy for this place and looks like a girl.

April 27.—Well, I was out from under rebel guard for an hour or so any way. Hurt my side though, and caught a little cold. Am sore somewhat. Have given up the idea of escaping. Think if Hendryx had been alone he would have gotten away. Is tougher than I am. A man caught stealing from one of his comrades and stabbed with a knife and killed. To show how little such things are noticed here, I will give the particulars as near as I could get them. There were five or six men stopping together in a sort of shanty. Two of them were speculators, and had some money, corn bread, &c., and would not divide with their comrades, who belonged to their own company and regiment. Some time in the night one of them got up and was stealing bread from a haversack belonging to his more prosperous neighbor, and during the operation woke up the owner, who seized a knife and stabbed the poor fellow dead. The one who did the murder spoke out and said: "Harry, I believe Bill is dead; he was just stealing from me and I run my knife into him." "Good enough for him," says Harry. The two men then got up and straightened out "Bill," and then both lay down and went to sleep. An occupant of the hut told me these particulars and they are true. This morning poor Bill lay in the hut until eight or nine oc'clock, and was then carried outside. The man who did the killing made no secret of it, but told it to all who wanted to know the particulars, who were only a few, as the occurrence was not an unusual one.

April 28.—Dr. Lewis is still getting worse with scurvy and dropsy combined. Limbs swollen to double their usual size—just like puff-balls. Raiders do about as they please, and their crimes would fill more paper than I have at my disposal.

April 30.—Very small rations given to us now. Not more than one quarter what we want to eat and that of the poorest quality. Splendid weather, but too warm; occasional rains. The Flying Dutchman (Wirtz) offers to give any two at a time twelve hours the start, and if caught to take the punishment he has for runaways. The offer is made to intimidate those thinking to escape. Half the men would take the consequences with two hours start.

May 1.—Warm. Samuel Hutton, of the 9th Mich. Cavalry, died last night; also Peter Christiancy and Joseph Sargent, of Co. D, 9th Mich., have died within a few weeks. Last evening 700 of the 85th New York arrived here. They were taken at Plymouth, N. C., with 1,400 others, making 2,100 in all. The balance are on the road to this place. Wrote a letter home to-day. Have not heard from the North for over six months. Dying off very fast.

May 2.—A crazy man was shot dead by the guard an hour ago. The guard dropped a piece of bread on the inside of the stockade, and the fellow went inside the dead line to get it and was killed. The bread wagon was raided upon as soon as it drove inside to-day and all the bread stolen, for which offense no more will be issued to-day. As I write Wirtz is walking about the prison revolver in hand, cursing and swearing. The men yell out "Hang him up!" "Kill the Dutch louse!" "Buck and gag him!" "Stone him to death!" &c., and he all the time trying to find out who it is insulting him so. "I vish I find out who calls me such insulting vords, I kill the dam Yankee as soon I eat my supper!" And, every few minutes a handful of dirt is thrown by some one. Wreaks his vengeance by keeping back rations from the whole camp.

May 3.—A rebel battery came to-day on the cars, and is being posted around the stockade. Ever since my introduction to Andersonville they have been constantly at work making their prison stronger, until now I believe it is impossible for a person to get away. Notwithstanding, there are men all the time at work in divers ways. Rebel officers now say that we are not going to be exchanged during the war, and as they can hold us now and no fear of escape, they had just as soon tell us the truth as not, and we must take things just as they see fit to give them to us. Tom McGill is well and hearty, and as black as any negro. Over 19,000 confined here now, and the death rate ninety or one hundred.

May 4.—Good weather. Gen. Howell Cobb and staff came among us to-day, and inspected the prison. Wirtz accompanied them pointing out and explaining matters. Gen. Winder, who has charge of all the prisoners of war in the South, is here, but has not been inside. Gen. Cobb is a very large and pompous looking man. None of the men dare address his highness. Three men out of every hundred allowed to go out after wood under a strong guard.

May 5.—Cold nights and warm days. Very unhealthy, such extremes. Small-pox cases carried out, and much alarm felt lest it should spread.

May 6.—Six months a prisoner to-day. Longer than any

GEORGE W. HENDRYX

six years of my previous life. It is wonderful how well I stand the hardships here. At home I was not very robust, in fact had a tendency to poor health; but there are not many in prison that stand it as well as I do. There are about eighty-five or ninety dying now per day, as near as I can find out. Of course there are stories to the effect that a hundred and fifty and two hundred die each day, but such is not the case. Have a code of reasoning that is pretty correct. Often wonder if I shall get home again, and come to the conclusion that I shall. My hopeful disposition does more for me than anything else. Sanders trades and dickers around and makes extra eatables for our mess. There is not a hog in the mess. Nearly every day some one is killed for some trifling offense, by the guards. Rather better food to-day than usual.

May 7.—A squad of Yankees taken outside to-day on parole of honor, for the purpose of baking meal into bread. George Hendryx is one of the number, and he will have enough to eat after this, which I am glad of. I could have gotten outside if I so chose, but curious to write down I don't want to go. George says he will try and send in something for us to eat, and I know he will, for a truer hearted fellow never lived.

May 8.—Awful warm and more sickly. About 3,500 have died since I came here, which is a good many, come to think of it—cooked rations of bread to-day. We get a quarter of a loaf of bread, weighing about six ounces, and four or five ounces of pork. These are small allowances, but being cooked it is better for us. Rebels are making promises of feeding us better, which we hope they will keep. There is nothing the matter with me now but lack of food. The scurvy symptoms which appeared a few weeks ago have all gone.

May 9.—Many rebels riding about camp on horseback. I listened to an animated conversation between an officer and two of our men. Mr. Rebel got talked all to pieces and hushed up entirely. He took it good naturedly, however, and for a wonder did not swear and curse us. It is a great treat to see a decent rebel. Am lonesome since Hendryx went outside. Men are continually going up to the dead line and getting shot. They do not get much sympathy, as they should know better.

May 10.—Capt. Wirtz very domineering and abusive. Is afraid to come into camp any more. There are a thousand men in here who would willingly die if they could kill him first. Certainly the worst man I ever saw. New prisoners coming in every day with good clothes, blankets, &c., and occasionally with considerable money. These are victims for the raiders who pitch into them for plunder. Very serious fights occur. Occasionally a party of new comers stick together and whip the raiders, who afterward rally their forces and the affair ends with the robbers victorious. Stones, clubs, knives, sling shots, &c., are used on these occasions, and sometimes the camp gets so stirred up that the rebels, thinking a break is intended, fire into the crowds gathered, and many are killed before quiet is again restored. Then Wirtz writes out an order and sends inside, telling he is prepared for any break, etc., etc. No less than five have died within a radius of thirty feet in the last twenty-four hours. Hendryx has a sore arm and in turning over last night I hurt it. He pitched in to me while I was in a sound sleep to pay me for it. Woke up in short order and we had it, rough and tumble. Tore down the tent poles—rolled around—scaring Lewis and all the rest. I am the stoutest, and soon get on top and hold him down, and keep him there until he quiets down, which is always in about five minutes. We have squabbles of this sort often, which don't do any particular harm. Always laugh, shake and make up afterwards. The Astor House Mess, or the heads rather, have gently requested that we do our fighting by daylight, and Sanders very forcibly remarked that should another scene occur as happened last night, he will take a hand in the business and lick us both. Battese laughed, for about the first time this summer. He has taken quite a shine to both Hendryx and myself. In the fore part of to-day's entry I should have stated that Hendryx has been sent inside, they not being quite ready for him at the cookhouse. He is a baker by trade.

May 11.—Rainy weather and cold nights. Men shiver and cry all night—groan and "holler." I lay awake sometimes for hours, listening to the guards yell out, "Post number one; ten o'clock and all's well!" And then Post No. 2 takes up the refrain, and it goes all around the camp, every one with a different sounding voice, squeaky, coarse, and all sorts. Some of them drawl out "H-e-r-e-'s y-e-r m-u-l-e!" and such like changes, instead of "All's well." Rumors of hard fighting about Richmond, and the rebels getting whipped, which of course they deny.

May 12.—Received a few lines from George Hendryx, who again went out to work on the outside last night. Wirtz with a squad of guards is about the camp looking for tunnels. Patrols also looking among the prisoners for deserters. A lame man, for telling of a tunnel, was pounded almost to death last night, and this morning they were chasing him to administer more punishment, when he ran inside the dead line claiming protection of the guard. The guard didn't protect worth a cent, but shot him through the head. A general hurrahing took place, as the rebel had only saved our men the trouble of killing him. More rumors of hard fighting about Richmond. Grant getting the best of it I reckon. Richmond surrounded and rebels evacuating the place. These are the rumors. Guards deny it.

May 13.—Rainy morning. We are guarded by an Alabama regiment, who are about to leave for the front. Georgia militia to take their places. Making preparations for a grand picnic outside, given by the citizens of the vicinity to the troops about to leave. I must here tell a funny affair that has happened to me, which, although funny is very annoying. Two or three days before I was captured I bought a pair of cavalry boots of a teamster named Carpenter. The boots were too small for him and just fitted me. Promised to pay him on "pay day," we not having been paid off in some time. We were both taken prisoners and have been in the same hundred ever since. Has dunned me now about 1,850 times, and has always been mad at not getting his pay. Sold the boots shortly after being captured and gave him half the receipts, and since that have paid him in rations and money as I could get it, until about sixty cents remain unpaid, and that sum is a sticker. He is my evil genius, and fairly haunts the life out of me. Whatever I may get trusted for in after life, it shall never be for a pair of boots. Carpenter is now sick with scurvy, and I am beginning to get the same disease hold of me again. Battese cut my hair which was about a foot long. Gay old cut. Many have long hair, which, being never combed, is matted together and full of vermin. With sunken eyes, blackened countenances from pitch pine smoke, rags and disease, the men look sickening. The air reeks with nastiness, and it is wonder that we live at all. When will relief come to us?

May 14.—A band of music from Macon yesterday to attend the picnic. A large crowd of women were present to grace the occasion. The grounds on which the festivities were held lay a mile off and in sight of all. In the evening a Bowery dance was one of the pleasures enjoyed. "The Girl I Left Behind Me," was about all they could play, and that very poorly.

May 15.—Sabbath day and hot. Would give anything for some shade to lay in. Even this luxury is denied us, and we are obliged to crawl around more dead than alive. Rumors that Sherman is marching towards Atlanta, and that place threatened. Kilpatrick said to be moving toward us for the purpose of effecting our release. Hope he will be more successful than in his attack on Richmond. Rebels have dug a deep ditch all around on the outside of the wall to prevent tunneling, and a guard walks in the bottom of the ditch. Banghart, of my Regiment, died to-day.

May 16.—Two men got away during the night and were brought back before noon. (Was going to say before dinner). The men are torn by the dogs, and one of them full of buck shot. A funny way of escape has just been discovered by Wirtz. A man pretends to be dead and is carried out on a stretcher and left with the row of dead. As soon as it gets dark, Mr. Dead-man jumps up and runs. Wirtz suspecting the trick took to watching, and discovered a "dead man" running away. An examination now takes place by the surgeon before being permitted out from under guard. I hear a number of men have gotten away by this method, and it seems very probable, as dead men are so plenty that not much attention is paid to them.

May 17.—Had a funny dream last night. Thought the rebels were so hard up for mules that they hitched up a couple of grayback lice to draw in the bread. Wirtz is watching out for Yankee tricks. Some one told him the other day that the Yankees were making a large balloon inside and some day would all rise up in the air and escape. He flew around as if mad, but could find no signs of a balloon. Says there is no telling what "te tam Yankee will do." Some prisoners came to-day who were captured at Dalton, and report the place in our possession, and the rebels driven six miles this side. Kilpatrick and Stoneman are both with Sherman and there are expectations of starting out on some mission soon, supposed to be for this place. Nineteen thousand confined here now and dying at the rate of ninety per day. Philo Lewis, of the 5th Michigan Cav., can live but a day or two. Talks continually of his wife and family in Ypsilanti, Mich. Has pictures of the whole family, which he has given me to take home to them, also a long letter addressed to his wife and children. Mr. Lewis used to be a teacher of singing in Ypsilanti. He is a fine looking man naturally, and a smart man, but he must go the way of thousands of others, and perhaps myself. One of his pupils is here confined. Philo Lewis must not be confounded with F. L. Lewis, the member of our mess. The latter, however, cannot live but a short time unless relief comes. Fine weather but very warm. The sandy soil fairly alive with vermin. If this place is so bad at this time of the year, what must it be in July, August and September? Every man will die, in my estimation, but perhaps we may be relieved before then. We'll try and think so anyway. New prisoners die off the fastest.

May 18.—We have some good singers in camp, and strange as it may seem, a good deal of singing is indulged in. There are some men that are happy as long as they can breathe, and such men smoothe over many rough places here. God bless a man who can sing in this place. A priest comes inside praying and chanting. A good man to come to such a place. Performs his duty the same to small-pox patients as to any other. Shall try and find out his name. Some of the wells dug by the Yanks furnish passable water, an improvement anyway on swamp water. Well water in great demand and sells readily for such trinkets as the men have to dispose of. Rebels building forts on the outside. Rebel officers inside trying to induce shoemakers, foundrymen, carpenters and wood choppers, to go out and work for the Confederacy. A very few accepted the offer. Well, life is sweet, and can hardly blame men for accepting the offer; still, I don't want to go, neither do ninety-nine out of every hundred. The soldiers here are loyal to the cause.

May 19.—Nearly twenty thousand men confined here now. New ones coming every day. Rations *very* small and *very* poor. The meal that the bread is made out of is ground, seemingly, cob and all, and it scourges the men fearfully. Things getting continually worse. Hundreds of cases of dropsy. Men puff out of human shape and are perfectly horrible to look at. Philo Lewis died to-day. Could not have weighed at the time of his death more than ninety pounds, and was originally a large man, weighing not less than one hundred and seventy. Jack Walker, of the 9th Mich. Cavalry, has received the appointment to assist in carrying out the dead, for which service he receives an extra ration of corn bread.

May 20.—Hendryx sent me in to-day from the outside a dozen small onions and some green tea. No person, on suddenly being lifted from the lowest depths of misery to peace and plenty, and all that money could buy, could feel more joyous or grateful than myself for those things. As the articles were handed in through the gate a crowd saw the transaction, and it was soon known that I had a friend on the outside who sent me in extras. I learn that a conspiracy is being gotten up on the outside, in which Hendryx is at the head, and they will try and overpower the guard and release the prisoners. If Capt. Wirtz only knew it, he has a very dangerous man in George Hendryx. Cram full of adventure, he will be heard from wherever he is.

May 21.—Still good weather and hot, with damp nights. Dr. Lewis lingers along in a miserable state of existence, and scurvy and dropsy doing their worst. His old messmates at the 9th Michigan regimental head-quarters little think of their favorite, story-telling, good fellows' condition now. We take as good care of him as possible under the circumstances. Two men shot to-day by the barbarians, and one of them has lain all the afternoon where he fell.

May 22.—No news of importance. Same old story. Am now a gallant washer-man. Battese, the Minnesota Indian, learn't me in the way of his occupation, made me a wash board by cutting creases in a piece of board, and I am fully installed. We have a sign out, made by myself on a piece of shingle: "WASHING." We get small pieces of bread for our labors, some of the sick cannot eat their bread, and not being able to keep clean, give us a job. Make probably a pound of bread two or three days in the week. Battese says: "I work, do me good; you do same." Have many applications for admission to the firm, and may enlarge the business.

May 23.—Rains very hard. Seems as if the windows of Heaven had opened up, in fact the windows out all together. It's a grand good thing for the camp, as it washes away the filth and purifies the air.

May 24.—Sherman coming this way, so said, towards Atlanta. It is thought the cavalry will make a break for us, but even if they do they cannot get us north. We are equal to no exertion. Men busy to-day killing swallows that fly low; partly for amusement, but more particularly for food they furnish. Are eaten raw before hardly dead. No, thank you, I will take no swallow.

May 25.—One thousand new prisoners came to-day from near Petersburg, Va. They give us encouraging news as to the termination of the spring campaign. Gen. Burnside said in a speech to his men that Petersburg would be taken in less than a month or Mrs. Burnside would be a widow. Every one hopeful. Getting warmer after the rain. Our squad has a very good well, and about one quarter water enough, of something a trifle better than swamp water. Man killed by the raiders near where we slept. Head all pounded to pieces with a club. Murders an every day occurrence.

May 26.—For the last three days I have had nearly enough to eat such as it is. My washing business gives me extra food. Have taken in a partner, and the firm now is Battese, Ransom

& Co. Think of taking in more partners, making Battese president, appointing vice presidents, secretaries, &c. We charge a ration of bread for admittance. Sand makes a very good soap. If we could get hold of a razor and open a barber shop in connection, our fortunes would be made. We are prolonging Lewis' life by trading for luxuries to give him. Occasionally a little real meat soup, with a piece of onion in it, etc. Am saving up capital to buy a pair of shears I know of. Molasses given us to-day, from two to four spoonfuls apiece, which is indeed a treat. Anything sweet or sour, or in the vegetable line, is the making of us. We have taken to mixing a little meal with water, putting in a little molasses and setting it in the sun to sour. Great trouble in the lack of vessels in which to keep it, and then too, after getting a dish partly well soured, some poor prisoner will deliberately walk up and before we can see him drink it all up. Men are fairly crazy for such things.

May 27.—We twist up pieces of tin, stovepipe, &c., for dishes. A favorite and common dish is half of a canteen. Our spoons are made of wood. Hardly one man in ten has a dish of any kind to put his rations of soup or molasses in, and often old shoes, dirty caps and the like are brought into requisition. Notwithstanding my prosperity in business the scurvy is taking right hold of me. All my old acquaintances visit us daily and we condole with one another. Fresh beef given us to-day, but in very small quantities with no wood or salt to put it into proper shape. No one can very well object to raw beef, however. Great trouble is in getting it to us before being tainted. I persistently let alone meat with even a suspicion of rottenness; makes no difference with nearly all here. We occasionally hear of the conspiracy of outside paroled Yankees. Time will tell if it amounts to anything.

May 28.—No more news. It really seems as if we're all to die here. My mouth getting sore from scurvy and teeth loose. New prisoners coming in every day and death rate increasing. I don't seem to get hardened to the situation and am shuddering all the time at the sights. Rainy weather.

May 29.—Sabbath day but not a pleasant one. Nearly a thousand just came in. Would seem to me that the rebels are victorious in their battles. New men are perfectly thunderstruck at the hole they have got into. A great many give right up and die in a few weeks, and some in a week. My limbs are badly swollen with scurvy and dropsy combined. Mouth also very sore. Battese digs for roots which he steeps up and I drink. Could give up and die in a short time but won't. Have got living reduced to a science.

May 30.—Another thousand came to-day and from the eastern army. Prison crowded. Men who came are from Siegel's corps in the Shenandoah Valley. The poor deluded mortals never heard of Andersonville before. Well, they hear of it now. Charlie Hudson, from some part of Ohio, took his canteen an hour ago and went to the swamp for water. He has not returned for the very good reason that he was shot while reaching up under the dead line to get the freshest water. Some one has pulled the body out of the water on to dry land where it will stay until to-morrow, when it will be piled with perhaps forty others on the dead wagon, carted off and buried like a dog. And this is the last of poor Charlie, who has enlivened us many an evening with his songs and stories. The Astor House Mess is very sad to-night.

May 31.—A rebel came inside to-day and enquired for me, in the tenth squad, first mess. I responded, wondering and fearful as to what they should want with me. Was happily surprised on going to the gate to see Hendryx with something in his hand for me. Seemed thunderstruck at my appearance and said I was looking bad. He was looking better than when he went out. Had brought me luxuries in the shape of ginger bread, onions and tea, and am happy. Geo. is a brick. Says it is against orders to send anything inside but he talked them over. Was afraid the raiders would waylay me before reaching the mess but they did not.

June 1.—Reported that the 51st Virginia Regt. is here for the purpose of conducting us north for exchange. Believe nothing of the kind. Prisoners come daily. E. P. Sanders, Rowe and myself carried our old friend Dr. Lewis to the hospital. He was immediately admitted and we came away feeling very sad, knowing he would live but a short time. The sick are not admitted until they are near death, and then there is no hope for them. Rainy day.

June 2.—Another dark, stormy day. Raiders playing the very devil. Muddy and sticky.

June 3.—New prisoners say that an armistice has been agreed upon for the purpose of effecting an exchange, and negotiating for peace. It may be so, and the authorities had good reasons for allowing us to stay here, but how can they pay for all the suffering? And now some negro prisoners brought inside. They belong to the 54th Massachusetts. Came with white prisoners. Many of the negroes wounded, as, indeed, there are wounded among all who come here now. No news from Hendryx or Lewis. Quite a number going out after wood to cook with. Hot and wet.

June 4.—Have not been dry for many days. Raining continually. Some men took occasion while out after wood, to overpower the guard and take to the pines. Not yet been brought back. *Very* small rations of poor molasses, corn bread and bug soup.

June 5.—Exchange rumors to the effect that transports are enroute for Savannah for the purpose of taking us home. Stick right to my washing however. A number of men taken out to be kept as hostages—so said. Raiders rule the prison. Am myself cross and feel like licking somebody, but Hendryx is gone and don't want to try to lick anybody else, fearing I might get licked myself. Some fun fighting him as it didn't make any difference which licked.

June 6.—Eight months a prisoner to-day. A lifetime has been crowded into these eight months. No rations at all. Am now a hair cutter. Have *hired* the shears. Enough to eat but not the right kind. Scurvy putting in its work, and symptoms of dropsy. Saw Hendryx at the bake house up stairs window, looking over the camp. Probably looking to see if he can locate his old comrades among the sea of human beings. Wirtz comes inside no more, in fact, does very few rebels. The place is too bad for them.

June 7.—Heard to-day that Hendryx had been arrested and in irons for inciting a conspiracy. Not much alarmed for him. He will come out all right. Still rainy. Have hard work keeping my diary dry. Nearly all the old prisoners who were captured with me are dead. Don't know of over 50 or 60 alive out of 800.

CHAPTER FIVE

From Bad to Worse

**The Astor House Mess Still Holds
Together, Although Depleted ✻ All More or
Less Diseased ✻ As the Weather Gets
Warmer the Death Rate Increases ✻ Dying Off
Like Sheep ✻ The End is Not Yet**

JUNE 8.—More new prisoners. There are now over 23,000 confined here, and the death rate 100 to 130 per day, and I believe more than that. Rations worse.

June 9.—It is said that a grand break will occur soon, and nearly the whole prison engaged in the plot. Spies inform the rebels of our intentions. Rains yet.

June 10.—The whole camp in a blaze of excitement. Plans for the outbreak known to Capt Wirtz. Some traitor unfolded the plans to him. Thirty or forty pieces of artillery pointed at us from the outside, and stockade covered with guards who shoot right and left. Thirty or forty outsiders sent inside, and they tell us how the affair was found out. A number of the ring leaders are undergoing punishment. Hendryx has made his escape, and not been heard of since yesterday. It is said he went away in full Confederate dress, armed, and furnished with a guide to conduct him. Dr. Lewis died to-day. Jack Walker told us about his death. Capt. Wirtz has posted up on the inside a notice for us to read. The following is the notice:

NOTICE

Not wishing to shed the blood of hundreds not connected with those who concocted a plan to force the stockade, and make in this way their escape. I hereby warn the leaders and those who formed themselves into a band to carry out this, that I am in possession of all the facts, and have made my arrangements accordingly, so to frustrate it. No choice would be left me but to open with grape and cannister on the stockade, and what effect this would have in this densely crowded place need not be told. Signed,

June 10, 1864.   H. WIRTZ.

June 11.—And so has ended a really colossal attempt at escape. George Hendryx was one of the originators of the plan. He took advantage of the excitement consequent upon its discovery and made good his escape and I hope will succeed in getting to our lines. It is the same old situation here only worse, and getting worse all the time. I am not very good at description, and find myself at fault in writing down the horrible condition we are in.

June 12.—Rained every day so far this month. A portion of the camp is a mud hole, and the men are obliged to lay down in it. Fort Pillow prisoners tell some hard stories against the Confederacy at the treatment they received after their capture. They came here nearly *starved to death,* and a good many were wounded after their surrender. They are mostly Tennesseans, and a "right smart sorry set." Battese has taken quite a fatherly interest in me. Keeps right on at the head of the washing and hair cutting business, paying no attention to anything outside of his work. Says: "We get out all right!"

June 13.—It is now as hot and sultry as it was ever my lot to witness. The cloudy weather and recent rains make everything damp and sticky. We don't any of us sweat though, particularly, as we are pretty well dried up. Laying on the ground so much has made sores on nearly every one here, and in many cases gangrene sets in and they are very bad off.

Have many sores on my body, but am careful to keep away the poison. To-day saw a man with a bullet hole in his head over an inch deep, and you could look down in it and see maggots squirming around at the bottom. Such things are terrible, but of common occurrence. Andersonville seems to be headquarters for all the little pests that ever originated—flies by the thousand millions. I have got into one bad scrape, and the one thing now is to get out of it. Can do nothing but take as good care of myself as possible, which I do. Battese works all the time at something. Has scrubbed his hands sore, using sand for soap.

June 14.—Mike Hoare stalks around, cheerful, black and hungry. We have long talks about our school days when little boys together. Mike is a mason by trade, and was solicited to go out and work for the rebels. Told them he would work on nothing but vaults to bury them in. Is a loyal soldier and had rather die here than help them, as, indeed, would a majority of the prisoners. To tell the truth, we are so near death and see so much of it, that it is not dreaded as much as a person would suppose. We stay here day after day, week after week, and month after month, seemingly forgotten by all our friends at the North, and then our sufferings are such that death is a relief in the view of a great many, and not dreaded to any extent. By four o'clock each day the row of dead at the gate would scare the life out of me before coming here, while now it is nothing at all, but the same thing over and over.

June 15.—I am sick: just able to drag around. My teeth are loose, mouth sore, with gums grown down in some places lower than the teeth and bloody, legs swollen up with dropsy and on the road to the trenches. Where there is so much to write about, I can hardly write anything. It's the same old story and must necessarily be repetition. Raiders now do just as they please, kill, plunder and steal in broad day light, with no one to molest them. Have been trying to organize a police force, but cannot do it. Raiders are the stronger party. Ground covered with maggots. Lice by the fourteen hundred thousand million infest Andersonville. A favorite game among the boys is to play at odd or even, by putting their hand inside some part of their clothing, pull out what they can conveniently get hold of and say "odd or even?" and then count up to see who beats. Think this is an original game here, never saw it at the North. Some of the men claim to have pet lice which they have trained. Am gradually growing worse. Nothing but the good care I have taken of myself has saved me thus far. I hope to last some time yet, and in the mean time relief may come. My diary about written through. It may end about the same time I do, which would be a fit ending.

June 16.—Old prisoners (some of them) will not credit the fact that there is plenty to eat at the North. They think because we are starved here, that it is so all over. They are crazy (as you may say) on the subject of food, and no wonder. In our dreams we see and eat bountiful repasts, and awake to the other extreme. Never could get a chance to talk with Capt. Wirtz, as he comes inside no more. Probably just as well. Is a thoroughly bad man, without an atom of humanity about him. He will get killed, should we ever be released, as there are a great many here who would consider it a Christian duty to rid the earth of his presence.

Disease is taking right hold of me now. Battese is an angel; takes better care of me than of himself. Although not in our mess or tent, he is nearly all the time with us. It is wonderful the powers of endurance he has. I have always been blessed with friends, and friends, too, of the right sort. Had quite a talk with Dorr Blakeman, a Jackson, Mich., boy. Was not much acquainted with him at home but knew his people. Is a thoroughly good fellow, and a sensible one. It is a relief to see any one who does not lose his head.

June 17.—Must nurse my writing material. A New York *Herald* in camp, which says an exchange will commence the 7th of July. Gen. Winder is on a visit to Andersonville. Is quite an aged man, and white haired. Very warm and almost suffocating. Seems as if the sun was right after us and belonged to the Confederacy. Chas. Humphrey, of Massachusetts, who has been in our hundred for months, has gone crazy; wanders about entirely naked, and not even a cap on his head. Many of the prisoners are crazy, and I only speak of those in our immediate proximity. Am in good spirits, notwithstanding my afflictions. Have never really thought yet that I was going to die in this place or in the Confederacy. Saw a new comer pounded to a jelly by the raiders. His cries for relief were *awful*, but none came. Must a few villains live at the expense of so many? God help us from these worse than rebels.

June 18.—Have now written two large books full; have another at hand. New prisoners who come here have diaries which they will sell for a piece of bread. No news to-day. Dying off as usual—more in numbers each day as the summer advances. Rebels say that they don't begin to have hot weather down here until about August. Well, it is plain to me that all will die. Old prisoners have stood it as long as they can, and are dropping off fast, while the new ones go anyhow. Some one stole my cap during the night. A dead neighbor furnished me with another, however. Fast as the men die they are stripped of their clothing so that those alive can be covered. Pretty hard, but the best we can do. Rebels are anxious to get hold of Yankee buttons. "Buttons with hens on," they enquire for. An insult to the American Eagle—but they don't know any better.

June 19.—A young fellow named Conely tramps around the prison with ball and chain on. His crime was trying to get away. I say he tramps around, he tramps away from the gate with it on at nine in the morning, and as soon as out of sight of the rebels he takes it off, and only puts it on at nine o'clock the next morning to report at the gate duly ironed off. They think, of course, that he wears it all the time. Jimmy Devers looks and is in a very bad way. Too bad if the poor fellow should die now, after being a prisoner almost a year. Talks a great deal about his younger brother in Jackson, named Willie. Says if he should die to be sure and tell Willie not to drink, which has been one of Jimmy's failings, and he sees now what a foolish habit it is. Michael Hoare stands it well. When a man is shot now it is called being "parolled."

June 20.—All the mess slowly but none the less surely succumbing to the diseases incident here. We are not what you may call hungry. I have actually felt the pangs of hunger more when I was a boy going home from school to dinner. But we are sick and faint and all broken down, feverish &c. It is starvation and disease and exposure that is doing it. Our stomachs have been so abused by the stuff called bread and soups, that they are diseased. The bread is coarse and musty. Believe that half in camp would die now if given rich food to eat.

June 21.—I am a fair writer, and am besieged by men to write letters to the rebel officers praying for release, and I do it, knowing it will do no good, but to please the sufferers. Some of these letters are directed to Capt. Wirtz, some to Gen. Winder, Jeff Davis and other officers. As dictated by them some would bring tears from a stone. One goes on to say he has been a prisoner of war over a year, has a wife and three children destitute, how much he thinks of them, is dying with disease, etc., etc. All kinds of stories are narrated, and handed to the first rebel who comes within reach. Of course they are never heard from. It's pitiful to see the poor wretches who think their letters will get them out, watch the gate from day to day, and always disappointed. Some one has much to answer for.

June 22.—The washing business progresses and is prosperous. One great trouble is, it is run too loose and we often get no pay. Battese, while a good worker, is no business man, and will do anybody's washing on promises, which don't amount to much. Am not able to do much myself, principally hanging out the clothes; that is, laying the shirt on one of the tent poles and then watching it till dry. All day yesterday I lay under the "coverlid" in the shade, hanging on to a string which was tied to the washing. If I saw a suspicious looking chap hanging around with his eyes on the washed goods, then gave a quick jerk and in she comes out of harm's way. Battese has paid for three or four shirts lost in this way, and one pair of pants. Pays in bread. A great many Irish here, and as a class, they stand hardships well. Jimmy Devers losing heart and thinks he will die. Capt. Wirtz has issued another order, but don't know what it is—to the effect that raiding and killing must be stopped, I believe. Being unable to get around as I used to, do not hear the particulars of what is going on, only in a general way. New men coming in, and bodies carried out. Is there no end but dying?

June 23.—My coverlid nobly does duty, protecting us from the sun's hot rays by day and the heavy dews at night. Have no doubt but it has saved my life many times. Never have heard anything from Hendryx since his escape. Either got away to our lines or shot. Rebels recruiting among us for men to put in their ranks. None will go—yes, I believe one Duffy has gone with them. Much fighting. Men will fight as long as they can stand up. A father fights his own son not ten rods from us. Hardly any are strong enough to do much damage except the raiders, who get enough to eat and are in better condition than the rest. Four or five letters were delivered to their owners. Were from their homes. Remarkable, as I believe this is the first mail since our first coming here. Something wrong. Just shake in my boots—shoes, I mean, (plenty of room) when I think what July and August will do for us. Does not seem to me as if any can stand it. After all, it's hard killing a man. Can stand most anything.

June 24.—Almost July 1st, when Jimmy Devers will have been a prisoner of war one year. Unless relief comes very soon he will die. I have read in my earlier years about prisoners in the revolutionary war, and other wars. It sounded noble and heroic to be a prisoner of war, and accounts of their adventures were quite romantic; but the romance has been knocked out of the prisoner of war business, higher than a kite. It's a fraud. All of the Astor House Mess now afflicted with scurvy and dropsy more or less, with the exception of Battese, and myself worst of any. Am fighting the disease, however, all the time, and the growth is but slight. Take exercise every morning and evening, when it is almost impossible for me to walk. Walk all over before the sun comes up, drink of Battese's medicine made of roots, keep clear of vermin, talk and even laugh, and if I do die, it will not be through neglect. Carpenter, the teamster who sold me the boots, is about gone, and thank the Lord he has received his sixty cents from me, in rations. Sorry for the poor fellow. Many who have all along stood it nobly now begin to go under. Wm. B. Rowe, our tall mess-mate, is quite bad off, still, he has an iron constitution, and will last some time yet.

June 25.—Another lead pencil wore down to less than an inch in length, and must skirmish around for another one. New men bring in writing material and pencils. To-day saw a New York *Herald* of date June 11th, nothing in it about exchange, however. That is all the news that particularly interests us, although accounts of recent battles are favorable to the Union side. Our guards are composed of the lowest element of the South—poor white trash. Very ignorant, much more so than the negro. Some of them act as if they never saw a gun before. The rebel adjutant does quite a business selling vegetables to those of the prisoners who have money, and has established a sutler stand not very far from our mess. Hub Dakin, an old acquaintance, is a sort of clerk, and gets enough to eat thereby. Hot! Hot! Raiders kill some one now every day. No restraint in the least. Men who were no doubt respectable at home, are now the worst villains in the world. One of them was sneaking about our quarters during the night, and Sanders knocked him about ten feet with a board. Some one of us must keep awake all the time, and on the watch, fearing to loose what little we have.

June 26.—The same old story, only worse, worse. It seems all the time it was as bad as could be, but is not. They die now like sheep—fully a hundred each day. New prisoners come inside in squads of hundreds, and in a few weeks are *all dead.* The change is too great and sudden for them. Old prisoners stand it the best. Found a Jackson, Michigan man, who says I am reported dead there. Am not, however, and may appear to them yet. Jimmy Devers is very bad with the scurvy and dropsy and will probably die if relief does not come. Sergt. Rowe also is afflicted; in fact all the mess except Battese. He does all the cooking now. He has made me a cane to walk with, brings water from the well, and performs nearly all the manual labor for us. He is a jewel, but a rough one.

June 27.—Raiders going on worse than ever before. A perfect pandemonium. Something must be done, and that quickly. There is danger enough from disease, without being killed by raiders. Any moment fifty or a hundred of them are liable to pounce upon our mess, knock right and left and take the very clothing off our backs. No one is safe from them. It is hoped that the more peacable sort will rise in their might and put them down. Our misery is certainly complete without this trouble added to it. We should die in peace anyway. Battese has called his Indian friends all together, and probably a hundred of us are banded together for self protection. The animal predominates. All restraint is thrown off and the very Old Harry is to pay. The farther advanced the summer, the death rate increases, until they die off by scores. I walk around to see friends of a few days ago and am told "dead." Men stand it nobly and are apparently ordinarily well, when all at once they go. Like a horse that will stand up until he drops dead. Some of the most horrible sights that can possibly be, are common every day occurrances. See men laying all around in the last struggles.

June 28.—It seems to me as if three times as many as ever before are now going off, still I am told that about one hundred and thirty die per day. The reason it seems worse, is because no sick are being taken out now, and they all die here instead of at the hospital. Can see the dead wagon loaded up with twenty or thirty bodies at a time, two lengths, just like four foot wood is loaded on to a wagon at the North, and away they go to the grave yard on a trot. Perhaps one or two will fall off and get run over. No attention paid to that; they are picked up on the road back after more. Was ever before in this world anything so terrible happening? Many entirely naked.

June 29.—Capt. Wirtz sent inside a guard of fifteen or twenty to arrest and take out quite a number of prisoners. They had the names and would go right to their quarters and take them. Some tell-tale traitor has been informing on them, for attempting to escape or something. Wirtz punishes very hard now; so much worse than a few months ago. Has numerous instruments of torture just outside the gate. Sores afflict us now, and the Lord only knows what next. Scurvy and scurvy sores, dropsy, not the least thing to eat that can be called fit for any one, much less a sick man, water that to drink is poison, no shelter, and surrounded by raiders liable to cut our throats any time. Surely, this is a go. Have been reading over the diary, and find nothing but grumbling and growlings. Had best enumerate some of the better things of this life. I am able to walk around the prison, although quite lame. Have black pepper to put in our soups. Am as clean perhaps as any here, with good friends to talk cheerful to. Then, too, the raiders will let us alone until about the last, for some of them will get killed when they attack the Astor House Mess. Am probably as well off as any here who are not raiders, and I should be thankful, and am thankful. Will live probably two or three months yet. "If t'weren't for hope the heart would break," and I am hopeful yet. A Pennsylvanian of German descent, named Van Tassel, and who has "sorter identified himself with us" for two or three months, died a few moments ago. The worst cases of the sick are again taken to the hospital—that is, a few of the worst cases. Many prefer to die among their friends inside. Henry Clayton also died to-day. Was at one time in charge of our Division, and an old prisoner. Mike Hoare still hangs on nobly, as also do many other of my friends and acquaintances. Dorr Blakeman stands it unusually well. Have had no meat now for ten days; nothing but one-third of a loaf of corn bread and half a pint of cow peas for each man, each day. Wood is entirely gone, and occasionally squads allowed to go and get some under guard. Rowe went out to-day, was not able to carry much, and that had to be divided between a hundred men. One of the most annoying things is being squadded over every few days, sick and all. It's an all day job, and have to stand out until we are all tired out, never getting any food on these days.

June 30.—A new prisoner fainted away on his entrance to Andersonville and is now crazy, a raving maniac. That is how our condition affected him. My pants are the worse for wear from repeated washings, my shirt sleeveless and feet stockingless; have a red cap without any front piece; shoes by some hocus-pocus are not mates, one considerable larger than the other. Wonder what they would think if I should suddenly appear on the streets in Jackson in this garb. Would be a circus; side show and all. But nights I have a grand old coverlid to keep off the wet. Raiders steal blankets and sell to the guards, which leaves all nearly destitute of that very necessary article. Often tell how I got my coverlid, to visitors. Have been peddling pea soup on the streets: "Ten cents in money or a dollar Confed for this rich soup! Who takes it?" And some wretch buys it. Anything in the way of food will sell, or water, if different from swamp water. Rebs making a pretense of fixing up sanitary privileges at the swamp, which amount to nothing. Strong talk of forming a police force to put down raiders and to enforce order. If successful it will prove of great benefit. Sanders, Rowe, Blakeman, Dakin and myself are among those who will take an active part, although the part I take cannot be very active. Half a dozen letters sent inside to prisoners, but no news in them that I can hear of. More hot and sultry, with occasional rains. The crazy man says nothing but "prayer" will save us. He has been sucking a bone now for about two weeks and pays more attention to that than to prayer.

July 1.—Matters must approach a crisis pretty soon with

the raiders. It is said that even the rebels are scared and think they will have no prisoners, should an exchange ever occur. John Bowen, a Corp. Christency, Hemmingway, Byron Goodsell and Pete Smith, old acquaintances, have all died within a few days. Jimmy Devers still lives, with wonderful tenacity to life. To-morrow he will have been a prisoner of war a year. Mike Hoare still keeps very well, but the most comical looking genius in the whole prison. Could make a fortune out of him on exhibition at the North. He says I look worse however. That may be, but not so comical. It's tragedy with the most of us. New guards are taking the place of the old ones, and it is said that Wirtz is going away. Hope so. Never have heard one word from Hendryx since his getting away. Sanders is trying to get outside as a butcher. He understands the business. "Dad" has been to Australia, and has told us all about that country. Have also heard all about Ireland and Scotland. Should judge they were fine countries. Rowe has been telling me of the advantage of silk underclothing, and in addition to visiting all the foreign countries, we shall have silk underwear. Rowe once lived in Boston, and I shall likewise go there.

July 2.—Almost the Glorious Fourth of July. How shall we celebrate? Know of no way except to pound on the bake tin, which I shall do. Have taken to rubbing my limbs, which are gradually become more dropsical. Badly swollen. One of my teeth came out a few days ago, and all are loose. Mouth very sore. Battese says: "We get away yet." Works around and always busy. If any news, he merely listens and don't say a word. Even he is in poor health, but never mentions it. An acquaintance of his says he owns a good farm in Minnesota.

Asked him if he was married—says: "Oh, yes." Any children? "Oh, yes." This is as far as we have got his history. Is very different from Indians in general. Some of them here are despisable cowards—worse than the negro. Probably one hundred negroes are here. Not so tough as the whites. Dead line being fixed up by the rebels. Got down in some places. Bought a piece of soap, first I have seen in many months. Swamp now in frightful condition from the filth of camp. Vermin and raiders have the best of it. Capt. Moseby still leads the villains.

CHAPTER SIX

The Raiders Put Down

**Andersonville on Its Metal * Leading
Raiders Arrested, Tried and Hung * Great
Excitement for a Few Days, Followed
by Good Order * Death Rate
Increases, However * The Astor House
Mess as Policemen**

JULY 3.—Three hundred and fifty new men from West Virginia were turned into this summer resort this morning. They brought good news as to successful termination of the war, and they also caused war after coming among us. As usual the raiders proceeded to rob them of their valuables and a fight occurred in which hundreds were engaged. The cut throats came out ahead. Complaints were made to Capt. Wirtz that this thing would be tolerated no longer, that these raiders must be put down or the men would rise in their might and break away if assistance was not given with which to preserve order. Wirtz flew around as if he had never thought of it before, issued an order to the effect that no more food would be given us until the leaders were arrested and taken outside for trial. The greatest possible excitement. Hundreds that have before been neutral and non-commital are now joining a police force. Captains are appointed to take charge of the squads which have been furnished with clubs by Wirtz. As I write, this middle of the afternoon, the battle rages. The police go right to raider headquarters knock right and left and make their arrests. Sometimes the police are whipped and have to retreat, but they rally their forces and again make a charge in which they are successful. Can lay in our shade and see the trouble go on. Must be killing some by the shouting. The raiders fight for their very life, and are only taken after being thoroughly whipped. The stockade is loaded with guards who are fearful of a break. I wish I could describe the scene to-day. A number killed. After each arrest a great cheering takes place. NIGHT.—Thirty or forty of the worst characters in camp have been taken outside, and still the good work goes on. No food to-day and don't want any. A big strapping fellow called Limber Jim heads the police. Grand old Michael Hoare is at the front and goes for a raider as quick as he would a rebel. Patrol the camp all the time and gradually quieting down. The orderly prisoners are feeling jolly.

July 4.—The men taken outside yesterday are under rebel guard and will be punished. The men are thoroughly aroused, and now that the matter has been taken in hand, it will be followed up to the letter. Other arrests are being made to-day, and occasionally a big fight. Little Terry, whom they could not find yesterday, was to-day taken. Had been hiding in an old well, or hole in the ground. Fought like a little tiger, but had to go. "Limber Jim" is a brick, and should be made a Major General if he ever reaches our lines. Mike Hoare is right up in rank, and true blue. Wm. B. Rowe also makes a good policeman, as does "Dad" Sanders. Battese says he "no time to fight, must wash." Jimmy Devers regrets that he cannot take a hand in, as he likes to fight, and especially with a club. The writer hereof does no fighting, being on the sick list. The excitement of looking on is most too much for me. Can hardly arrest the big graybacks crawling around. Capt. Moseby is one of the arrested ones. His right name is Collins and he has been in our hundred all the time since leaving Richmond. Has got a good long neck to stretch. Another man whom I have seen a good deal of, one Curtiss, is also arrested. I haven't mentioned poor little Bullock for months, seems to me. He was most dead when we first came to Andersonville, and is still alive and tottering around. Has lost his voice entirely and is nothing but a skeleton. Hardly enough of him for disease to get hold of. Would be one of the surprising things on record if he lives through it, and he seems no worse than months ago. It is said that a court will be formed of our own men to try the raiders. Any way, so they are punished. All have killed men, and they themselves should be killed. When arrested, the police had hard work to prevent their being lynched. Police more thoroughly organizing all the time. An extra amount of food this P. M., and police get extra rations, and three out of our mess is doing pretty well, as they are all willing to divide. They tell us all the encounters they have, and much interesting talk. Mike has some queer experiences. Rebel flags at half mast for some of their great men. Just heard that the trial of raiders will begin to-morrow.

July 5.—Court is in session outside and raiders being tried by our own men. Wirtz has done one good thing, but it's a question whether he is entitled to any credit, as he had to be threatened with a break before he would assist us. Rations again to-day. I am quite bad off with my diseases, but still there are so many thousands so much worse off that I do not complain much, or try not to however.

July 6.—Boiling hot, camp reeking with filth, and no sanitary privileges; men dying off over a hundred and forty per day. Stockade enlarged, taking in eight or ten more acres, giving us more room, and stumps to dig up for wood to cook with. Mike Hoare is in good health; not so Jimmy Devers. Jimmy has now been a prisoner over a year, and poor boy, will probably die soon. Have more mementoes than I can carry, from those who have died, to be given to their friends at home. At least a dozen have given me letters, pictures &c., to take North. Hope I shan't have to turn them over to some one else.

July 7.—The court was gotten up by our own men and from our own men; Judge, jury, counsel. &c. Had a fair trial, and were even defended, but to no purpose. It is reported that six have been sentenced to be hung, while a good many others are condemned to lighter punishment, such as setting in the stocks, strung up by the thumbs, thumb screws, head hanging, etc. The court has been severe, but just. Mike goes out to-morrow to take some part in the court proceedings. The prison seems a different place altogether; still, dread disease is here, and mowing down good and true men. Would seem to me that three or four hundred died each day, though officially but one hundred and forty odd is told. About twenty-seven thousand, I believe, are here now in all. No new ones for a few days. Rebel visitors, who look at us from a distance. It is said the stench keeps all away who have no business here and can keep away. Washing business good. Am negotiating for a pair of pants. Dislike fearfully to wear dead men's clothes, and haven't to any great extent.

July 8.—Oh, how hot, and oh, how miserable. The news that six have been sentenced to be hanged is true, and one of them is Moseby. The camp is thoroughly under control of the police now, and it is a heavenly boon. Of course there is some stealing and robbery, but not as before. Swan, of our mess, is sick with scurvy. I am gradually swelling up and growing weaker. But a few more pages in my diary. Over a hundred and fifty dying per day now, and twenty six thousand in camp. Guards shoot now very often. Boys, as guards, are the most cruel. It is said that if they kill a Yankee, they are given a thirty days furlough. Guess they need them as soldiers too much to allow of this. The swamp now is fearful, water perfectly reeking with prison offal and poison. Still men drink it and die. Rumors that the six will be hung inside. Bread to-day and it is so coarse as to do more hurt than good to a majority of the prisoners. The place still gets worse. Tunneling is over with; no one engages in it now that I know of. The prison is a success as regards safety; no escape except by death, and very many take advantage of that way. A man who has preached to us (or tried to) is dead. Was a good man I verily believe, and from Pennsylvania. It's almost impossible for me to get correct names to note down; the last named man was called "the preacher," and I can find no other name for him. Our quartette of singers a few rods away is disbanded. One died, one nearly dead, one a policeman and the other cannot sing alone, and so where we used to hear and enjoy good music evenings, there is nothing to attract us from the groans of the dying. Having formed a habit of going to sleep as soon as the air got cooled off and before fairly dark, I wake up at two or three o'clock and stay awake. I then take in all the horrors of the situation. Thousands are groaning, moaning and crying, with no bustle of the daytime to drown it. Guards every half hour call out the time and post, and there is often a shot to make one shiver as if with the ague. Must arrange my sleeping hours to miss getting owly in the morning. Have taken to building air castles of late, on being exchanged. Getting loony, I guess, same as all the rest.

July 9.—Battese brought me some onions, and if they ain't

good then no matter; also a sweet potato. One half the men here would get well if they only had something in the vegetable line to eat, or acids. Scurvy is about the most loathsome disease, and when dropsy takes hold with the scurvy, it is terrible. I have both diseases but keep them in check, and it only grows worse slowly. My legs are swollen, but the cords are not contracted much, and I can still walk very well. Our mess all keep clean, in fact are obliged to or else turned adrift. We want none of the dirty sort in our mess. Sanders and Rowe enforce the rules, which is not much work, as all hands are composed of men who prefer to keep clean. I still do a little washing, but more particularly hair cutting, which is easier work. You should see one of my hair cuts. Nobby! Old prisoners have hair a foot long or more, and my business is to cut it off, which I do without regards to anything except to get it off. I should judge that there are one thousand rebel soldiers guarding us, and perhaps a few more, with the usual number of officers. A guard told me to-day that the Yanks were "gittin licked," and they didn't want us exchanged; just as soon we should die here as not; a Yank asked him if he knew what exchange meant; said he knew what shootin' meant, and as he began to swing around his old shooting iron we retreated in among the crowd. Heard that there were some new men belonging to my regiment in another part of the prison; have just returned from looking after them and am all tired out. Instead of belonging to the 9th Michigan Cavalry, they belong to the 9th Michigan Infantry. Had a good visit and quite cheered with their accounts of the war news. Some one stole Battese's wash board and he is mad; is looking for it— may bust up the business. Think Hub Dakin will give me a board to make another one. Sanders owns the jack-knife, of this mess, and he don't like to lend it either; borrow it to carve on roots for pipes. Actually take solid comfort "building castles in the air," a thing I have never been addicted to before. Better than getting blue and worrying myself to death. After all, we may get out of this dod-rotted hole. Always an end of some sort to such things.

July 10.—Have bought of a new prisoner quite a large (thick I mean,) blank book so as to continue my diary. Although it's a tedious and tiresome task, am determined to keep it up. Don't know of another man in prison who is doing likewise. Wish I had the gift of description that I might describe this place. Know that I am not good at such things, and have more particularly kept track of the mess which was the Astor House Mess on Belle Isle, and is still called so here. Thought that Belle Isle was a very bad place, and used about the worst language I knew how to use in describing it, and so find myself at fault in depicting matters here as they are. At Belle Isle we had good water and plenty of it, and I believe it depends more upon water than food as regards health. We also had good pure air from up the James River. Here we have the very worst kind of water. Nothing can be worse or nastier than the stream drizzling its way through this camp. And for air to breathe, it is what arises from this foul place. On all four sides of us are high walls and tall trees, and there is apparently no wind or breeze to blow away the stench, and we are obliged to breathe and live in it. Dead bodies lay around all day in the broiling sun, by the dozen and even hundreds, and we must suffer and live in this atmosphere. It's too horrible for me to describe in fitting language. There was once a very profane man driving a team of horses attached to a wagon in which there were forty or fifty bushels of potatoes. It was a big load and there was a long hill to go up. The very profane man got off the load of potatoes to lighten the weight, and started the team up the hill. It was hard work, but they finally reached the top and stopped to rest. The profane man looked behind him and saw that the end board of the wagon had slipped out just as he had started, and there the potatoes were, scattered all the way along up the hill. Did the man make the very air blue with profanity? No, he sat down on a log feeling that he couldn't do the subject justice and so he remarked: "No! it's no use, I can't do it justice." While I have no reason or desire to swear, I certainly cannot do this prison justice. It's too stupendous an undertaking. Only those who are here will ever know what Andersonville is.

AN ACCOUNT OF THE HANGING

July 11.—This morning lumber was brought into the prison by the rebels, and near the gate a *gallows* erected for the purpose of executing the six condemned Yankees. At about ten o'clock they were brought inside by Capt. Wirtz and some guards, and delivered over to the police force. Capt. Wirtz then said a few words about their having been tried by our own men and for us to do as we choose with them, that he washed his hands of the whole matter, or words to that effect. I could not catch the exact language, being some little distance away. I have learned by enquiry, their names, which are as follows: John Sarsfield, 144th New York; Wil-

liam Collins, alias "Moseby," Co. D, 88th Pennsylvania;
Charles Curtiss, Battery A, 5th Rhode Island Artillery; Pat
Delaney, Co. E, 83d Pennsylvania; A. Munn, U. S. Navy,
and W. R. Rickson of the U. S. Navy. After Wirtz made
his speech he withdrew his guards, leaving the condemned
at the mercy of 28,000 enraged prisoners who had all been
more or less wronged by these men. Their hands were tied behind them, and one by one they mounted the scaffold. Curtiss,
who was last, a big stout fellow, managed to get his hands
loose and broke away and ran through the crowd and down
toward the swamp. It was yelled out that he had a knife in
his hand, and so a path was made for him. He reached the
swamp and plunged in, trying to get over on the other side,
presumably among his friends. It being very warm he over
exerted himself, and when in the middle or thereabouts, col-
lapsed and could go no farther. The police started after him,
waded in and helped him out. He pleaded for water and it
was given him. Then led back to the scaffold and helped to
mount up. All were given a chance to talk. Munn, a good
looking fellow in marine dress, said he came into the prison
four months before perfectly honest, and as innocent of
crime as any fellow in it. Starvation, with evil companions,
had made him what he was. He spoke of his mother and
sisters in New York, that he cared nothing as far as he
himself was concerned, but the news that would be carried
home to his people made him want to curse God he had ever
been born. Delaney said he would rather be hung than live
here as the most of them lived, on their allowance of rations.
If allowed to steal could get enough to eat, but as that was
stopped had rather hang. Bid all good bye. Said his name

was not Delaney and that no one knew who he really was, therefore his friends would never know his fate, his Andersonville history dying with him. Curtiss said he didn't care a — only hurry up and not be talking about it all day; making too much fuss over a very small matter. William Collins alias Moseby, said he was innocent of murder and ought not to be hung; he had stolen blankets and rations to preserve his own life, and begged the crowd not to see him hung as he had a wife and child at home, and for their sake to let him live. The excited crowd began to be impatient for the "show" to commence as they termed it. Sarsfield made quite a speech; he had studied for a lawyer; at the outbreak of the rebellion he had enlisted and served three years in the army, been wounded in battle, furloughed home, wound healed up, promoted to first sergeant and also commissioned; his commission as a lieutenant had arrived but had not been mustered in when he was taken prisoner; began by stealing parts of rations, gradually becoming hardened as he became familiar with the crimes practiced; evil associates had helped him to go down hill and here he was. The other did not care to say anything. While the men were talking they were interrupted by all kinds of questions and charges made by the crowd, such as "don't lay it on too thick, you villain," "get ready to jump off," "cut it short," "you was the cause of so and so's death," "less talk and more hanging," &c., &c. At about eleven o'clock they were all blindfolded, hands and feet tied, told to get ready, nooses adjusted and the plank knocked from under. Moseby's rope broke and he fell to the ground, with blood spurting from his ears, mouth and nose. As they was lifting him back to the swinging off place he revived and begged for his life, but no use, was soon dangling with the rest, and died very hard. Munn died easily, as also did Delaney, all the rest died hard and particularly Sarsfield who drew his knees nearly to his chin and then straightened them out with a jerk, the veins in his neck swelling out as if they would burst. It was an awful sight to see, still a necessity. Moseby, although he said he had never killed any one, and I don't believe he ever did deliberately kill a man, such as stabbing or pounding a victim to death, yet he has walked up to a poor sick prisoner on a cold night and robbed him of blanket, or perhaps his rations and if necessary using all the force necessary to do it. These things were the same as life to the sick man, for he would invariably die. The result has been that many have died from his robbing propensities. It was right that he should hang, and he did hang most beautifully and Andersonville is the better off for it. None of the rest denied that they had killed men, and probably some had murdered dozens. It has been a good lesson; there are still bad ones in camp but we have the strong arm of the law to keep them in check. All during the hanging scene the stockade was covered with rebels, who were fearful a break would be made if the raiders should try and rescue them. Many citizens too were congregated on the outside in favorable positions for seeing. Artillery was pointed at us from all directions, ready to blow us all into eternity in short order; Wirtz stood on a high platform in plain sight of the execution and says we are a hard crowd to kill our own men. After hanging for half an hour or so the six bodies were taken down and carried outside. In noting down the speeches made by the condemned men, have used my own language; in substance it is the same as told by them. I occupied a near position to the hanging and saw it all from first to last, and stood there until they were taken down and carried away. Was a strange sight to see and the first hanging I ever witnessed. The raiders had many friends who crowded around and denounced the whole affair and but for the police there would have been a riot; many both for and against the execution were knocked down. Some will talk and get into trouble thereby; as long as it does no good there is no use in loud talk and exciting arguments; is dangerous to advance any argument, men are so ready to quarrel. Have got back to my quarters thoroughly prostrated and worn out with fatigue and excitement, and only hope that to-day's lesson will right matters as regards raiding. Battese suspended washing long enough to look on and see them hang and grunted his approval. Have omitted to say that the good Catholic priest attended the condemned. Rebel negroes came inside and began to take down the scaffold; prisoners took hold to help them and resulted in its all being carried off to different parts of the prison to be used for kindling wood, and the rebels get none of it back and are mad. The ropes even have been gobbled up, and I suppose sometime may be exhibited at the north as mementoes of to-day's proceedings. Mike Hoare assisted at the hanging. Some fears are entertained that those who officiated will get killed by the friends of those hanged. The person who manipuated the "drop," has been taken outside on parole of honor, as his life would be in danger in here. Jimmy thanks God that he has lived to see justice done the raiders; he is about gone—nothing but skin and bone and can hardly move hand or foot; rest of the mess moderately well. The extra rations derived from our three mess-mates as policemen, helps wonderfully to prolong life. Once in a while some of them gets a chance to go outside on some duty and buy onions or sweet potatoes which is a great luxury.

July 12.—Good order has prevailed since the hanging. The men have settled right down to the business of dying, with no interruption. I keep thinking our situation can get no worse, but it does get worse every day and not less than one hundred and sixty die each twenty-four hours. Probably one-fourth or one-third of these die inside the stockade, the balance in the hospital outside. All day and up to four o'clock P. M., the dead are being gathered up and carried to the south gate and placed in a row inside the dead line. As the bodies are stripped of their clothing in most cases as soon as the breath leaves, and in some cases before, the row of dead presents a sickening appearance. Legs drawn up and in all shapes. They are black from pitch pine smoke and laying in the sun. Some of them lay there for twenty hours or more, and by that time are in a horrible condition. At four o'clock a four or six mule wagon comes up to the gate and twenty or thirty bodies are loaded on to the wagon and they are carted off to be put in trenches, one hundred in each trench, in the cemetery, which is eighty or a hundred rods away. There must necessarily be a great many whose names are not taken. It is the orders to attach the name, company and regiment to each body, but it is not always done. I was invited to-day to dig in a tunnel, but had to decline. My digging days are over. Must dig now to keep out of the ground, I guess. It is with difficulty now that I can walk, and only with the help of two canes.

July 13.—Can see in the distance the cars go poking along

by this station, with wheezing old engines, snorting along. As soon as night comes a great many are blind, caused by sleeping in the open air, with moon shining in the face. Many holes are dug and excavations made in camp. Near our quarters is a well about five or six feet deep, and the poor blind fellows fall into this pit hole. None seriously hurt, but must be quite shaken up. Half of the prisoners have no settled place for sleeping, wander and lay down wherever they can find room. Have two small gold rings on my finger, worn ever since I left home. Have also a small photograph album with eight photographs in. Relics of civilization. Should I get these things through to our lines they will have quite a history. When I am among the rebels I wind a rag around my finger to cover up the rings, or else take them and put in my pocket. Bad off as I have been, have never seen the time yet that I would part with them. Were presents to me, and the photographs have looked at about one-fourth of the time since imprisonment. One prisoner made some buttons here for his little boy at home, and gave them to me to deliver, as he was about to die. Have them sewed on to my pants for safe keeping.

July 14.—We have been too busy with the raiders of late to manufacture any exchange news, and now all hands are at work trying to see who can tell the biggest yarns. The weak are feeling well to-night over the story that we are all to be sent North this month, before the 20th. Have not learned that the news came from any reliable source. Rumors of midsummer battles with Union troops victorious. It's "bite dog, bite bear," with most of us prisoners; we don't care which licks, what we want is to get out of this pen. Of course, we all care

EXECUTION OF UNION PRISONERS BY THE REGULATORS

and want our side to win, but it's tough on patriotism. A court is now held every day and offenders punished, principally by buck and gagging, for misdemeanors. The hanging has done worlds of good, still there is much stealing going on yet, but in a sly way, not openly. Hold my own as regards health. The dreaded month of July is half gone, almost, and a good many over one hundred and fifty die each day, but I do not know how many. Hardly any one cares enough about it to help me any in my inquiries. It is all self with the most of them. A guard by accident shot himself. Have often said they didn't know enough to hold a gun. Bury a rebel guard every few days within sight of the prison. Saw some women in the distance. Quite a sight. Are feeling quite jolly to-night since the sun went down. Was visited by my new acquaintances of the 9th Michigan Infantry, who are comparatively new prisoners. Am learning them the way to live here. They are very hopeful fellows and declare the war will be over this coming fall, and tell their reasons very well for thinking so. We gird up our loins and decide that we will try to live it through. Rowe, although often given to despondency, is feeling good and cheerful. There are some noble fellows here. A man shows exactly what he is in Andersonville. No occasion to be any different from what you really are. Very often see a great big fellow in size, in reality a baby in action, actually sniveling and crying, and then again you will see some little runt, "not bigger than a pint of cider," tell the big fellow to "brace up" and be a man. Stature has nothing to do as regards nerve, still there are noble big fellows as well as noble little ones. A Sergt. Hill is judge and jury now, and dispenses justice to evil doers with impartiality. A farce is made of defending some of the arrested ones. Hill inquires all of the particulars of each case, and sometimes lets the offenders go as more sinned against than sinning. Four receiving punishment.

July 15.—Blank cartridges were this morning fired over the camp by the artillery, and immediately the greatest commotion outside. It seems that the signal in case a break is made, is cannon firing. And this was to show us how quick they could rally and get into shape. In less time than it takes for me to write it, all were at their posts and in condition to open up and kill nine-tenths of all here. Sweltering hot. Dying off one hundred and fifty-five each day. There are twenty-eight thousand confined here now.

July 16.—Well, who ever supposed that it could be any hotter; but to-day is more so than yesterday, and yesterday more than the day before. My coverlid has been rained on so much and burned in the sun, first one and then the other, that it is getting the worse for wear. It was originally a very nice one, and home made. Sun goes right through it now, and reaches down for us. Just like a bake oven. The rabbit mules that draw in the rations look as if they didn't get much more to eat than we do. Driven with one rope line, and harness patched up with ropes, strings, &c. Fit representation of the Confederacy. Not much like U. S. Army teams. A joke on the rebel adjutant has happened. Some one broke into the shanty and tied the two or three sleeping there, and carried off all the goods. Tennessee Bill, (a fellow captured with me) had charge of the affair, and is in disgrace with the adjutant on account of it. Every one is glad of the robbery. Probably there was not ten dollars worth of things in there, but they asked outrageous prices for everything. Adjt. very mad, but no good. Is a small, sputtering sort of fellow.

July 17.—Cords contracting in my legs and very difficult for me to walk—after going a little ways have to stop and rest and am faint. Am urged by some to go to the hospital but don't like to do it; mess say had better stay where I am, and Battese says shall not go, and that settles it. Jimmy Devers anxious to be taken to the hospital but is pursuaded to give it up. Tom McGill, another Irish friend, is past all recovery; is in another part of the prison. Many old prisoners are dropping off now this fearful hot weather; knew that July and August would thin us out; cannot keep track of them in my disabled condition. A fellow named Hubbard with whom I have conversed a good deal, is dead; a few days ago was in very good health, and it's only a question of a few days now with any of us. Succeeded in getting four small onions about as large as hickory nuts, tops and all for two dollars Confederate money. Battese furnished the money but won't eat an onion; ask him if he is afraid it will make his breath smell? It is said that two or three onions or a sweet potato eaten raw daily will cure the scurvy. What a shame that such things are denied us, being so plenty the world over. Never appreciated such things before but shall hereafter. Am talking as if I expected to get home again. I do.

July 18.—Time slowly dragging itself along. Cut some wretches's hair most every day. Have a sign out "Hair Cutting," as well as "Washing," and by the way, Battese has a new wash board made from a piece of the scaffold lumber. About half the time do the work for nothing, in fact not more than one in three or four pays anything—expenses not much though, don't have to pay any rent. All the mess keeps their hair cut short which is a very good advertisement. My eyes getting weak with other troubles. Can just hobble around. Death rate more than ever, reported one hundred and sixty-five per day; said by some to be more than that, but 165 is about the figure. Bad enough without making any worse than it really is. Jimmy Devers most dead and begs us to take him to the hospital and guess will have to. Every morning the sick are carried to the gate in blankets and on stretchers, and the worst cases admitted to the hospital. Probably out of five or six hundred half are admitted. Do not think any lives after being taken there; are past all human aid. Four out of every five prefer to stay inside and die with their friends rather than go to the hospital. Hard stories reach us of the treatment of the sick out there and I am sorry to say the cruelty emanates from our own men who act as nurses. These dead beats and bummer nurses are the same bounty jumpers the U. S. authorities have had so much trouble with. Do not mean to say that all the nurses are of that class but a great many of them are.

July 19.—There is no such thing as delicacy here. Nine out of ten would as soon eat with a corpse for a table as any other way. In the middle of last night I was awakened by being kicked by a dying man. He was soon dead. In his struggles he had floundered clear into our bed. Got up and moved the body off a few feet, and again went to sleep to dream of the hideous sights. I can never get used to it as some do. Often wake most scared to death, and shuddering from head to foot. Almost dread to go to sleep on this account. I am getting worse and worse, and prison ditto.

July 20.—Am troubled with poor sight together with

scurvy and dropsy. My teeth are all loose and it is with difficulty I can eat. Jimmy Devers was taken out to die to-day. I hear that McGill is also dead. John McGuire died last night, both were Jackson men and old acquaintances. Mike Hoare is still policeman and is sorry for me. Does what he can. And so we have seen the last of Jimmy. A prisoner of war one year and eighteen days. Struggled hard to live through it, if ever any one did. Ever since I can remember have known him. John Maguire also, I have always known. Everybody in Jackson, Mich., will remember him, as living on the east side of the river near the wintergreen patch, and his father before him. They were one of the first families who settled that country. His people are well-to-do, with much property. Leaves a wife and one boy. Tom McGill is also a Jackson boy and a member of my own company. Thus you will see that three of my acquaintances died the same day, for Jimmy cannot live until night I don't think. Not a person in the world but would have thought either one of them would kill me a dozen times enduring hardships. Pretty hard to tell about such things. Small squad of poor deluded Yanks turned inside with us, captured at Petersburg. It is said they talk of winning recent battles. Battese has traded for an old watch and Mike will try to procure vegetables for it from the guard. That is what will save us if anything.

July 21.—And rebels are still fortifying. Battese has his hands full. Takes care of me like a father. Hear that Kilpatrick is making a raid for this place. Troops (rebel) are arriving here by every train to defend it. Nothing but corn bread issued now and I cannot eat it any more.

July 22.—A petition is gotten up signed by all the sergeants in the prison, to be sent to Washington, D. C., *begging* to be released. Capt. Wirtz has consented to let three representatives go for that purpose. Rough that it should be necessary for us to *beg* to be protected by our government.

July 23.—Reports of an exchange in August. Can't stand it till that time. Will soon go up the spout.

July 24.—Have been trying to get into the hospital, but Battese won't let me go. Geo. W. Hutchins, brother of Charlie Hutchins of Jackson, Mich., died to-day—from our mess. Jimmy Devers is dead.

July 25.—Rowe getting very bad. Sanders ditto. Am myself much worse, and cannot walk, and with difficulty stand up. Legs drawn up like a triangle, mouth in terrible shape, and dropsy worse than all. A few more days. At my earnest solicitation was carried to the gate this morning, to be admitted to the hospital. Lay in the sun for some hours to be examined, and finally my turn came and I tried to stand up, but was so excited I fainted away. When I came to myself I lay along with the row of dead on the outside. Raised up and asked a rebel for a drink of water, and he said: "Here, you Yank, if you ain't dead, get inside there!" And with his help was put inside again. Told a man to go to our mess and tell them to come to the gate, and pretty soon Battese and Sanders came and carried me back to our quarters; and here I am, completely played out. Battese flying around to buy me something good to eat. Can't write much more. Exchange rumors.

July 26.—Ain't dead yet. Actually laugh when I think of the rebel who thought if I wasn't dead I had better get inside. Can't walk a step now. Shall try for the hospital no more. Had an onion.

July 27.—Sweltering hot. No worse than yesterday. Said that two hundred die now each day. Rowe very bad and Sanders getting so. Swan dead, Gordon dead, Jack Withers dead, Scotty dead, a large Irishman who has been near us a long time is dead. These and scores of others died yesterday and day before. Hub Dakin came to see me and brought an onion. He is just able to crawl around himself.

July 28.—Taken a step forward toward the trenches since yesterday, and am worse. Had a wash all over this morning. Battese took me to the creek; carries me without any trouble.

July 29.—Alive and kicking. Drank some soured water made from meal and water.

July 30.—Hang on well, and no worse.

CHAPTER SEVEN

Moved Just in Time

**Removed from Andersonville to the
Marine Hospital, Savannah * Getting Through
the Gate * Battese has Saved Us *
Very Sick, But by no Means Dead Yet *
Better and Humane Treatment**

AUG. 1.—Just about the same. My Indian friend says: "We all get away."

Aug. 2.—Two hundred and twenty die each day. No more news of exchange.

Aug. 3.—Had some good soup, and feel better. All is done for me that can be done by my friends. Rowe and Sanders in almost as bad a condition as myself. Just about where I was two or three weeks ago. Seem to have come down all at once. August goes for them.

Aug. 4.—Storm threatened. Will cool the atmosphere. Hard work to write.

Aug. 5.—Severe storm. Could die in two hours if I wanted to, but don't.

Aug. 12.—Warm. Warm. Warm. If I only had some shade to lay in, and a glass of lemonade.

Aug. 13.—A nice spring of cold water has broken out in camp, enough to furnish nearly all here with drinking water. God has not forgotten us. Battese brings it to me to drink.

Aug. 14.—Battese very hopeful, as exchange rumors are afloat. Talks more about it than ever before.

Aug. 15.—The water is a God-send. Sanders better and Rowe worse.

Aug. 16.—Still in the land of the living. Capt. Wirtz is sick and a Lieut. Davis acting in his stead.

Aug. 17.—Hanging on yet. A good many more than two hundred and twenty-five die now in twenty-four hours. Messes that have stopped near us are all dead.

Aug. 18.—Exchange rumors.

Aug. 19.—Am still hoping for relief. Water is bracing some up, myself with others. Does not hurt us.

Aug. 20.—Some say three hundred now die each day. No more new men coming. Reported that Wirtz is dead.

Aug. 21.—Sleep nearly all the time except when too hot to do so.

Aug. 22.—Exchange rumors.

Aug. 23.—Terribly hot.

Aug. 24.—Had some soup. Not particularly worse, but Rowe is, and Sanders also.

Aug. 25.—In my exuberance of joy must write a few lines. Received a letter from my brother, George W. Ransom, from Hilton Head.* Contained only a few words.

Aug. 26.—Still am writing. The letter from my brother has done good and cheered me up. Eye sight very poor and writing tires me. Battese sticks by; such disinterested friendship is rare. Prison at its worst.

Aug. 27.—Have now written nearly through three large books, and still at it. The diary am confident will reach my people if I don't. There are many here who are interested and will see that it goes North.

Aug. 28.—No news and no worse; set up part of the time. Dying off a third faster than ever before.

Aug. 29.—Exchange rumors afloat. Any kind of a change would help me.

Aug. 30.—Am in no pain whatever, and no worse.

Aug. 31.—Still waiting for something to turn up. My In-

* My brother supposed me dead, as I had been so reported; still, thinking it might not be so, every week or so he would write a letter and direct to me as a prisoner of war. This letter, very strangely, reached its destination.

dian friend says: "good news yet." Night.—The camp is full of exchange rumors.

Sept. 1.—Sanders taken outside to butcher cattle. Is sick but goes all the same. Mike sick and no longer a policeman. Still rumors of exchange.

Sept. 2.—Just about the same; rumors afloat does me good. Am the most hopeful chap on record.

Sept. 3.—Trade of my rations for some little luxury and manage to get up quite a soup. Later.—Sanders sent in to us a quite large piece of fresh beef and a little salt; another Godsend.

Sept. 4.—Anything good to eat lifts me right up, and the beef soup has done it.

Sept. 4.—The beef critter is a noble animal. Very decided exchange rumors.

Sept. 5.—The nice spring of cold water still flows and furnishes drinking water for all; police guard it night and day so to be taken away only in small quantities. Three hundred said to be dying off each day.

Sept. 6.—Hurrah! Hurrah!! Hurrah!!! Can't holler except on paper. Good news. Seven detachments ordered to be ready to go at a moment's notice. Later.—*All who cannot walk must stay behind.* If left behind shall die in twenty-four hours. Battese says *I shall go.* Later.—Seven detachments are going out of the gate; all the sick are left behind. Ours is the tenth detachment and will go to-morrow so said. The greatest excitement; men wild with joy. Am worried fearful that I cannot go, but Battese says I shall.

Sept. 7.—Anxiously waiting the expected summons. Rebels say as soon as transportation comes, and so a car whistle is music to our ears. Hope is a good medicine and am sitting up and have been trying to stand up but can't do it; legs too crooked and with every attempt get faint. Men laugh at the idea of my going, as the rebels are very particular not to let any sick go, still Battese say I am going. MOST DARK.— Rebels say we go during the night when transportation comes. Battese grinned when this news came and can't get his face straightened out again.

MARINE HOSPITAL, SAVANNAH, GA., *Sept. 15, 1864.*—A great change has taken place since I last wrote in my diary. Am in heaven now compared with the past. At about midnight, September 7th, our detachment was ordered outside at Andersonville, and Battese picked me up and carried me to the gate. The men were being let outside in ranks of four, and counted as they went out. They were very strict about letting none go but the well ones, or those who could walk. The rebel adjutant stood upon a box by the gate, watching very close. Pitch pine knots were burning in the near vicinity to give light. As it came our turn to go Battese got me in the middle of the rank, stood me up as well as I could stand, and with himself on one side and Sergt. Rowe on the other began pushing our way through the gate. Could not help myself a particle, and was so faint that I hardly knew what was going on. As we were going through the gate the adjutant yells out: "Here, here! hold on there, that man can't go, hold on there!" and Battese crowding right along outside. The adjutant struck over the heads of the men and tried to stop us, but my noble Indian friend kept straight ahead, hallooing: "He all right, he well, he go!" And so I got outside, and adjutant having too much to look after to follow me. After we were outside, I was car-

BATTESE, *the Minnesota Indian*

ried to the railroad in the same coverlid which I fooled the
rebel out of when captured, and which I presume has saved
my life a dozen times. We were crowded very thick into box
cars. I was nearly dead, and hardly knew where we were or
what was going on. We were two days in getting to Savannah.
Arrived early in the morning. The railroads here run in the
middle of very wide, handsome streets. We were unloaded,
I should judge, near the middle of the city. The men as they
were unloaded, fell into line and were marched away. Battese
got me out of the car, and laid me on the pavement. They then
obliged him to go with the rest, leaving me; would not let him
take me. I lay there until noon with four or five others, without any guard. Three or four times negro servants came to us
from houses near by, and gave us water, milk and food. With
much difficulty I could set up, but was completely helpless. A
little after noon a wagon came and *toted* us to a temporary
hospital in the outskirts of the city, and near a prison pen they
had just built for the well ones. Where I was taken it was
merely an open piece of ground, having wall tents erected
and a line of guards around it. I was put into a tent and lay
on the coverlid. That night some gruel was given to me, and
a nurse whom I had seen in Andersonville looked in, and my
name was taken. The next morning, September 10th, I woke
up and went to move my hands, and could not do it; could not
move either limb so much as an inch. Could move my head
with difficulty. Seemed to be paralyzed, but in no pain whatever. After a few hours a physician came to my tent, examined
and gave me medicine, also left medicine, and one of the
nurses fed me some soup or gruel. By night I could move my
hands. Lay awake considerable through the night thinking.

Was happy as a clam in high tide. Seemed so nice to be under a nice clean tent, and there was such cool pure air. The surroundings were so much better that I thought now would be a good time to die, and I didn't care one way or the other. Next morning the doctor came, and with him Sergt. Winn. Sergt. Winn I had had a little acquaintance with at Andersonville. Doctor said I was terribly reduced, but he thought I would improve. Told them to wash me. A nurse came and washed me, and Winn brought me a white cotton shirt, and an old but clean pair of pants; my old clothing, which was in rags, was taken away. Two or three times during the day I had gruel of some kind. I don't know what. Medicine was given me by the nurses. By night I could move my feet and legs a little. The cords in my feet and legs were contracted so, of course, that I couldn't straighten myself out. Kept thinking to myself, "am I really away from that place Andersonville?" It seemed too good to be true. On the morning of the 12th, ambulances moved all to the Marine Hospital, or rather an orchard in same yard with Marine Hospital, where thirty or forty nice new tents have been put up, with bunks about two feet from the ground, inside. Was put into a tent. By this time could move my arms considerable. We were given vinegar weakened with water, and also salt in it. Had medicine. My legs began to get movable more each day, also my arms, and to-day I am laying on my stomach and writing in my diary. Mike Hoare is also in this hospital. One of my tentmates is a man named Land, who is a printer, same as myself. I hear that Wm. B. Rowe is here also, but haven't seen him.

Sept. 16.—How I do sleep; am tired out, and seems to me I can just sleep till doomsday.

Sept. 17.—Four in each tent. A nurse raises me up, sitting posture, and there I stay for hours, dozing and talking away. Whiskey given us in very small quantities, probably half a teaspoonful in half a glass of something. I don't know what. Actually makes me drunk. I am in no pain whatever.

Sept. 18.—Surgeon examined me very thoroughly to-day. Have some bad sores caused by laying down so much; put something on them that makes them ache. Sergt. Winn gave me a pair of socks.

Sept. 19.—A priest gave me some alum for my sore mouth. Had a piece of sweet potato, but couldn't eat it. Fearfully weak. Soup is all I can eat, and don't always stay down.

Sept. 20.—Too cool for me. The priest said he would come and see me often. Good man. My left hand got bruised in some way and rebel done it up. He is afraid gangrene will get in sore. Mike Hoare is quite sick.

Sept. 21.—Don't feel as well as I did some days ago. Can't eat; still can use my limbs and arms more.

Sept. 22.—Good many sick brought here. Everybody is kind, rebels and all. Am now differently sick than at any other time. Take lots of medicine, eat nothing but gruel. Surgeons are very attentive. Man died in my tent. Oh, if I was away by myself, I would get well. Don't want to see a sick man. That makes me sick.

Sept. 23.—Shall write any way; have to watch nurses and rebels or will lose my diary. Vinegar reduced I drink and it is good; crave after acids and salt. Mouth appears to be actually sorer than ever before, but whether it is worse or not can't say. Sergt. Winn says the Doctor says that I must be very careful if I want to get well. How in the old Harry can I be careful? They are the ones that had better be careful and give me the right medicine and food. Gruel made out of a dish cloth to eat.

Sept. 24.—Arrow root soup or whatever you may call it; don't like it; makes me sick. Priest spoke to me. Cross and peevish and they say that is a sure sign will get well. Ain't sure but shall be a Catholic yet. Every little while get out the old diary from under the blanket and write a sentence. Never was made to be sick—too uneasy. This will do for to-day.

CHAPTER EIGHT

Hospital Life

**A Gradual Improvement in Health ✻
Good Treatment Which is Opportune ✻
Parting With Relics to Buy Luxuries ✻ Daly,
the Teamster at Andersonville, Killed ✻
A Visit from Battese, the Indian**

SEPT. 25.—Can eat better—or drink rather; some rebel general dead and buried with honors outside. Had another wash and general clean up; ocean breezes severe for invalids. Am visited twice a day by the rebel surgeon who instructs nurses about treatment. Food principally arrow root; have a little whiskey. Sleep great deal of the time. Land, my acquaintance and mess-mate, is lame from scurvy, but is not weak and sick as I am. When I think of anything, say: "Land, put her down," and he writes what I tell him. Everything clean here, but then any place is clean after summering in Andersonville. Don't improve much and sometimes not at all; get blue sometimes; nature of the beast suppose; other sick in the tent worry and make me nervous.

Sept. 26.—Am really getting better and hopeful. Battese has the two first books of my diary; would like to see him. Was mistaken about Rowe being in the hospital; he is not, but I hear is in the big stockade with bulk of prisoners. Say we were removed from Andersonville for the reason that our troops were moving that way. Well, thank heaven they moved that way. Mike Hoare, the irrepressible Irishman, is hobbling around and in our tent about half the time; is also getting well. Quite a number die here not having the constitution to rally. This is the first hospital I was ever in. My old coverlid was washed and fumigated the first day in hospital. Am given very little to eat five or six times a day; washed with real soap, an improvement on sand. Half a dozen rebel doctors prowling around, occasionally one that needs dressing down, but as a general thing are very kind. Can see from my bunk a large live oak tree which is a curiosity to me. Although it is hot weather the evenings are cool, in fact cold; ocean breezes. A discussion on the subject has set me down as weighing about ninety-five; I think about one hundred and five or ten pounds; weighed when captured one hundred and seventy-eight; boarding with the Confederacy does not agree with me. The swelling about my body has all left me. Sergt. Winn belongs to the 100th Ohio; he has charge of a ward in this hospital.

Sept. 27.—Getting so I can eat a little and like the gruel. Have prided myself all during the imprisonment on keeping a stiff upper lip while I saw big strong men crying like children; cruelty and privations would never make me cry—always so mad, but now it is different and weaken a little sometimes all to myself. Land, my sick comrade, writes at my dictation.

Sept. 28.—Sent word to Battese by a convalescent who is being sent to the large prison, that I am getting well. Would like to see him. Am feeling better. Good many Union men in Savannah. Three hundred sick here, with all kinds of diseases —gangrene, dropsy, scurvy, typhoid and other fevers, diarrhea, &c. Good care taken of me. Have medicine often, and gruel. Land does the writing.

Sept. 29.—Yes, I am better, but poor and weak. Feeling hungry more now, and can take nourishment quite often. Mike Hoare calls to see me. He is thinking of escape. Should think a person might escape from here when able. I shall get well now. Sweet potatoes for sale. Like to see such things, but cannot eat them. Rebel officer put his hand on my head a few minutes ago and said something; don't know what. It is said the Yankees can throw shell into Savannah from their gunboats down the river. Sergeant Winn comes to see me and cheers me up. Winn is a sutler as well as nurse, that is, he buys eatables from the guards and other rebels, and sells to our men. Number of marines and sailors in the building adjoining our hospital; also some Yankee officers sick. Winn makes quite a little money. They have soap here to wash with. The encouraging talk of ending the war soon helps me to get well.

Sept. 30.—Am decidedly better and getting quite an appetite but can get nothing but broth, gruel, &c. Mouth very bad. Two or three teeth have come out, and can't eat any hard food any way. They give me quinine, at least I think it is quinine. Good many visitors come here to see the sick, and they look like union people. Savannah is a fine place from all accounts of it. Mike is getting entirely over his troubles and talks continually of getting away, there are a great many Irish about here, and they are principally Union men. Mike wishes I was able to go with him. Nurses are mostly marines who have been sick and are convalescent. As a class they are good fellows, but some are rough ones. Are very profane. The cords in my legs loosening up a little. Whiskey and water given me to-day, also weakened vinegar and salt. Am all the time getting better. LATER.—My faithful friend came to see me to-day. Was awful glad to see him. He is well. A guard came with him. Battese is quite a curiosity among the Savannah rebels. Is a very large, broad shouldered Indian, rather ignorant, but full of common sense and very kind hearted. Is allowed many favors.

Oct. 1.—A prisoner of war nearly a year. Have stood and went through the very worst kind of treatment. Am getting ravenously hungry, but they won't give me much to eat. Even

143

Mike won't give me anything. Says the doctors forbid it. Well, I suppose it is so. One trouble with the men here who are sick, they are too indolent and discouraged, which counteracts the effect of medicines. A dozen or twenty die in the twenty-four hours. Have probably half tablespoonful of whiskey daily, and it is enough. Land is a good fellow. (I wrote this last sentence myself, and Land says he will scratch it out.—Ransom). A high garden wall surrounds us. Wall is made of stone. Mike dug around the corners of the walls, and in out-of-the way places, and got together a mess of greens out of pusley. Offered me some and then wouldn't let me have it. Meaner than pusley. Have threatened to lick the whole crowd in a week.

Oct. 2.—Coming cool weather and it braces me right up. Sailors are going away to be exchanged. Ate some sweet potato to-day, and it beats everything how I am gaining. Drink lots of gruel, and the more I drink the more I want. Have vinegar and salt and water mixed together given me, also whiskey, and every little while I am taking something, either food or medicine, and the more I take the more I want. Am just crazy for anything, no matter what. Could eat a mule's ear. Eat rice and vegetable soup. All the talk that I hear is to the effect that the war is most over. Don't want to be disturbed at all until I am well, which will not be very long now. All say if I don't eat too much will soon be well. Mike lives high. Is an ingenious fellow and contrives to get many good things to eat. Gives me anything that he thinks won't hurt me. Setting up in my bunk. Have washed all over and feel fifty per cent. better. Just a-jumping toward convalescence.

Oct. 3.—The hospital is crowded now with sick; about thirty die now each day. Men who walked away from Andersonville, and come to get treatment, are too far gone to rally, and die. Heard Jeff. Davis' speech read to-day. He spoke of an exchange soon. I am better where I am for a few weeks yet. Number of sailors went to-day. Knaw onion, raw sweet potato. Battese here, will stay all day and go back to-night. Says he is going with marines to be exchanged. Give him food, which he is loth to eat although hungry. Says he will come to see me after I get home to Michigan.

Oct. 4.—Am now living splendid; vegetable diet is driving off the scurvy and dropsy, in fact the dropsy has dropped out but the effect remains. Set up now part of the time and talk like a runaway horse until tired out and then collapse. Heard that all the prisoners are going to be sent to Millen, Ga. Wrote a few lines directed to my father in Michigan. Am now given more food but not much at a time. Two poor fellows in our tent do not get along as well as I do, although Land is doing well and is going to be a nurse. The hospital is not guarded very close and Mike Hoare cannot resist the temptation to escape. Well, joy go with him. Dosed with quinine and beastly to take. Battese on his last visit to me left the two first books of my diary which he had in his posession. There is no doubt but he has saved my life, although he will take no credit for it. It is said all were moved from Andersonville to different points; ten thousand went to Florence, ten thousand to Charleston and ten thousand to Savannah; but the dead stay there and will for all time to come. What a terrible place and what a narrow escape I had of it. Seems to me that fifteen thousand died while I was there; an army almost and as many men as inhabit a city of fifty thousand population.

Oct. 5.—All in Andersonville will remember Daly, who used to drive the bread wagon into that place. He came to Savannah with us and was in this hospital; a few days ago he went away with some sailors to be exchanged. Soon after leaving Savannah he fell off the cars and was killed, and a few hours after leaving here was brought back and buried; it is said he had been drinking. Getting better every day, eat right smart. Mike waiting for a favorable chance to escape and in the meantime is getting well; heard that Battese has gone away with sailors to our lines. It's wonderful the noticeable change of air here from that at Andersonville—wonder that any lived a month inhaling the poison. If some of those good fellows that died there, Jimmy Devers, Dr. Lewis, Swain, McGuire and scores of others, had lived through it to go home with me, should feel better. Have a disagreeable task to perform—that of going to see the relatives of fifteen or twenty who died and deliver messages. Rebel surgeons act as if the war was most over, and not like very bad enemies. Fresh beef issued to those able to eat it which is not me; can chew nothing hard, in fact cannot chew at all. Am all tired out and will stop for to-day.

Oct. 7.—Havn't time to write much; busy eating. Mouth getting better, cords in my legs loosening up. Battese has not gone; was here to-day and got a square meal. Don't much think that I have heretofore mentioned the fact that I have two small gold rings, which has been treasured carefully all during my imprisonment. They were presents to me before leaving home; it is needless to say they were from lady friends. Have worn them part of the time and part of the time they have been secreted about my clothes. Yankee rings are in great demand by the guards; crave delicacies and vegetables so much that think I may be pardoned for letting them go now, and as Mike says he can get a bushel of sweet potatoes for them, have told him to make the trade, and he says will do it. Sweet potatoes sliced up and put in a dish and cooked with a piece of beef and seasoned, make a delicious soup. There are grayback lice in the hospital, just enough for company's sake—should feel lonesome without them. Great many visitors come to look at us and from my bunk can see them come through the gate; Yankees are a curiosity in this Southern port, as none were ever kept here before; I hear that the citizens donate bread and food to the prisoners.

Oct. 8.—Talk of Millen, about ninety miles from here. Mike will trade off the rings to-night. Owe Sergt. Winn $12 for onions and sweet potatoes, Confederate money however; a dollar Confed. is only ten cents in money. Hub Dakin, from Dansville, Mich., is in this hospital. It is said Savannah will be in our hands in less than two months. Some Irish citizens told Mike so. Union army victorious everywhere. Going on twelve months a prisoner of war. Don't want to be exchanged now; could not stand the journey home; just want to be let alone one month and then home and friends. Saw myself in a looking glass for the first time in ten months and am the worst looking specimen—don't want to go home in twelve years unless I look different from this; almost inclined to disown myself. Pitch pine smoke is getting peeled off; need skinning. Eye sight improving with other troubles. Can't begin to read a newspaper and with difficulty write a little at a time. Can hear big guns every morning from down the river; it is said to be Yankee gunboats bidding the city of Savannah "good morning."

Oct. 9.—The reason we have not been exchanged is because if the exchange is made it will put all the men held by the union forces right into the rebel army, while the union prisoners of war held by the rebels are in no condition to do service; that would seem to me to be a very poor reason. Rowe and Bullock are in the main prison I hear, and well; it is one of the miracles that Bullock lived as he was ailing all through Andersonville. Brass buttons with hens on (eagles) are eagerly sought after by the guards. Mike still harping on escape, but I attend right to the business of getting enough to eat. Although can't eat much have the appetite all the same. The rebel M. D., by name Pendleton, or some such name, says if I am not careful will have a relapse, and is rather inclined to scold; says I get along all together too fast, and tells the nurse and Mike and Land, that I must not eat but little at a time and then only such food as he may direct, and if I don't do as he says, will put me in the main building away from my friends. Says it is suicide the way some act after a long imprisonment. Well, suppose he is right and I must go slow. Names of Yankee officers marked on the tents that have occupied them as prisoner of war before us.

Oct. 10.—Mike traded off the gold rings for three pecks of sweet potatoes and half a dozen onions; am in clover. Make nice soup out of beef, potatoe, bread, onion and salt; can trade a sweet potatoe for most anything. Mike does the cooking and I do the eating; he won't eat my potatoes, some others do though and without my permission. 'Tis ever thus, wealth brings care and trouble. Battese came to-day to see me and

gave him some sweet potatoes. He is going away soon, the
rebels having promised to send him with next batch of
sailors; is a favorite with rebels. Mike baking bread to take
with him in his flight. Set now at the door of the tent on a
soap box; beautiful shade trees all over the place. Am in the
5th Ward, tent No. 12; coverlid still does me good service.
Many die here but not from lack of attention or medicine.
They haven't the vitality to rally after their sufferings at
Andersonville. Sisters of Charity go from tent to tent looking
after men of their own religion; also citizens come among us.
Wheat bread we have quite often and is donated by citizens.
Guards walk on the outside of the wall and only half a dozen
or so on the inside, two being at the gate; not necessary to
guard the sick very close. Should judge the place was some
fine private residence before being transformed into the
Marine Hospital. Have good water. What little hair I have
is coming off; probably go home bald-headed.

Oct. 12.—Still getting better fast, and doctor says too fast.
Now do nearly all the diary writing. Hardly seems possible
that our own Yankee gunboats are so near us, so near that
we can hear them fire off their guns, but such is the case. Reports have it that the Johnny Rebels are about worsted. Has
been a hard war and cruel one. Mike does all my cooking
now, although an invalid. He trades a sweet potato for
vinegar, which tastes the best of anything, also have other
things suitable for the sick, and this morning had an egg. My
gold rings will put me in good health again. All the time
medicine, that is, three or four times a day; and sores on my
body are healing up now for the first time. Mouth, which was
one mass of black bloody swellings on the inside, is now

white and inflamation gone, teeth however, loose, and have lost four through scurvy, having come out themselves. My eyes, which had been trying to get in out of sight, are now coming out again and look more respectable. Battese was taken prisoner with eighteen other Indians; they all died but one beside himself.

Oct. 14.—Did not write any yesterday. A man named Hinton died in our tent at about two o'clock this morning, and his bunk is already filled by another sick man. None die through neglect here; all is done that could reasonably be expected. The pants with those buttons on to be taken North for a little boy whose father died in Andersonville, were taken away from me when first taken to the hospital. Have also lost nearly all the relics, pictures and letters given me to take North. For a week or ten days could take care of nothing. Winn took charge of the book that I am writing in now and Battese had the other two books, and now they are all together safe in my charge. Wonder if any one will ever have the patience or time to read it all? Not less than a thousand pages of finely written crow tracks, and some places blurred and unintelligible from being wet and damp. As I set up in my bunk my legs are just fitted for hanging down over the side, and have not been straightened for three or four months. Rub the cords with an ointment furnished me by physician and can see a change for the better. Legs are blue, red and shiny and in some places the skin seems calloused to the bone.

Oct. 15.—Richard is getting to be himself again. A very little satisfies me as regards the upward tendency to health and liberty. Some would think to look at me almost helpless and a prisoner of war, that I hadn't much to feel glad about.

Well, let them go through what I have and then see. Citizens look on me with pity when I should be congratulated. Am probably the happiest mortal any where hereabouts. Shall appreciate life, health and enough to eat hereafter. Am anxious for only one thing, and that is to get news home to Michigan of my safety. Have no doubt but I am given up for dead, as I heard I was so reported. Drizzling rain has set in. Birds chipper from among the trees. Hear bells ring about the city of Savannah. Very different from the city of Richmond; there it was all noise and bustle and clatter, every man for himself and the devil take the hindmost, while here it is quiet and pleasant and nice. Every one talks and treats you with courtesy and kindness. Don't seem as if they could both be cities of the Confederacy. Savannah has probably seen as little of real war or the consequence of war, as any city in the South.

Oct. 18.—Every day since last writing I have continued to improve, and no end to my appetite. Now walk a trifle with the aid of crutches. Coming cool, and agrees with me. Have fresh beef issued to us. Mike not yet gone. Battese went some days ago with others to our lines, at least it was supposed to our lines. Hope to see him sometime. Many have gangrene. Millen still talked of. See city papers every day, and they have a discouraged tone as if their cause were on its last legs. Mike goes to-night for sure, he says. Think if I was in his place would not try to get away, we are so comfortable here. Still liberty is everything, and none know what it is except those deprived of it. It's a duty, we think, to escape if possible, and it seems possible to get away from here. Rebel guards that I sometimes come in contact with are marines, who belong to rebel gunboats stationed in the mouth of Savannah River and are on duty here for a change from boat life. They seem a kindly set, and I don't believe they would shoot a prisoner if they saw him trying to get away.

Oct. 19.—Last night I talked with a guard while Mike Hoare went out of his tunnel and got away safely from the hospital. The guard was on the inside and I hobbled to where he was and engaged him in conversation and Mike crawled away. It seems that Mike learned of some Union Irish citizens in the city and his idea is to reach them which he may do, as there are scarcely any troops about the city, all being to the front. Now I am alone, best friends all gone one way or the other. The only acquaintances here now are Land and Sergt. Winn, with whom I became acquainted in Andersonville. Not like my other friends though. It is said there are half a dozen hospitals similar to this in Savannah which are filled with Andersonville wrecks. They have need to do something to redeem themselves from past conduct. Don't believe that it is the Confederacy that is taking such good care of us, but it is the city of Savannah; that is about the way it is as near as I can find out.

Oct. 22.—Lieut. Davis commands the prison in Savannah. Is the same individual who officiated at Andersonville during Wirtz's sickness last summer. He is a rough but not a bad man. Probably does as well as he can. Papers state that they will commence to move the prisoners soon to Millen, to a Stockade similar to the one at Andersonville. I am hobbling about the hospital with the help of two crutches. Have not heard a word from old Mike, or Battese or any one that I ever heard of before, for some days. Sweet potatoes building me up with the luxuries they are traded for. Had some rice in my soup. Terrible appetite, but for all that don't eat a great deal. Have three sticks propped up at the mouth of our tent, with a little fire under it, cooking food. Men in tent swear because smoke goes inside. Make it all straight by giving them some soup. Rebel surgeons all smoke, at least do while among us. Have seen prisoners who craved tobacco more than food, and said of the two would prefer tobacco. I never have used tobacco in any form.

Oct. 24.—Did not write yesterday. Jumping right along toward health if not wealth. Discarded crutches and have now two canes. Get around considerable, a little at a time. It is said that they want Yankee printers who are prisoners of war to go and work in the printing offices in the city on parole of honor(?). Will not do it. Am all right where I am for a month yet, and by that time expect to go to our lines. Hub Dakin in hospital now. Priests still come and go. Convalescent shot and wounded by the guards, the first I have heard of being hurt since I came to this place. A small-pox case discovered in hospital and created great excitement. Was removed. Was loitering near the gate, when an Irish woman came through it with her arms full of wheat bread. All those able to rushed up to get some of it and forty hands were pleading for her favors. After picking her men and giving away half a dozen loaves her eyes lighted on me and I secured a large loaf. She was a jolly, good natured woman, and it is said that she keeps a bake shop. My bad looks stood me in well this time. As beautiful bread as I ever saw.

Oct. 25.—Am feeling splendid and legs doing nobly, and even taking on fat. Am to be a gallant nurse as soon as

able, so Sergt. Winn says. Most of the men as soon as convalescent are sent to big prison, but Winn has spoken a good
word for me. Papers say the prison at Millen, Ga., is about
ready for occupancy, and soon all will be sent there, sick and
all. Nights cool and need more covering than we have. I am
congratulated occasionally by prisoners who saw me in Andersonville. They wonder at my being alive. Rains.

Oct. 26.—Time passes now fast; most a year since captured. When the Rebs once get hold of a fellow they hang
on for dear life. Talk that all are to be vaccinated any way,
whether they want to or not. Don't suppose it will do any
harm if good matter is used. Vaccinate me if they want to.
Walk better every day. Sometimes I overdo a little and feel
bad in consequence. Land is "right smart," in fact, so smart
that he will have to go to the big stockade pretty soon.

Oct. 27.—A rebel physician (not a regular one), told me
that it looked very dark for the Confederacy just now; that
we need have no fears but we would get home very soon now,
which is grand good news. I have no fears now but all will
turn out well. Everything points to a not far away ending of
the war, and all will rejoice, rebels and all.

Oct. 28.—Am feeling splendid, and legs most straight.
Getting fat fast. Am to be a nurse soon. Reported that they
are moving prisoners to Millen. Over a thousand went yesterday. About ten thousand of the Andersonville prisoners came
to Savannah, ten thousand went to Florence and ten to
Charleston, S. C. Only the sick were left behind there, and it
is said they died like sheep after the well ones went away.
Great excitement among the Gray-coats. Some bad army

MICHAEL HOARE

news for them, I reckon. Negroes at work fortifying about the city.

Oct. 29.—I suppose we must be moved again, from all reports. Savannah is threatened by Union troops, and we are to be sent to Millen, Ga. Am sorry, for while I remain a prisoner would like to stay here, am getting along so nicely and recovering my health. It is said, however, that Millen is a good place to go to, and we will have to take the consequences whatever they may be. Can eat now anything I can get hold of, provided it can be cooked up and made into the shape of soup. Mouth will not admit of hard food. This hospital is not far from the Savannah jail, and when the gate is open we can see it. It is said that some one was hung there not long ago. Papers referred to it and I asked a guard and he nodded "Yes." Have seen one "hanging bee," and never want to see another one. Last of my three pecks of sweet potatoes almost gone. For a dollar, Confed., bought two quarts of guber peas (pea-nuts), and now I have got them can't eat them. Sell them for a dollar per quart—two dollars for the lot. It is thus that the Yankee getteth wealth. Have loaned one cane to another convalescent and go around with the aid of one only. Every day a marked improvement. Ain't so tall as I "used to was." Some ladies visited the hospital to-day to see live Yankees, who crowded around. They were as much of a curiosity to us as we were to them.

Oct. 30.—It is said prisoners from main prison are being removed every day, and the sick will go last. Quite a batch of the nearest well ones were sent from here to-day to go with the others. Am to be a nurse pretty soon. Don't think I could nurse a sick cat, still it's policy to be one. Winn tells me that he has made money dickering at trade with the rebels and prisoners. He has trusted me to twelve dollars worth of things and says he don't expect or want pay. The twelve dollars amounts to only one dollar and twenty cents in our money. The surgeon who has had charge of us has been sent away to the front. It seems he had been wounded in battle and was doing home duty until able to again go to his command. Shall always remember him for his kind and skillful treatment. Came round and bid us all good bye, and sick sorry to lose him. Are now in charge of a hospital steward, who does very well. The atmosphere here makes gentlemen of everybody. Papers say that the city must be fortified, and it is being done. Considerable activity about the place. Trains run through at all hours of the night, evidently shifting their troops to other localities. LATER—Since the surgeon went away the rebels are drinking up our whiskey, and to-night are having a sort of carnival, with some of the favorite nurses joining in; singing songs, telling stories, and a good time generally. They are welcome to my share.

Oct. 31.—Reported that the well prisoners have all left this city for Millen and we go to-night or to-morrow. I am duly installed as nurse, and walk with only one cane. Legs still slightly drawn up. Hub Dakin, Land and myself now mess together. Am feeling very well. Will describe my appearance. Will interest me to read in after years, if no one else. Am writing this diary to please myself, now. I weigh one hundred and seventeen pounds, am dressed in rebel jacket, blue pants with one leg torn off and fringed about half way between my knee and good sized foot, the same old pair of mismatched shoes I wore in Andersonville, very good pair of stockings, a "biled" white shirt, and a hat which is a compromise between a clown's and the rebel white partially stiff hat; am poor as a tad-pole, in fact look just about like an East Tennesseean, of the poor white trash order. You might say that I am an "honery looking cuss" and not be far out of the way. My cheeks are sunken, eyes sunken, sores and blotches both outside and inside my mouth, and my right leg the whole length of it, red, black and blue and tender of touch. My eyes, too, are very weak, and in a bright sun I have to draw the slouch hat away down over them. Bad as this picture is, I am a beauty and picture of health in comparison to my appearance two months ago. When taken prisoner was fleshy, weighing about one hundred and seventy or seventy-five, round faced, in fact an overgrown, ordinary, green-looking chap of twenty. Had never endured any hardships at all and was a spring chicken. As has been proven however, I had an iron constitution that has carried me through, and above all a disposition to make the best of everything no matter how bad, and considerable will power with the rest. When I think of the thousands and thousands of thorough-bred soldiers, tough and hearty and capable of marching thirty, forty, and even fifty miles in twenty-four hours and think nothing of it, I wonder and kept wondering that it can be so, that I am alive and gaining rapidly in health and strength. Believe now that no matter where we are moved to, I shall continue to improve, and get well. Succumbed only at the last in Andersonville, when no one could possibly keep well. With this general inventory of myself and the remark that I haven't a red cent, or even a Confederate shin-plaster, will put up my diary and get ready to go where ever they see fit to send us, as orders have come to get ready. LATER—We are on the Georgia Central Railroad, en-route for Millen, Ga., which is ninety miles from Savannah, and I believe north. Are in box cars and very crowded with sick prisoners. Two nurses, myself being one of them, have charge of about a hundred sick. There are, however, over six hundred on the train.

CHAPTER NINE

Removed to Millen

**Another Change, and not a Bad One ∗
Almost a Hostage of War ∗ Election Day
and a Vote for Little Mac ∗ One Year
a Prisoner of War**

CAMP LAWTON, Millen, Ga., Nov. 1.—Arrived at our destination not far from midnight, and it was a tedious journey. Two died in the car I was in. Were taken from the cars to this prison in what they call ambulances, but what I call lumber wagons. Are now congregated in the south-east corner of the stockade under hastily put up tents. This morning we have drawn rations, both the sick and the well, which are good and enough. The stockade is similar to that at Andersonville, but in a more settled country, the ground high and grassy, and through the prison runs a stream of good pure water, with no swamp at all. It is apparently a pleasant and healthy location. A portion of the prison is timber land, and the timber has been cut down and lays where it fell, and the men who arrived before us have been busily at work making shanties and places to sleep in. There are about six thousand prisoners here, and I should judge there was room for twelve or fifteen thousand. Men say they are given food twice each day, which consists of meal and fresh beef in rather small quantities, but good and wholesome. The rebel officer in command is a sociable and kindly disposed man, and the guards are not strict, that is, not cruelly so. We are told that our stay here will be short. A number of our men have been detailed to cook the food for the sick, and their well being is looked to by the rebel surgeon as well as our own men. The same surgeon who for the last ten days had charge of us in Savannah has charge of us now. He does not know over and above much but on the whole does very well. Barrels of molasses (nigger toe) have been rolled inside and it is being issued to the men, about one-fourth of a pint to each man, possibly a little more. Some of the men, luxuriantly, put their allowances together and make molasses candy of it. One serious drawback is the scarcity of dishes, and one man I saw draw his portion in his two hands, which held it until his comrade could find a receptacle for it.

Nov. 2.—Have seen many of my old comrades of Andersonville, among whom is my tried friend Sergt. Wm. B. Rowe; were heartily glad to see one another; also little Bullock who has improved wonderfully in appearance. Everyone is pleased with this place and are cheerful, hoping and expecting to be released before many weeks; they all report as having been well treated in Savannah and have pleasant recollections of that place; from what could be seen of the city by us prisoners it seems the handsomest one in America. Should judge it was a very wealthy place. My duties as nurse are hard, often too much so for my strength, yet the enforced exercise does me good and continue to improve all the time. A cane will be necessary to my locomotion for a long time as am afraid myself permanently injured; my cane is not a gold headed one; it is a round picket which has been pulled off some fence. Very cheering accounts of the war doings. All who want to can take the oath of allegiance to the Confederacy and be released; am happy to say though that out of all here, but two or three has done so, and they are men who are a detriment to any army. The weather now is beautiful, air refreshing, water ditto; all happy and contented and await coming events with interest. Part of the brook, the lower part, is planked and sides boarded up for sanitary privileges; water has also been damned up and a fall made which carries off the filth with force. Plenty of wood to do cooking with and the men putter around with their cooking utensils such as they have. Sort of prize fight going on now.

Nov. 3.—About a hundred convalescents were taken outside to-day to be sent away to our lines the officials told us. At a later hour the commander came inside and said he wanted twelve men to fall into line and they did so, myself being one of the twelve; he proceeded to glance us over and on looking at me said: "Step back out of the ranks, I want only able bodied men." I stepped down and out considerably chagrinned, as the general impression was that they were to go to our lines with the convalescents who had been taken outside before. He marched off the twelve men and it then leaked out that they were to be sent to some prison to be held as hostages until the end of the war. Then I felt better. It is said all the sick will be taken outside as soon as they get quarters fixed up to accommodate them. Think that I shall resign my position as nurse. Would rather stay with the "boys." Land is no longer with the sick but has been turned into the rank and file, also Dakin. Dakin, Rowe and Land are all together, and if the sick are taken outside I shall join my old comrades and mess with them. But few die now; quite a number died from the removal, but now all seem to be on the mend. I am called, contrary to my expectations, a good nurse; certainly have pity for the poor unfortunates, but lack the strength to take care of them. It needs good strong men to act as nurses.

Nov. 4.—The fine weather still continues. Just warm enough, and favorable for prisoners. Food now we get but once a day—not all we want, but three times as much as issued at Andersonville and of good quality. The officer in command, as I have said before, is a kind-hearted man, and on his appearance inside he was besieged by hundreds of applications for favors and for the privilege of going outside on parole of honor. He began granting such favors as he could, but has been besieged too much and now stays outside. Has, however, put up a letter box on the inside so that letters will reach him, and every day it is filled half full. Occasionally he takes to a letter and sends inside for the writer of it, and that one answered is the occasion of a fresh batch, until it is said that the poor man is harrassed about as much as the President of the United States is for fat offices. As I have before remarked in my diary, the Yankee is a queer animal.

Nov. 5.—Hostages taken out. Everything is bright and pleasant and I see no cause to complain, therefore won't. To-morrow is election day at the North; wish I was there to vote—which I ain't. Will here say that I am a War Democrat to the backbone. Not a very stiff one, as my backbone is weak.

Nov. 6.—One year ago to-day captured. Presidential election at the North between Lincoln and McClellan. Some one fastened up a box, and all requested to vote, for the fun of the thing. Old prisoners haven't life enough to go and vote; new prisoners vote for present administration. I voted for McClellan with a hurrah, and another hurrah, and still another. Had this election occurred while we were at Andersonville, four-fifths would have voted for McClellan. We think ourselves shamefully treated in being left so long as prisoners of war. Abe Lincoln is a good man and a good President, but he is controlled by others who rule the exchange business as well as most other things. Of course our likes and dislikes make no difference to him or any one else. Yes, one year ago to-day captured. A year is a good while, even when pleasantly situated, but how much longer being imprisoned as we have been. It seems a lifetime, and I am twenty years older than a year ago. Little thought that I was to remain all this time in durance vile. Improving in health, disposition and everything else. If both breeches legs were of the same length should be supremely happy. Should make a bon-fire to-night if I wasn't afraid of celebrating a defeat. Had lots of fun hurrahing for "Little Mac."

Nov. 7.—A rather cold rain wets all who have not shelter. Many ladies come to see us; don't come through the gate, but look at us through that loophole. Any one with money can buy extras in the way of food, but, alas, we have no money. Am now quite a trader—that is, I make up a very thin dish of soup and sell it for ten cents, or trade it for something. Am ravenously hungry now and can't get enough to eat. The disease has left my system, the body demands food, and I have to exert my speculative genius to get it. Am quite a hand at such things and well-calculated to take care of myself. A man belonging to the Masonic order need not stay here an hour. It seems as if every rebel officer was of that craft, and a prisoner has but to make himself known to be taken care of. Pretty strong secret association that will stand the fortunes of war. That is another thing I must do when I get home—join the Masons. No end of things for me to do: visit all the foreign countries that prisoners told me about, and not forgetting to take in Boston by the way, wear silk underclothing, join the Masons, and above all educate myself to keep out of rebel prisons. A person has plenty of time to think here, more so than in Andersonville; there it was business to keep alive. Small alligator killed at lower part of the stream.

Nov. 8.—All eager for news. Seems as if we were on the eve of something. So quiet here that it must predict a storm. Once in a while some pesky rebel takes it upon himself to tell us a lot of lies to the effect that our armies are getting beaten; that England joins the Confederacy to whip out the North; that there is no prospect of ending the war; that we are not going to be exchanged at all, but remain prisoners, etc., etc. If he is a good talker and tells his story well it makes us all blue and down hearted. Then, pretty soon, we are told more joyful news which we are ready to believe, and again take heart and think of the good times coming. Would like to hear the election news. Wonder who is elected? Feel stronger every day, and have a little flesh on my bones. As the weather gets cool, we are made painfully aware of the fact that we are sadly deficient in clothing. Will freeze if compelled to stay through the winter. Coverlid still does duty although disabled by past experience, same as all of us. We talk over the many good traits of Battese and others who are separated from us by death and otherwise. The exploits of Hendryx we will never tire of narrating. What a meeting when we can get together in future years, and talk over the days we have lived and suffered together. Exchange rumors fill the air. One good sign—the rebels are making no more improvements about this prison; they say we are not to stay here long. We hear that our troops are marching all through the South. Guess that is the reason why they think of moving us all the time. All right, Johnny Rebels, hope we are an elephant on your hands. Jeff Davis denounced by the papers, which is a good sign. Occasionally get one in camp, and read it all up. No library here. Not a scrap of anything to read; principal occupation looking for stray news.

Nov. 9.—This diary would seem to treat of two things principally, that of food and exchange. Try to write of something else, but my thoughts invariably turn to these two subjects. Prisoners of war will know how to excuse me for thus writing. A dead line has also been fixed up in Camp Lawton, but thus far no one has been shot. Rebel doctors inside examining men who may be troubled with disease prison life might aggravate. Those selected are taken outside and either put in hospitals or sent to our lines. Yankee ingenuity is brought into play to magnify diseases, and very often a thoroughly well man will make believe that he is going to die in less than a week unless taken away. Have laughed for an hour at the way a fellow by the name of Sawyer fooled them. The *modus operandi* will hardly bear writing in these pages, but will do to tell. Have made a raise of another pair of pants with both legs of the same length, and I discard the old ones to a "poor" prisoner. An advantage in the new pair is that there is plenty of room, too, from being three or four sizes too large, and the legs as long as the others were short. My one suspender has a partner now, and all runs smoothly. Although Bullock is fleshing up and getting better in health, he is a wreck and always will be. Seems to be a complete change in both body and mind. He was a favorite in our regiment, well known and well liked. Rowe is the same stiff, stern patrician as of old, calmly awaiting the next turn in the wheel of fortune.

Nov. 10.—Pleasant and rather cool. My hair is playing

me pranks. It grows straight up in the air and only on the topmost part of my head. Where a man is generally bald, it's right the other way with me. If there is anything else that can happen to make me any more ridiculous, now is the time for it to appear. About all I lack now is to have an eye gouged out. A friend says that the reason my hair grows the way it does is because I have been scared so much, and it has stuck up straight so much, that it naturally has a tendency that way. Perhaps that is it. If I thought we were to stay here for any length of time would open up a hair cutting shop; but should hate to get nicely started in business and a trade worked up, then have an exchange come along and knock the whole thing in the head. We are not far from the railroad track, and can listen to the cars going by. Very often Confederate troops occupy them and they give the old familiar rebel yell. Once in a while the Yanks get up steam enough to give a good hurrah back to them. Seems to be a good deal of transferring troops now in the South. I watch all the movements of the rebels and can draw conclusions, and am of the opinion that Mr. Confederacy is about whipped and will soon surrender. It certainly looks that way to me. Rumors that we are to be moved.

Nov. 11.—Very well fed. There it goes again. Had determined not to say anything more about how we were fed, and now I have done it. However, I was not grumbling about it any way. Will merely add that I have an appetite larger than an elephant. Will also say that there are rumors of exchange, for a change—a subject that has been spoken of before. Cannot possibly refrain from saying that I am feeling splendidly and worth a hundred dead men yet. Have two dollars in Confederate money and if I can sell this half canteen of dish-water soup shall have another dollar before dark. "Who takes it? Ah, here ye are! Sold again; business closed for to-night, gentlemen. Early in the morning shall have a fresh supply of this delicious soup, with real grease floating on top." Shutters put up and we settle down for the night without depositing in the bank. Shan't go to sleep until ten or eleven o'clock, but lay and think, and build those air castles that always fall with a crash and bury us in the debris. Often hear the baying of hounds from a distance, through the night—and such strange sounds to the Northern ear. Good night. In rather a sentimental mood. Wonder if she is married?

Nov. 12.—Everything quiet and running smoothly. Waiting for something. Have just heard the election news—Mr. Lincoln again elected, and "Little Mac" nowhere. Just about as I expected. Returns were rather slow in coming in, evidently waiting for the Camp Lawton vote. Well, did what I could for George; hurrahed until my throat was sore and stayed so for a week; know that I influenced twenty or thirty votes, and now can get no office because the political opponent was elected. 'Tis ever thus. Believe I would make a good postmaster for this place. There is none here and should have applied immediately, if my candidate had been elected. More sick taken away on the cars; rebels say to be exchanged. Appears to be a sort of mystery of late, and can't make head nor tail of their movements. Would not be surprised at any hour to receive news to get ready for our lines. Don't know that I have felt so before since my imprisonment. Have lived rather high to-day on capital made yesterday and early this morning. Just my way—make a fortune and then spend it.

Nov. 13.—To-day had an incident happen to me; hardly an incident, but a sort of an adventure. When I was nurse on one or two occasions helped the hospital steward make out his report to his superiors, and in that way got a sort of reputation for knowing how to do these things a little better than the ordinary run of people, and rebels in particular. A rebel sergeant came inside at just about nine o'clock this morning and looked me up and said I was wanted outside, and so went. Was taken to a house not far from the stockade, which proved to be the officers head-quarters. There introduced to three or four officers, whose names do not occur to me, and informed that they were in need of some one to do writing and assist in making out their army papers, and if I would undertake the job, they would see that I had plenty to eat, and I should be sent North at the first opportunity. I respectfully, gently and firmly declined the honor, and after partaking of quite a substantial meal, which they gave me thinking I would reconsider my decision, was escorted back inside. Many thought me very foolish for not taking up with the offer. My reasons for not doing so are these: I would be clearly working for the Confederacy; can see no real difference in it from actually entering their army. If I occupied that position it would relieve some rebel of that duty, and he could stay in the ranks and fight our men. That is one reason. Another is the fact that instead of their letting me go to our lines with the first that went, I would be the very last to go, as they would need me to do duty for them until the last moment. Was always willing to do extra duty for our own men, such as issuing clothing on Belle Isle, also my nursing the sick or in any way doing for them, but when it comes to working in any way for any rebel, I shall beg to be excused. Might have gone out and worked in the printing offices in Savannah had I so wished, as they were short of men all the time, in fact could hardly issue their papers on account of the scarcity of printers. And so I am still loyal to the Stars and Stripes and shall have no fears at looking my friends in the face when I do go home.

Nov. 14.—The kaleidoscope has taken another turn. Six hundred taken away this forenoon; don't know where to. As I was about the last to come to Millen, my turn will not come for some days if only six hundred are taken out each day. Rebels say they go straight to our lines, but their being heavily guarded and every possible precaution taken to prevent their escape, it does not look like our lines to me. Probably go to Charleston; that seems to be the jumping off place. Charleston, for some reason or other, seems a bad place to go to. Any city familiar with the war I want to avoid. Shall hang back as long as I can, content to let well enough alone. Some of my friends, of which Bullock is one, flanked out with those going off. What I mean by "flanked out" is crowding in when it is not their turn and going with the crowd. Hendryx and I did that when we left Belle Isle, and we brought up in Andersonville. Will let those do the flanking who want to, I don't.

Nov. 15.—At about six or seven o'clock last night six hundred men were taken away, making in all twelve hundred for the day; another six hundred are ready to go at a moment's notice. I don't know what to think. Can hardly believe they go to our lines. Seems almost like a funeral procession to me, as they go through the gate. Rowe and Hub Dakin talk of going to day, if any go, having decided to flank. I have concluded to wait until it is my turn to go. If it is an exchange there is no danger but all will go, and if not an exchange would rather be here than any place I know of now. LATER —Eight hundred have gone, with Rowe and Dakin in the crowd, and I am here alone as regards personal friends. Could not be induced to go with them. Have a sort of presentiment that all is not right. STILL LATER—Six hundred more have gone, making 2,600 all together that have departed, all heavily guarded.

Nov. 16.—A decided thinness in our ranks this morning. Still house keeping goes right along as usual. Rebels not knowing how to figure give us just about the same for the whole prison as when all were here. Had a talk with a rebel sergeant for about an hour. Tried to find out our destination and could get no satisfaction, although he said we were going to our lines. Told him I was a Mason, Odd-fellow, had every kind of religion (in hopes to strike his), and flattered him until I was ashamed of myself. In a desultory sort of way he said he "reckoned we war goin' nawth." Well, I will write down the solution I have at last come to, and we will see how near right I am after a little. Our troops, Sherman or Kilpatrick or some of them, are raiding through the South, and we are not safe in Millen, as we were not safe in Andersonville, and as was plainly evident we were not safe in Savannah. There is the whole thing in a nutshell, and we will see. Six hundred gone today.

Nov. 17.—It is now said that the prisoners are being moved down on the coast near Florida. That coincides with my own view, and I think it very probable. Will try and go about to-morrow. Hardly think I can go to-day. LATER.—The to-day's batch are going out of the gate. Makes me fairly crazy to wait, fearful I am missing it in not going. This lottery way of living is painful on the nerves. There are all kinds of rumors. Even have the story afloat that now the raid is over that drove us away from Andersonville, we are going back there to stay during the war. That would be a joke. However, I stick to my resolution that the rebels don't really know themselves where we are going. They move us because we are not safe here. They are bewildered. Believing this am in a comparatively easy state of mind. Still I worry. Haven't said a word in a week about my health. Well, I am convalescing all the time. Still lame, and always expect to be; can walk very well though, and feeling lively for an old man.

Nov. 18.—None being taken away to-day, I believe on account of not getting transportation. Notice that rebel troops are passing through on the railroad and immense activity among them. Am now well satisfied of the correctness of my views as regards this movement. Have decided now to stay here until the last. Am getting ready for action however. Believe we are going to have a warm time of it in the next few months. Thank fortune I am as well as I am. Can stand considerable now. Food given us in smaller quantities, and hurriedly so too. All appears to be in a hurry. Cloudy, and rather wet weather, and getting decidedly cooler. My noble old coverlid is kept rolled up and ready to accompany me on my travels at any moment. Have my lame and stiff leg in training. Walk all over the prison until tired out so as to strengthen myself. Recruiting officers among us trying to induce prisoners to enter their army. Say it is no exchange for during the war, and half a dozen desert and go with them. Even if we are not exchanged during the war, don't think we will remain prisoners long.

Nov. 19.—A car load went at about noon, and are pretty well thinned out. Over half gone—no one believes to our lines now; all hands afraid of going to Charleston. Believe I shall try and escape on the journey, although in no condition to rough it. Am going to engineer this thing to suit myself and have a little fun. Would like to be out from under rebel guard once more. When I can look around and not see a prison wall and a gun ready to shoot me, I shall rejoice. Have edged up to another comrade and we bunk together. Said comrade is Corporal Smith, belonging to an Indiana regiment. While he is no great guns, seems quite a sensible chap and a decided improvement on many here to mess with. The nights are cool, and a covering of great benefit. My being the owner of a good blanket makes me a very desirable comrade to mess with. Two or three together can keep much warmer than one alone. It is said that a number of outsiders have escaped and taken to the woods. Another load goes to-night or early in the morning. My turn will come pretty soon. Nothing new in our situation or the prospects ahead. Food scarce, but of good quality. More go and I go to-morrow.

Nov. 20.—None as yet gone to-day and it is already most night. My turn would not come until to-morrow, and if none go at all to-day I will probably not get away until about day after to-morrow. Shan't flank out, but await my turn and go where fate decrees. Had a falling out with my companion

BAPTISM IN THE PEN

Smith, and am again alone walking about the prison with my coverlid on my shoulders. Am determined that this covering protects none but thoroughly good and square fellows. LATER—Going to be a decidedly cold night, and have "made up" with two fellows to sleep together. The going away is the all absorbing topic of conversation. Received for rations this day a very good allowance of hard tack and bacon. This is the first hard-tack received since the trip to Andersonville, and is quite a luxury. It is so hard that I have to tack around and soak mine up before I am able to eat it. There is a joke to this. Will again go to bed as I have done the last week, thinking every night would be the last at Camp Lawton.

Nov. 21.—Got up bright and early, went to the creek and had a good wash, came back, after a good walk over the prison, and ate my two large crackers and small piece of bacon left over from yesterday, and again ready for whatever may turn up. Lost my diminutive cake of soap in the water and must again take to sand to scrub with, until fortune again favors me. Men are very restless and reckless, uncertainty making them so. Try my very best not to have any words or trouble with them, but occasionally get drawn into it, as I did this morning. Came out solid however. Is pretty well understood that I can take care of myself. NOON. —Five hundred getting ready to go; my turn comes to-morrow, and then we will see what we will see. Decided rumors that Sherman has taken Atlanta and is marching toward Savannah, the heart of the Confederacy. All in good spirits for the first time in a week.

CHAPTER TEN

Escape, but Not Escape

**Moved from Camp Lawton After a Sojourn
of Twenty Days ✳ Destination Blackshear,
Georgia ✳ Jump Off the Cars and
Out from Rebel Guard for Six Days ✳ A
Hungry Time, but a Good One ✳ Captured
and Make the Acquaintance of Two Other
Runaways, with whom I Cast My Fortunes**

❦

Nov. 22.—And now my turn has come, and I get off with the next load going to-day. My trunk is packed and baggage duly checked; shall try and get a "lay over" ticket, and rusticate on the road. Will see the conductor about it. A nice cool day with sun shining brightly—a fit one for an adventure and I am just the boy to have one. Coverlid folded up and thrown across my shoulder, lower end tied as only a soldier knows how. My three large books of written matter on the inside of my thick rebel jacket, and fastened in. Have a small book which I keep at hand to write in now. My old hat has been exchanged for a red zouave cap, and I look like a red-headed woodpecker. Leg behaving beautifully. My latest comrades are James Ready and Bill Somebody. We have decided to go and keep together on the cars. One of them has an apology for a blanket and the two acting in conjunction keep all three warm nights. LATER.—On the cars, in vicinity of Savannah en route for Blackshear, which is pretty well south and not far from the Florida line. Are very crowded in a close box car and fearfully warm. Try to get away to-night.

IN THE WOODS NEAR DOCTORTOWN STATION, No. 5, Ga., Nov. 23.—A change has come over the spirit of my dreams. During the night the cars ran very slow, and sometimes stopped for hours on side tracks. A very long, tedious night, and all suffered a great deal with just about standing room only. Impossible to get any sleep. Two guards at each side door, which are open about a foot. Guards were passably decent, although strict. Managed to get near the door, and during the night talked considerable with the two guards on

181

the south side of the car. At about three o'clock this A.M., and after going over a long bridge which spanned the Altamaha River and in sight of Doctortown, I went through the open door like a flash and rolled down a high embankment. Almost broke my neck, but not quite. Guard fired a shot at me, but as the cars were going, though not very fast, did not hit me. Expected the cars to stop but they did not, and I had the inexpressible joy of seeing them move off out of sight. Then crossed the railroad track going north, went through a large open field and gained the woods, and am now sitting on the ground leaning up against a big pine tree *and out from under rebel guard!* The sun is beginning to show itself in the east and it promises to be a fine day. Hardly know what to do with myself. If those on the train notified Doctortown people of my escape they will be after me. Think it was at so early an hour that they might have gone right through without telling any one of the jump off. Am happy and hungry and considerably bruised and scratched up from the escape. The happiness of being here, however, overbalances everything else. If I had George Hendryx with me now would have a jolly time, and mean to have as it is. Sun is now up and it is warmer; birds chippering around, and chipmunks looking at me with curiosity. Can hear hallooing off a mile or so, which sounds like farmers calling cattle or hogs or something. All nature smiles—why should not I?—and I do. Keep my eyes peeled, however, and look all ways for Sunday. Must work farther back toward what I take to be a swamp a mile or so away. Am in a rather low country although apparently a pretty thickly settled one; most too thickly populated for me, judging from the signs of the times. It's now about dinner time, and I have traveled two or three miles from the railroad track, should judge and am in the edge of a swampy forest, although the piece of ground on which I have made my bed is dry and nice. Something to eat wouldn't be a bad thing. Not over sixty rods from where I lay is a path evidently travelled more or less by negroes going from one plantation to another. My hope of food lays by that road. Am watching for passers by. LATER.—A negro boy too young to trust has gone by singing and whistling, and carrying a bundle and a tin pail evidently filled with somebody's dinner. In as much as I want to enjoy this out-door Gypsy life, I will not catch and take the dinner away from him. That would be the heighth of foolishness. Will lay for the next one traveling this way. The next one is a dog and he comes up and looks at me, gives a bark and scuds off. Can't eat a dog. Don't know how it will be to-morrow though. Might be well enough for him to come around later. Well, it is most dark and will get ready to try and sleep. Have broken off spruce boughs and made a soft bed. Have heard my father tell of sleeping on a bed of spruce, and it is healthy. Will try it. Not a crust to eat since yesterday forenoon. Am educated to this way of living though, and have been hungryer. Hope the pesky alligators will let me alone. If they only knew it, I would make a poor meal for them. Thus closes my first day of freedom and it is *grand*. Only hope they may be many, although I can hardly hope to escape to our lines, not being in a condition to travel.

Nov. 24.—Another beautiful morning, a repetition of yesterday, opens up to me. It is particularly necessary that I procure sustenance wherewith life is prolonged, and will change my head-quarters to a little nearer civilization. Can hear some one chopping not a mile away. Here goes. LATER.— Found an old negro fixing up a dilapidated post and rail fence. Approached him and enquired the time of day. (My own watch having run down.) He didn't happen to have his gold watch with him, but reckoned it was nigh time for the horn. Seemed scared at the apparition that appeared to him, and no wonder. Forgave him on the spot. Thought it policy to tell him all about who and what I was, and did so. Was very timid and afraid, but finally said he would divide his dinner as soon as it should be sent to him, and for an hour I lay off a distance of twenty rods or so, waiting for that dinner. It finally came, brought by the same boy I saw go along yesterday. Boy sat down the pail and the old darkey told him to scamper off home—which he did. Then we had dinner of rice, cold yams and fried bacon. It was a glorious repast, and I succeeded in getting quite well acquainted with him. We are on the Bowden plantation and he belongs to a family of that name. Is very fearful of helping me as his master is a strong Secesh., and he says would whip him within an inch of his life if it was known. Promise him not to be seen by any one and he has promised to get me something more to eat after it gets dark. LATER.—After my noonday meal went back toward the low ground and waited for my supper, which came half an hour ago and it is not yet dark. Had a good supper of boiled seasoned turnips, corn bread and sour milk, the first milk I have had in about a year. Begs me to go off in the morning, which I have promised to do. Says for me to go two or three miles on to another plantation owned by LeCleye, where there are good negroes who will feed me.

Thanked the old fellow for his kindness. Says the war is about over and the Yanks expected to free them all soon. It's getting pretty dark now, and I go to bed filled to overflowing; in fact, most too much so.

Nov. 25.—This morning got up cold and stiff; not enough covering. Pushed off in the direction pointed out by the darky of yesterday. Have come in the vicinity of negro shanties and laying in wait for some good benevolent colored brother. Most too many dogs yelping around to suit a runaway Yankee. Little nigs and the canines run together. If I can only attract their attention without scaring them to death, shall be all right. However, there is plenty of time, and won't rush things. Time is not valuable with me. Will go sure and careful. Don't appear to be any men folks around; more or less women of all shades of color. This is evidently a large plantation; has thirty or forty negro huts in three or four rows. They are all neat and clean to outward appearances. In the far distance and toward what I take to be the main road is the master's residence. Can just see a part of it. Has a cupola on top and is an ancient structure. Evidently a nice plantation. Lots of cactus grows wild all over, and is bad to tramp through. There is also worlds of palm leaves, such as five cent fans are made of. Hold on there, two or three negro men are coming from the direction of the big house to the huts. Don't look very inviting to trust your welfare with. Will still wait, McCawber like, for something to turn up. If they only knew the designs I have on them, they would turn pale. Shall be ravenous by night and go for them. I am near a spring of water, and lay down flat and drink. The Astor House Mess is moving around for a change; hope

I won't make a mess of it. Lot of goats looking at me now, wondering, I suppose, what it is. Wonder if they butt? Shoo! Going to rain, and if so I must sleep in one of those shanties. Negroes all washing up and getting ready to eat, with doors open. No, thank you; dined yesterday. Am reminded of the song: "What shall we do, when the war breaks the country up, and scatters us poor darkys all around." This getting away business is about the best investment I ever made. Just the friendliest fellow ever was. More than like a colored man, and will stick closer than a brother if they will only let me. Laugh when I think of the old darky of yesterday's experience, who liked me first rate only wanted me to go away. Have an eye on an isolated hut that looks friendly. Shall approach it at dark. People at the hut are a woman and two or three children, and a jolly looking and acting negro man. Being obliged to lay low in the shade feel the cold, as it is rather damp and moist. LATER.—Am in the hut and have eaten a good supper. Shall sleep here to-night. The negro man goes early in the morning, together with all the male darky population, to work on fortifications at Fort McAllister. Says the whole country is wild at the news of approaching Yankee army. Negro man named "Sam" and woman "Sady." Two or three negroes living here in these huts are not trustworthy, and I must keep very quiet and not be seen. Children perfectly awe struck at the sight of a Yankee. Negroes very kind but afraid. Criminal to assist me. Am five miles from Doctortown. Plenty of "gubers" and yams. Tell them all about my imprisonment. Regard the Yankees as their friends. Half a dozen neighbors come in by invitation, shake hands with me, scrape the floor with their feet, and rejoice most to death at the good times coming. "Bress de Lord," has been repeated hundred of times in the two or three hours I have been here. Surely I have fallen among friends. All the visitors donate of their eatables, and although enough is before me to feed a dozen men, I give it a tussle. Thus ends the second day of my freedom, and it is glorious.

Nov. 26.—An hour before daylight "Sam" awoke me and said I must go with him off a ways to stay through the day. Got up, and we started. Came about a mile to a safe hiding place, and here I am. Have plenty to eat and near good water. Sam will tell another trusty negro of my whereabouts, who will look after me, as he has to go away to work. The negroes are very kind, and I evidently am in good hands. Many of those who will not fight in the Confederate army are hid in these woods and swamps, and there are many small squads looking them up with dogs and guns to force them into the rebel ranks. All able bodied men are conscripted into the army in the South. It is possible I may be captured by some of these hunting parties. It is again most night and have eaten the last of my food. Can hear the baying of hounds and am skeery. Shall take in all the food that comes this way in the meantime. Sam gave me an old jack knife and I shall make a good bed to sleep on, and I also have an additional part of a blanket to keep me warm. In fine spirits and have hopes for the future. Expect an ambassador from my colored friends a little later. LATER.—The ambassador has come and gone in the shape of a woman. Brought food; a man told her to tell me to go off a distance of two miles or so, to the locality pointed out, before daylight, and wait there until called upon to-morrow. Rebel guards occupy the main roads, and very unsafe.

Nov. 27.—Before daylight, came where I now am. Saw alligators—small ones. This out in the woods life is doing me good. Main road three miles away, but there are paths running everywhere. Saw a white man an hour ago. Think he was a skulker hiding to keep out of the army, but afraid to hail him. Many of these stay in the woods day times, and at night go to their homes, getting food. Am now away quite a distance from any habitation, and am afraid those who will look for me cannot find me. Occasionally hear shots fired; this is a dangerous locality. Have now been out four days and fared splendidly. Have hurt one of my ankles getting through the brush; sort of sprain, and difficult to travel at all. No water near by and must move as soon as possible. Wild hogs roam around through the woods, and can run like a deer. Palm leaves grow in great abundance, and are handsome to look at. Some of them very large. Occasionally see lizards and other reptiles, and am afraid of them. If I was a good traveler I could get along through the country and possibly to our lines. Must wander around and do the best I can however. Am armed with my good stout cane and the knife given me by the negro; have also some matches, but dare not make a fire lest it attract attention. Nights have to get up occasionally and stamp around to get warm. Clear, cool nights and pleasant. Most too light, however, for me to travel. The remnants of yesterday's food, have just eaten. Will now go off in an easterly direction in hopes of seeing the messenger.

Nov. 28.—No one has come to me since day before yesterday. Watched and moved until most night of yesterday but could see or hear no one. Afraid I have lost communication. In the distance can see a habitation and will mog along that way. Most noon. LATER.—As I was poking along through some light timber, almost ran into four Confederates with guns. Lay down close to the ground and they passed by me not more than twenty rods away. Think they have heard of my being in the vicinity and looking me up. This probably accounts for not receiving any visitor from the negroes. Getting very hungry, and no water fit to drink. Must get out of this community as fast as I can. Wish to gracious I had two good legs. LATER.—It is now nearly dark and I have worked my way as near direct north as I know how. Am at least four miles from where I lay last night. Have seen negroes, and white men, but did not approach them. An completely tired out and hungry, but on the edge of a nice little stream of water. The closing of the fifth day of my escape. Must speak to somebody tomorrow, or starve to death. Good deal of yelling in the woods. Am now in the rear of a hovel which is evidently a negro hut, but off quite a ways from it. Cleared ground all around the house so I can't approach it without being too much in sight. Small negro boy playing around the house. Too dark to write more.

Nov. 29.—The sixth day of freedom, and a hungry one. Still where I wrote last night, and watching the house. A woman goes out and in but cannot tell much about her from this distance. No men folks around. Two or three negro boys playing about. Must approach the house, but hate to. NOON. —Still right here. Hold my position. More than hungry. Three days since I have eaten anything, with the exception of a small pototoe and piece of bread eaten two days ago and left from the day before. That length of time would have been nothing in Andersonville, but now being in better health demand eatables, and it takes right hold of this wandering sinner. Shall go to the house towards night. A solitary woman lives there with some children. My ankle from the sprain and yesterday's walking is swollen and painful. Bathe it in water, which does it good. Chickens running around. Have serious meditations of getting hold of one or two of them after they go to roost, then go farther back into the wilderness, build a fire with my matches and cook them. That would be a royal feast. But if caught at it, it would go harder with me than if caught legitimately. Presume this is the habitation of some of the skulkers who return and stay home nights. Believe that chickens squawk when being taken from the roost. Will give that up and walk boldly up to the house.

CHAPTER ELEVEN

Re-Captured

Home Guards Gobble Me Up * Well Treated and Well Fed * Taken to Doctortown and From Thence to Blackshear * The Two Buck Boys as Runaways * Ride on a Passenger Train Prospects Ahead

DOCTORTOWN STATION, No. 5, *Nov. 30.*—Ha! Ha! My boy, you are a prisoner of war again. Once more with a blasted rebel standing guard over me, and it all happened in this wise: Just before dark I went up to that house I spoke of in my writings yesterday. Walked boldly up and rapped at the door; and what was my complete astonishment when a white woman answered my rapping. Asked me what I wanted, and I told her something to eat. Told me to come in and set down. She was a dark looking woman and could easily be mistaken from my hiding place of the day for a negro. Began asking me questions. Told her I was a rebel soldier, had been in the hospital sick and was trying to reach home in the adjoining county. Was very talkative; told how her husband had been killed at Atlanta, &c. She would go out and in from a shanty kitchen in her preparation of my supper. I looked out through a window and saw a little darky riding away from the house, a few minutes after I went inside. Thought I had walked into a trap, and was very uneasy. Still the woman talked and worked, and I talked, telling as smoothe lies as I knew how. For a full hour and a half sat there, and she all the time getting supper. Made up my mind that I was the same as captured, and so put on a bold face and made the best of it. Was very well satisfied with my escapade anyway, if I could only get a whack at that supper before the circus commenced. Well, after a while heard some hounds coming through the woods and towards the house. Looked at the woman and her face pleaded guilty, just as if she had done something very mean. The back door of the house was open and pretty soon half a dozen large blood hounds bounded into the room and began snuffing me over; about this time the woman began to cry. Told her I understood the whole thing and she need not make a scene over it. Said she knew I was a Yankee and had sent for some men at Doctortown. Then five horsemen surrounded the house, dismounted and four of them came in with guns cocked prepared for a desperate encounter. I said: "Good evening, gentlemen." "Good evening," said the foremost, "We are looking for a runaway Yankee prowling around here." "Well," says I, "You needn't look any farther, you have found him." "Yes, I see," was the answer. They all sat down, and just then the woman said "supper is ready and to draw nigh." Drawed as nigh as I could to that supper and proceeded to take vengeance on the woman. The fellows proved to be home guards stationed here at Doctortown. The woman had mounted the negro boy on a horse just as soon as I made my appearance at the house and sent for them. They proved to be good fellows. Talked there at the house a full hour on the fortunes of war, &c. Told them of my long imprisonment and escape and all about myself. After a while we got ready to start for this place. One rebel rode in front, one on each side and two in the rear of me. Was informed that if I tried to run they would shoot me. Told them no danger of my running, as I could hardly walk. They soon saw that such was the case after going a little way, and sent back one of the men to borrow the woman's horse. Was put on the animal's back and we reached Doctortown not far from midnight. As we were leaving the house the woman gave me a bundle; said in it was a shirt and stockings. Told her she had injured me enough and I would take them. No false delicacy will prevent my taking a shirt. And so my adventure has ended and have enjoyed it hugely. Had plenty to eat with the exception of the two days, and at the last had a horseback ride. How well I was reminded of my last ride when first taken prisoner and at the time I got the coverlid. In the bundle was a good white shirt, pair of stockings, and a chunk of dried beef of two pounds or so. One of the captors gave me ten dollars in Confederate money. Now am in an old vacant building and guarded and it is the middle of the afternoon. Many citizens have visited me and I tell the guard he ought to charge admission; money in it. Some of the callers bring food and are allowed to give it to me, and am stocked with more than can conveniently carry. Have had a good wash up, put on my clean white shirt with standing collar, and new stockings and am happy. Doctortown is a small village with probably six or eight hundred population, and nigger young ones by the scores. Am treated kindly and well, and judge from conversations that I hear, that the battles are very disastrous to the rebels and that the war is pretty well over. All the negroes are hard pressed, fortifying every available point to contest the advance of the Union Army. This is cheering news to me. My escape has given me confidence in myself, and I shall try it again the first opportunity. A woman has just given me a bottle of milk and two dollars in money. Thanked her with my heart in my mouth. Having been captured and brought to this place, am here waiting for them to get instructions as to what they shall do with me. They say I will probably be sent to the prison at Blackshear, which is forty or fifty miles away. Think I should be content to stay here with plenty to eat. Am in a good clean room in a dwelling. Can talk with any one who chooses to come and see me. The room was locked during the night, and this morning was thrown open, and I can wander through three rooms. Guard is off a few rods where he can see all around the house. Occasionally I go out doors and am having a good time. LATER.—Have seen a Savannah paper which says Sherman and his hosts are marching toward that city, and for the citizens to rally to repel the invader. My swollen ankle is being rubbed to-day with ointment furnished by an old darky. I tell you there are humane people the world over, who will not see even an enemy suffer if they can help it. While I have seen some of the worst people in the South, I have also seen some of the very best, and those, too, who were purely southern people and rebels. There are many pleasant associations connected with my prison life, as well as some directly to the opposite.

Dec. 1.—Still at Doctortown, and the town is doctoring me up "right smart." There is also a joke to this, but a weak one. The whole town are exercised over the coming of the Yankee army, and I laugh in my sleeve. Once in a while some poor ignorant and bigoted fellow amuses himself cursing me and the whole U. S. army. Don't talk back much, having too much regard for my bodily comfort. Orders have come to put me on a train for Blackshear. Have made quite a number of friends here, who slyly talk to me encouragingly. There are many Union people all through the South, although they have not dared to express themselves as such, but now they are more decided in their expressions and actions. Had a canteen of milk, and many other luxuries. Darkys are profuse in their gifts of small things. Have now a comb, good jack knife, and many little nicknacks. One old negress brought

me a chicken nicely roasted. Think of that, prisoners of war,
roast chicken! Shall jump off the cars every twenty-rods hereafter. Tried to get a paper of the guard, who was reading the
latest, but he wouldn't let me see it. Looks rather blue himself, and I surmise there is something in it which he don't
like. All right, old fellow, my turn will come some day.
Young darky brought me a cane, which is an improvement
on my old one. Walk now the length of my limit with an old
fashioned crook cane and feel quite proud. LATER.—Got all
ready to take a train due at 3:30, and it didn't stop. Must wait
until morning. Hope they won't stop for a month.

BLACKSHEAR, GA., *Dec. 2.*—In with the same men whom I
deserted on the cars. We are near the Florida line. Was put
in a passenger train at Doctortown and rode in style to this
place. On the train were two more Yanks named David and
Eli S. Buck, who are Michigan men. They were runaways
who had been out in the woods nearly three months and were
in sight of our gunboats when recaptured. Belong to the 6th
Michigan Cavalry. David Buck was one of Kilpatrick's scouts;
a very smart and brave fellow, understands living in the
woods, and thoroughly posted. We have mutually agreed to
get away the first chance, and shall get to our lines. David
Buck used to attend school at Leoni, Mich., and was educated
for a preacher. They are cousins. We three Yankees were
quite a curiosity to the passengers on the train that brought us
to this place. Some of them had evidently never seen a Yankee
before, and we were stared at for all we were worth. Some
smarties were anxious to argue the point with us in a rather
"we have got you" style. David Buck is a good talker, and
satisfactorily held up our end of the war question; in fact, I

thought talked them all out on their own grounds. The ladies in particular sneered and stared at us. Occasionally we saw some faces which looked as if they were Union, and we often got a kind word from some of them. The railroads are in a broken down condition, out of decent repair, and trains run very slow. The Confederacy is most assuredly hard up, and will go to pieces some of these days. My out door life of the few days I roamed through the woods, was just jolly. Being out from under rebel guard made me the happiest chap imaginable. Knew that I couldn't escape to our lines, as I was not able to travel much, and my sole business was to remain a tramp as long as possible, and to get enough to eat, which I did. The negroes, and especially the field hands, are all Union darkys, and fed me all I wanted as a general thing. Made a mistake in going to the house of a white woman for food.

Dec. 3.—Blackshear is an out-of-the-way place, and shouldn't think the Yankee army would ever find us here. The climate is delightful. Here it is December and at the North right in the middle of winter, and probably good sleighing, and cold; while here it is actually warm during the day time, and at night not uncomfortably cold. The Buck boys are jolly good fellows, and full of fun. Seem to have taken a new lease of life myself. Both of them are in good health and fleshy, and open for an escape any hour. And we don't stay here but a few days, the guards say. Why not keep us on the cars and run us around the country all the time? There is no wall or anything around us here, only guards. Encamped right in the open air. Have food once a day, just whatever they have to give us. Last night had sweet potatoes. I am getting considerably heavier in weight, and must weigh one hundred and forty pounds or more. Still lame, however, and I fear permanently so. Teeth are firm in my mouth now, and can eat as well as ever, and oh! such an appetite. Would like to see the pile of food that I couldn't eat. Found Rowe and Bullock, and Hub Dakin. They are well, and all live in jolly expectancy of the next move. The old coverlid still protects my person. The Bucks have also each a good blanket, and we are comfortable. Some fresh beef given us to-day; not much, but suppose all they have got. Guard said he wished to God he was one of us prisoners instead of guarding us.

Dec. 4.—Another delightfully cool morning. There are not a great many guards here to watch over us, and it would be possible for all to break away without much trouble. The men, however, are so sure of liberty that they prefer to wait until given legitimately. Would like to have seen this guard hold us last summer at Andersonville. Fresh meat again to-day. Rebels go out to neighboring plantations and take cattle, drive them here, and butcher for us to eat. Rice is also given us to eat. Have plenty of wood to cook with. Have traded off the old mis-mated pair of brogans for a smaller and good pair, and feel quite like a dandy. Have some money to buy extras. Have plenty of food yet from that given me at Doctortown. Divide with the Bucks, or rather, it is all one common mess, and what any one owns belongs equally to the others. Rebels glum and cross, and sometimes we laugh at them, and then they swear and tell us to shut up or they will blow our heads off. Blackshear is a funny name and it is a funny town, if there is any, for as yet I haven't been able to see it. Probably a barn and a hen-coop comprise the place. Cars go thundering by as if the Yanks were after them. About every train loaded with troops. Go first one way and then the other. Think they are trying to keep out of the way themselves.

Dec. 5.—Guard said that orders were not to talk with any of the prisoners, and above all not to let us get hold of any newspapers. No citizens are allowed to come near us. That shows which way the wind blows. Half a dozen got away from here last night, and guards more strict to-day, with an increased force. Going to be moved, it is said, in a few days. Why don't they run us right into the ocean? That wouldn't do though, our gunboats are there. Well, keep us then, that is punishment enough. Do what you are a mind to. You dare not starve us now, for we would break away. In fact, although under guard, we are masters of the situation. Can see an old darky with an ox hitched to a cart with harness on, the cart loaded with sugar cane. This is quite a sugar country, it is said. On the road here saw the famous palmetto tree in groves. Live-oaks are scattered all over, and are a funny affair. Persimmon and pecan trees also abound here. We are pretty well south now, spending the winter. But few die now; no more than would naturally die in any camp with the same numbers. It is said that some men get away every night, and it is probably so.

Dec. 6.—Thirteen months ago to-day captured—one year and one month. Must be something due me from Uncle Sam in wages, by this time. All come in a lump when it does come. No great loss without small gain, and while I have been suffering the long imprisonment my wages have been accumulating. Believe that we are also entitled to ration money while in prison. Pile it on, you can't pay us any too much for this business. This is the land of the blood hound. Are as common as the ordinary cur at the North. Are a noble looking dog except when they are after you, and then they are beastly. Should think that any one of them could whip a man; are very large, strong, and savage looking. Should think it would be hard for the negro to run away. See no horses about here at all— all mules and oxen, and even cows hitched up to draw loads. I walk the prison over forty times a day. Everybody knows me, and I hail and am hailed as I walk around, and am asked what I think of the situation. Tell them of my escape and the good time I had, which incites them to do likewise the first opportunity. Occasionally a man here who growls and grumbles, and says and thinks we will never get away, &c. Some would find fault if they were going to be hung. Should think they would compare their condition with that of six months ago and be contented.

Dec. 7.—Another day of smiling weather. Still call our mess the Astor House Mess. It is composed of only three— the Bucks and myself. I am the only one of the original mess here, and it is still the most prosperous and best fed of any. We are all the time at work at something. Have a good piece of soap, and have washed our clothing throughout, and are clean and neat for prisoners of war. Eli S. Buck is a large fellow, and a farmer when at home. Both are young, and from the same neighborhood. As I have said before, are cousins, and think a great deal of one another, which is good to see. Relatives rarely get along together in prison as well as those who are not related. There were brothers in Andersonville who would not mess together. Seems funny, but such is the case. Should like to see myself throwing over a brother for any one else. Guards denounce Jeff Davis as the author of their misfortunes. We also denounce him as the author of ours, so we are agreed on one point. Going to move. The "mess" will escape *en masse* at the first move, just for the sake of roaming the woods. With the Bucks in company with me, shall have a good time, and we can undoubtedly soon reach our troops in as much as they are raiding through the South. Dave Buck is the acknowledged leader of us. He prays; think of that.

Dec. 8.—There are many men of many minds here. That used to be a favorite copy at writing school in Jackson, Mich. "Many men of many minds, many birds of many kinds." How a person's thoughts go back to the old boyhood days in such a place as this. Happiest times of life are those of youth, but we didn't know it. Everybody told us so, but we didn't believe it; but now it is plain. Every one, I think, has that experience. We all see where we might have done different if we only had our lives to live over, but alas, it is not to be. A majority of the men here have about half enough to eat. Our mess has enough to eat, thanks to our own ingenuity. Now expect to go away from here every day. Have borrowed a needle, begged some thread, and have been sewing up my clothing; am well fixed up, as are also the Bucks. Am quite handy with the needle, and it is difficult to make some of them believe I am not a tailor by trade. If I always keep my ways mended as I do my clothes, I shall get along very well. Eli has come with four large yams bought of a guard and we will proceed to cook and eat a good supper, and then go to bed and perhaps dream of something pleasant to remember the next day. Rumors of all kinds in camp, and rebels say something is up that will interest us, but I can get no satisfaction as to what it is. Drew cuts for the extra potato, and Dave won, and he cut that article of food into three pieces and we all had a share. Good boy.

Dec. 9.—Still in Blackshear, and quiet. Many incidents happened when I was out in the wood, and I am just crazy to get there once more. Look at the tall trees in sight, and could hug them. My long sickness and the terrible place in which I was confined so long, and my recovering health, and the hope now of getting entirely well and recovering my liberty, has made a new man of me—a new lease of life, as it were. The Bucks are the best of fellows, and having money which they use for my benefit the same as their own, we get along swimmingly. One of these days my Northern friends and relatives will hear from me. Am getting over my lameness, and have an appetite for more than my supply of food. Certainly had a good constitution to stand all that has been passed through, during which time thousands and thousands died, of apparently better health than myself. Of all my many messmates and friends in prison, have lost track of them all; some died, in fact nearly all, and the balance scattered, the Lord only knows where. What stories we can talk over when we meet at the North. This Blackshear country is rather a nice section. Warm and pleasant, although rather low. Don't know where we are located, but must be not far from the coast.

Dec. 10.—The grand change has come and a car load of prisoners go away from here to-day. Although the Bucks and myself were the last in prison, we are determined to flank out and go with the first that go. Our destination is probably Charleston, from what I can learn. We three will escape on the road, or make a desperate effort to do so, anyway. Can walk much better now than ten days ago, and feel equal to the emergency. Fine weather and in good spirits, although many here are tired of being moved from place to place. More guards have come to take charge of us on the road, and it looks very discouraging for getting away, although "Dave" says we will make it all right. Place great reliance in him, as he has caution as well as the intention to escape. So like Hendryx, and added to it has more practical quiet common sense. Eli Buck and myself acknowledge him as leader in all things. Now comes the tug of war.

Dec. 11.—We flanked out this morning, or rather paid three fellows two dollars apiece for their turn to go. Are now thirty miles from Blackshear; have been unloaded from the cars and are encamped by the side of the railroad track for the night. Most dark. Rebel soldiers going by on the trains, with hoots and yells. We are strongly guarded, and it augurs not for us to get away to-night. Our best hold is jumping from the cars. Ride on open platform cars with guards standing and sitting on the sides, six guards to each car. About sixty prisoners ride on each car, and there are thirty or forty cars. Were given rations yesterday, but none to-day. It is said we get nothing to eat to-night, which is bad; more so for the other prisoners than ourselves. Low country we come through, and swampy. Bucks think we may get away before morning, but I doubt it. Rebs flying around lively, and Yanks going for them I guess.

Dec. 12.—Routed up at an early hour and loaded on to the cars, which stood upon a side track, and after being loaded have been here for six mortal hours. Small rations given us just before loading up. All are cramped up and mad.

We will more than jump the first opportunity. We go to Charleston, via Savannah. Wish they would hurry up their old vehicles for transportation. Being doubled up like a jack knife makes my legs stiff and sore, and difficult to use my limbs from cramped position. Worth four hundred dollars a day to see the rebel troops fly around. Would give something to know the exact position now of both armies. Guards are sleepy and tired out from doing double duty, and I think we can get away if they move us by night, which I am afraid they won't do. Bucks jubilant and confident, consequently so am I.

CHAPTER TWELVE

A Successful Escape

**Jump Off the Cars Near Savannah ✻ Find
Friendly Negroes ✻ Travel by Night and
Rest by Day ✻ Good Times
with Many Adventures ✻ A Morning Bath ✻
Almost Run into Rebel Pickets**

IN THE WOODS, *Dec. 13.*—How does that sound for a location to date from? Yesterday long toward night our train started from its abiding place and rolled slowly toward its destination, wherever that might be. When near Savannah, not more than a mile this side, David Buck jumped off the cars and rolled down the bank. I jumped next and Eli Buck came right after me. Hastily got up and joined one another, and hurried off in an easterly direction through the wet, swampy country. A number of shots were fired at us, but we were surprised and glad to find that none hit us, although my cap was knocked off by a bullet hitting the fore-piece. Eli Buck was also singed by a bullet. It seemed as if a dozen shots were fired. Train did not stop, and we ran until tired out. Knew that we were within a line of forts which encircle Savannah, going all the way around it and only twenty rods or so apart. It was dark when we jumped off, and we soon came in the vicinity of a school house in which was being held a negro prayer meeting. We peeked in at the windows, but dared not stop so near our jumping off place. Worked around until we were near the railroad again and guided by the track going south—the same way we had come. It was very dark. Dave Buck went ahead, Eli next and myself last, going Indian file and very slow. All at once Dave stopped and whispered to us to keep still, which you may be sure we did. Had come within ten feet of a person who was going directly in the opposite direction and also stopped, at the same time we did. Dave Buck says: "Who comes there?" A negro woman says "it's me," and he walked up close to her and asked where she was going. She says: "Oh! I knows you; you are Yankees and has jumped off de cars." By this time we had come up even with Dave and the woman. Owned up to her that such was the case. She said we were her friends, and would not tell of us. Also said that not twenty rods ahead there was a rebel picket, and we were going right into them. I think if I ever wanted to kiss a woman, it was that poor, black, negro wench. She told us to go about thirty rods away and near an old shed, and she would send us her brother; he would know what to do. We went to the place designated and waited there an hour, and then we saw two dusky forms coming through the darkness, and between them a wooden tray of food consisting of boiled turnips, corn bread and smoked bacon. We lay there behind that old shed and ate and talked, and talked and ate, for a full hour more. The negro, "Major," said he was working on the forts, putting them in order to oppose the coming of the Yankees, and he thought he could get us through the line before morning to a safe hiding place. If we all shook hands once we did fifty times, all around. The negroes were fairly jubilant at being able to help genuine Yankees. Were very smart colored people, knowing more than the ordinary run of their race. Major said that in all the forts was a reserve picket force, and between the forts the picket. He said pretty well south was a dilapidated fort which had not as yet been repaired any, and that was the one to go through or near, as he did not think there was any picket there. "Bress de Lord, for yo' safety," says the good woman. We ate all they brought us, and then started under the guidance of Major at somewhere near midnight. Walked slow and by a roundabout way to get to the fort and was a long time about it, going through a large turnip patch and over and through hedges. Major's own safety as much as ours depended upon the trip. Finally came near the fort and discovered there were rebels inside and a picket off but a few rods. Major left us and crawled slowly ahead to reconnoitre; returned in a few minutes and told us to follow. We all climbed over the side of the fort, which was very much out of repair. The reserve picket was asleep around a fire which had nearly gone out. Major piloted us through the fort, actually stepping over the sleeping rebels. After getting on the outside there was a wide ditch which we went through. Ditch was partially full of water. We then went way round near the railroad again, and started south, guided by the darky, who hurried us along at a rapid gait. By near day light we were five or six miles from Savannah, and then stopped for consultation and rest. Finally went a mile further, where we are now laying low in a swamp, pretty well tired out and muddy beyond recognition. Major left us at day light, saying he would find us a guide before night who would show us still further. He had to go back and work on the forts. And so I am again loose, a free man, with the same old feeling I had when in the woods before. We got out of a thick settled country safely, and again await developments. Heard drums and bugles playing reveille this morning in many directions, and "We are all surrounded." David Buck is very confident of getting away to our lines. Eli thinks it is so if Dave says so, and I don't know, or care so very much. The main point with me is to stay out in the woods as long as I can. My old legs have had a hard time of it since last night and ache, and are very lame. It's another beautiful and cold day, this 13th of

December. Biting frost nights, but warmer in the day time. Our plan is to work our way to the Ogechee River, and wait for the Stars and Stripes to come to us. Major said Sherman was marching right toward us all the time, driving the rebel army with no trouble at all. Told us to keep our ears open and we would hear cannon one of these days, possibly within a week. The excitement of the last twenty-four hours has worn me out, and I couldn't travel to-day if it was necessary. Have a plenty to eat, and for a wonder I ain't hungry for anything except things we haven't got. Dave is happy as an oyster, and wants to yell. Where they are so confident I am satisfied all will be well. As soon as it comes night we are going up to some negro huts less than a mile off, where we hope and expect that Major has posted the inmates in regard to us. The railroad is only a short distance off, and the river only three or four miles. As near as we know, are about twenty miles from the Atlantic coast. Tell the boys it may be necessary for me to stay here for two or three days to get recruited up, but they think three or four miles to-night will do me good. Don't like to burden them and shall try it.

Dec. 14.—We are now three miles from yesterday's resting place, and near the Miller plantation. Soon as dark last night we went to the negro huts and found them expecting us. Had a jubilee. No whites near, but all away. The Buck boys passed near here before when out in the woods, and knew of many darkys who befriended them. Had a surfeit of food. Stayed at the huts until after midnight, and then a woman brought us to this place. To-night we go to Jocko's hut, across the river. A darky will row us across the Little Ogechee to Jocko's hut, and then he will take us in tow. It is a rice country about here, with canals running every way. Negroes all tickled to death because Yankees coming. I am feeling better than yesterday, but difficult to travel. Tell the boys they had better leave me with the friendly blacks and go ahead to our lines, but they won't. Plenty to eat and milk to drink, which is just what I want. The whites now are all away from their homes and most of the negroes. Imagine we can hear the booming of cannon, but guess we are mistaken. Dave is very entertaining and good company. Don't get tired of him and his talk. Both of them are in rebel dress throughout, and can talk and act just like rebels. Know the commanders of different rebel regiments. They say that when out before they on different occasions mixed with the Southern army, without detection. Said they didn't wonder the widow woman knew I was a Yankee. Ain't up to that kind of thing.

Dec. 15.—Jocko's hut was not across the river as I supposed and wrote yesteday, but on the same side we were on. At about ten o'clock last night we went to his abiding place as directed and knocked. After a long time an old black head was stuck out of the window with a nightcap on. The owner of the head didn't know Jocko or anything about him; was short and crusty; said: "Go way from dar!" Kept talking to him and he scolding at being disturbed. Said he had rheumatics and couldn't get out to let us in. After a long time opened the door and we set down on the door step. Told him we were Yankees and wanted help. Was the funniest darky we have met yet. Would give something for his picture as he was framed in his window in the moonlight talking to us, with the picturesque surroundings, and us Yankees trying to win him over to aid us. Finally owned up that he was Jocko, but said he couldn't row us across the river. He was lame and could not walk, had no boat, and if he had the river was so swift he couldn't get us across, and if it wasn't swift, the rebels would catch him at it and hang him. Talked a long time and with much teasing. By degrees his scruples gave way, one at a time. Didn't know but he might row us across if he only had a boat, and finally didn't know but he could find a boat. To get thus far into his good graces took at least three hours. Went looking around and found an old scow, fixed up some old oars, and we got in; before doing so however, he had warmed up enough to give us some boiled sweet potatoes and cold baked fish. Rowed us way down the river and landed us on the noted Miller plantation and a mile in rear of the negro houses. Jocko, after we forced our acquaintance on him with all kind of argument, proved to be a smart able bodied old negro, but awful afraid of being caught helping runaways. Would give something for his picture as he appeared to us looking out of his cabin window. Just an old fashioned, genuine negro, and so black that charcoal would make a white mark on him. Took us probably three miles from his hut, two miles of water and one of land, and then started back home after shaking us a dozen times by the hand, and "God blessing us." Said "Ole Massa Miller's niggers all Union niggers," and to go up to the huts in broad day light and they would help us. No whites at home on the plantation. We arrived where Jocko left us an hour or so before daylight, and lay down to sleep until light. I woke up after a while feeling wet, and found the tide had risen and we were surrounded with water; woke up the boys and scrambled out of that in a hurry, going through two feet of water in some places. The spot where we had laid down was a higher piece of ground than that adjoining. Got on to dry land and proceeded to get dry. At about ten o'clock Dave went up to the negro huts and made himself known, which was hard work. The negroes are all afraid that we are rebels and trying to get them into a scrape, but after we once get them thoroughly satisfied that we are genuine Yanks they are all right, and will do anything for us. The negroes have shown us the big house, there being no whites around, they having left to escape the coming Yankee army. We went up into the cupola and looked way off on the ocean, and saw our own noble gunboats. What would we give to be aboard of them? Their close proximity makes us discuss the feasibility of going down the river and out to them, but the negroes say there are chain boats across the river farther down, and picketed. Still it makes us anxious, our being so near, and we have decided to go down the river to-night in a boat and see if we can't reach them. It is now the middle of the afternoon and we lay off from the huts eighty rods, and the negroes are about to bring us some dinner. During the night we traveled over oyster beds by the acre, artificial ones, and they cut our feet. Negroes say there are two other runaways hid a mile off and they are going to bring them to our abiding place. LATER. —Negroes have just fed us with corn bread and a kind of fish about the size of sardines, boiled by the kettle full, and they are nice. Fully as good as sardines. Think I know now where nearly all the imported sardines come from. Negroes catch them by the thousands, in nets, put them in kettles, and cook them a few minutes, when they are ready to eat. Scoop them out of the creeks. The two other runaways are here with us. They are out of the 3d Ohio Cavalry. Have been out in the woods for two weeks. Escaped from Blackshear and traveled this far. I used to know one of them in Savannah. We do not take to them at all, as they are not of our kind. Shall separate to-night, they going their way and we going ours. Have secured a dug-out boat to go down the Ogechee River with to-night. The negroes tell us of a Mr. Kimball, a white man, living up the country fifteen miles, who is a Union man, and helps runaways, or any one of Union proclivities. He lays up the river, and our gunboats lay down the river. Both have wonderful charms for us, and shall decide before night which route to take. Are on rice plantation, and a valuable one. Before the "wah" there were over fifteen hundred negroes on this place. Cotton is also part of the production. Have decided to go down the river and try to reach our gunboats. It's a very hazardous undertaking, and I have my doubts as to its successful termination.

Dec. 16.—Another adventure, and a red hot one. Started down the river in our dug-out boat somewhere near midnight. Ran down all right for an hour, frequently seeing rebel pickets and camp fires. Saw we were going right into the lion's mouth, as the farther down the more rebels. All at once our boat gave a lurch and landed in a tree top which was sticking out of the water, and there we were, swaying around in the cold water in the middle or near the middle of the Ogechee. Dave went ashore and to a negro hut, woke up the inmates, and narrated our troubles. A negro got up, and with another boat came to the rescue. Were about froze with the cold and wet. Said not more than a mile farther down we would have run right into a chain boat, with pickets posted on it. It really

DAVID BUCK

seems as if a Divine providence were guiding us. After getting
a breakfast of good things started off toward the Big Ogechee
River, and have traveled three or four miles. Are now encamped, or rather laying down, on a little hillock waiting for
evening, to get out of this vicinity which is a dangerous one.
In our river escapade lost many of our things, but still hang to
my coverlid and diary. There are three or four houses in
view, and principally white residences, those of the poor white
trash order, and they are the very ones we must avoid. Have
caught cold and am fearfully out of traveling condition, but
must go it now. A mistake in coming down the river. Am
resting up, preparatory to traveling all night up the country.
No chance of getting out by the coast. Have enough food to
last all day and night, and that is a good deal. Can't carry
more than a day's supply. Have now been out in the woods,
this is the fourth day, and every day has been fresh adventures
thick and fast. If I could only travel like my comrades, would
get along. Bucks praise me up and encourage me to work
away, and I do. For breakfast had more of those imported
sardines. Storm brewing of some sort and quite chilly. Saw
rebel infantry marching along the highway not more than
eighty rods off. Hugged the ground very close. Dogs came
very near us, and if they had seen us would have attracted
the rebels' attention. Am writing with a pencil less than an
inch long. Shall print this diary and make my everlasting fortune, and when wealthy will visit this country and make every
negro who has helped us millionaires. Could not move from
here half a mile by daylight without being seen, and as a
consequence we are feeling very sore on the situation. Don't
know but I shall be so lame to-night that I cannot walk at all,

and then the boys must leave me and go ahead for themselves. However, they say I am worth a hundred dead men yet, and will prod me along like a tired ox. Dave goes now bareheaded, or not quite so bad as that, as he has a handkerchief tied over his head. The programme now is to go as straight to Mr. Kimball's as we can. He is probably twenty miles away; is a white Union man I spoke of a day or so ago in this same diary. Will stick to him like a brother. Can hear wagons go along the road toward Savannah, which is only thirteen or fourteen miles away. LATER.—Most dark enough to travel and I have straightened up and am taking an inventory of myself. Find I can walk with the greatest difficulty. The boys argue that after I get warmed up I will go like a top, and we will see.

Dec. 17.—And another day of vicissitudes. We traveled last night about four miles, piloted by a young negro. It was a terrible walk to me; slow and painful. Were fed, and have food for to-day. Are now about three miles from a canal which we must cross before another morning. Negroes say "Sherman most here" and "Bress de Lord!" Mr. Kimball lives nine miles away and we must reach him some way, but it seems an impossibility for me to go so far. Are now in a high and fine country, but too open for us. Have to lay down all day in the bushes. David is a thorough scout. Goes crawling around on his hands and knees taking in his bearings. Troops are encamped on the main road. Every cross road has its pickets, and it is slow business to escape running into them. Eli S. Buck has a sore throat and is hoarse. Pretty good jaunt for him, tough as he is. Shall have no guide to-night, as Dave thinks he can engineer us all right in the right direction. Some thinks he will leave us both and reach Kimball's to-night, and then come back and see us through. Guess I will be on hand to go along however.

Dec. 18.—Six days of freedom and what a sight of hardship, sweetened by kind treatment and the satisfaction of being out from under guard. We traveled last night some four miles and now are in a very precarious position. When almost daylight we came to the canal, and found cavalry pickets all along the tow-path; walked along until we came to a lock. A cavalryman was riding his horse up and down by the lock. At the lock there was a smoldering fire. It was absolutely necessary that we get across before daylight. As the mounted picket turned his horse's head to go from us, Dave slid across the tow-path and went across the timbers which formed the lock, and by the time the picket turned around to come back Dave was hid on the opposite shore. At the next trip of the rebel Eli went the same as Dave. The third one to go was myself, and I expected to get caught, sure. Could not go as quiet as the rest, and was slower. Thought the picket saw me when half way across but kept right on going, and for a wonder made it all right. Was thoroughly scared for the first time since jumping off the train. Am very nervous. All shook hands when the picket turned about to go back the fourth time. Getting light in the east and we must move on, as the country is very open. Dare not travel over half a mile, and here we are hid almost in a woman's door yard, not over thirty rods from her very door. Are in some evergreen bushes and shrubs. It's now most noon, and have seen a rather elderly lady go out and in the house a number of times. The intrepid Dave is going up to the house to interview the lady soon. LATER.—Dave crawled along from our hiding place until he came to the open ground, and then straightened boldly up and walked to the house. In fifteen minutes he came back with some bread and dried beef, and said the woman was a Union woman and would help us. Her daughter slept at her uncle's a mile off last night, and expected her back soon, and perhaps the uncle, who is a violent Secesh, with her. Said for us to lay low. LATER.—The daughter came home on horseback and alone. Could see the old lady telling the daughter about us and pointing our way. About the middle of the afternoon the old lady started out toward us. Behind her came a young darky, and behind the darky came another darky; then a dog, then a white boy, then a darky, and then the daughter. Old lady peeked in, and so did the rest except the grown up girl, who was too afraid. Finally came closer, and as she got a good view of us she says: "Why, mother, they look just like anybody else." She had never seen a Yankee before. Brought us some more food, and after dark will set a table for us to come to the house and eat. Her name is Mrs. Dickinson. They went back to the house and we proceeded to shake hands with one another. During the afternoon five rebel soldiers came to the house, one at a time. It is now most dark and we are about ready to go to the house and eat. Mr. Kimball lives only four miles away.

Dec. 19.—We are now less than half a mile from Mr. Kimball's. After dark last night we went to Mrs. Dickinson's house and partook of a splendid supper. I wrote a paper directed to the officer commanding the first Yankee troops that should arrive here telling what she had done for us runaway Yankees. She talked a great deal, and I thought was careless leaving the front door open. Three or four times I

got up and shut that door. We had taken off our blankets
and other wraps and left them in a sort of a kitchen, and
were talking in the best room. I heard the gate click, and on
looking out saw two rebel officers coming to the house and
not six rods off. We jumped into the other room and out of the
back door and behind a corn house, bare headed. The officers
were asked into the front room by the daughter. They asked
who the parties were who ran out of the backway. She said she
reckoned no one. They kept at her and jokingly intimated
that some of her skulking lovers had been to see her. She kept
talking back and finally said: "Mother, did any one just go
away?" And the old lady said: "Why, yes, brother Sam and
his 'boy' just went off home." Them confounded rebels had
come to see the girl and spent the evening, and we shivering
out in the cold. Joked her for an hour and a half about her
lovers and we hearing every word. Finally they got up and
bid her good night, saying they would send back some men to
guard the house and keep her lovers away. Just as soon as
they were down the road a ways, the daughter came out very
frightened and said for us to hurry off, as they would send
back troops to look for us. Hurried into the house, got our
things and some dried beef, and started off toward Mr.
Kimball's house. Reached here just before daylight and lay
down back of the house about eighty rods, in the corner of
the fence, to sleep a little before morning. Just at break of
day heard some one calling hogs. David got up and went
toward an old man whom we knew was our friend Kimball.
Came to us, and was glad to shake hands with genuine
Yankees. Said one of his neighbors was coming over early to
go with him to hunt some hogs, and for us to go farther off

and stay until night, and he would think up during the day what to do with us. Did not want anything to eat. Came to this place where we now are, and feeling that our journey was most ended. Mr. Kimball said that Sherman was not over fifty miles off, and coming right along twenty miles per day, and our plan was to hide and await coming events. Mr. Kimball is an old man, probably sixty years old, white haired and stooped shouldered. He had five sons, all drafted into the rebel army. All refused to serve. Two have been shot by the rebels, one is in some prison for his Union proclivities, and two are refugees. The old man has been imprisoned time and again, his stock confiscated, property destroyed, and all together had a hard time of it. Still he is true blue, a Union man to the back bone. Really think our troubles coming to an end. Kimball said: "Glory to God, the old Stars and Stripes shall float over my house in less than a week!" It's a noble man who will stand out through all that he has, for his principles, when his interests are all here. Is not only willing, but glad to help us, and says anything he has is ours, if it will help us toward our escape. LATER.—Have been laying all day watching Kimball's house. Along in the morning the neighbor spoken of came to Kimball's, and they both went off on horseback to shoot hogs. The swine here roam over a large territory and become most wild, and when they want fresh pork they have to go after it with a gun. You may be sure the hunters did not come near us with Mr. Kimball for a guide. A negro boy went with them with a light wagon and mule attached. Near noon they returned with some killed hogs in the wagon. At three or four o'clock the old man came down where we were "to look after his boys," he said. Is in the best of spirits. Says we are to hide to-night where he tells us, and stay until our troops reach us. That is jolly good news for me, as I hate to travel. Said come to the house after dark and he would have a supper prepared for us, and has just left us. LATER.—Have just eaten a splendid supper at Kimball's and getting ready to travel three miles to a safe hiding place.

Dec. 20.—Well, we are just well fixed and happy. After partaking of a royal repast last night, served in an out-building near the main building of the Kimball home, we were directed to this place which is on the banks of the Big Ogechee river, in a most delightful spot. While we were at Kimball's he had negro sentinels stationed at different points on the plantation to announce the coming of any rebel soldiers or citizens that might see fit to come near. He gave us an axe, a quart of salt, a ham too big to carry conveniently, and all the sweet potatoes we could drag along; also a butcher knife. Went with us a mile as guide and then told us so we found the place pointed out. Also gave us some shelled corn to bait hogs and told Dave how to make a deadfall to catch them. We left the main road going directly west until we came to a fence, then turned to the left and followed the line of the fence, and when we had got to the end of it kept straight ahead going through a swampy low section. After a while came to higher and dry land and to the banks of the river. Is a sort of an island, and as I said before, a very pretty and pleasant spot. Out in the river grows tall canebrake which effectually hides us from any one going either up or down the river. Tall pines are here in abundance and nice grass plats, with as handsome palm clusters as ever I saw. Are going to build us a house to keep off the cold and rain. Have matches and a rousing fire cooked our breakfast of nice ham and sweet potatoes. We also roasted some corn and had corn coffee. Any quantity of hogs running around and Dave is already thinking of a trap to catch them. It will be necessary for we are making that ham look sick. Eat so much breakfast that we can hardly walk and don't know but will commit suicide by eating. Buzzards fly around attracted by the cooking. Are as large and look like turkeys. Our government should give to Mr. Kimball a fortune for his patriotism and sacrifices to the Union cause. About eight miles above is a long bridge across the river and there it is thought a big fight will take place when Sherman attempts to cross, and so we will know when they approach, as we could hear a battle that distance. NIGHT.—We have built the cosyest and nicest little house to lay in. Cut poles with the axe and made a frame, and then covered the top with palm leaves just like shingles on a house at the north, then fixed three sides the same way, each leaf overlapping the other, and the fourth side open to a fire and the river. The water is cold and clear and nice to drink; just like spring water. Have eaten the ham half up; ditto potatoes. The increased prosperity makes me feel well bodily, and mentally am more so. It is still the Astor House Mess. We all cook, and we all eat. Dave prays to-night as he does every night and morning, and I ain't sure but all through the day. Is a thorough Christian if ever there was one. I also wrote a letter for Mr. Kimball to the commanding Union officer who may first approach these parts. In it I told how he had befriended us and others. We heard boats going by on the river to-day. At such times all we do is to keep still, as no one can see us.

Rebels are too busy to look for us or any one else. All they can do now to take care of themselves. Eli is making up our bed, getting ready to turn in. I have just brought a tin pail of nice water and we all drink. Take off our shoes for the first time in some days. A beautiful night—clear and cold. And thus ends another day, and we are in safety.

Dec. 21.—Got up bright and early. Never slept better. Getting rested up. We talk continually. Both Bucks are great talkers, especially David. Cooked and ate our breakfast, and would you believe it the ham is all gone. Incredible, the amount of food we eat. Wonder it don't make us all sick. Sweet potatoes getting low. Dave fixing up his deadfall for hogs. Has rolled some heavy logs together forty rods away from our house, and fixed up a figure four spring-trap, with the logs for weight to hold down the animal which may be enticed into it. Has scattered corn in and around the trap, and we wait for developments. Hogs are very shy of us and surroundings. Are apparently fat and in good order. Plenty of roots and shack which they eat, and thrive thereon. Buzzards are very curious in regard to us. They light on the limbs in the trees, and if their support is a dead limb it breaks and makes a great noise in the still woods. Two or three hundred all together make a terrible racket, and scare us sometimes. The weather is very fine, and this must be a healthy climate. Dave is going out to-day to look around. As I have said before, he is a scout and understands spying around, and won't get caught. If we had a fish hook and line or a net of some sort could catch fish to eat. That would be a grand sport as we can see nice large fish in the water. The main road is away about one and a half miles we think by the sound of the teams which occasionally rumble along. Ofter hear shouting on the road as if cattle were being driven along toward Savannah. Once in a while we hear guns fired off, but it is no doubt hogs being killed. We also hear folks going up and down the river, but cannot see them. After dark we have no fire as that would expose us, it is so much plainer to be seen in the night. The river is wide; should think a third of a mile, as we can view it from away up the stream. The cane that grows in the river is the same as we have for fish poles at the North, and are shipped from the South. Have added some repairs to the house and it is now water tight, we think. Made a bed of soft boughs, and with our three blankets have a good sleeping place. Dave got a tall cane and fastened up on the house, and for a flag fastened on a piece of black cloth—the best we could do. That means no quarter; and it is just about what we mean, too. Don't believe we would be taken very easy now. I am getting fat every day, yet lame, and have come to the conclusion that it will be a long time before I get over it. The cords have contracted so in my right leg that they don't seem to stretch out again to their original length. That scurvy business came very near killing me. LATER.—I also went out of our hiding place, and saw away out in a field what I took to be a mound where sweet potatoes were buried. Came back and got a pair of drawers, tied the bottom of the legs together, and sallied forth. The mound of potatoes was a good way back from the house, although in plain sight. I crawled up, and began digging into it with a piece of canteen. Very soon had a hole in, and found some of the nicest potatoes that you can imagine, of the red variety, which I believe are the genuine Southern yam. Filled the drawers cram full, filled my pockets and got all I could possibly carry, then closed up the hole and worked my way back to camp. Eli was alone, Dave not having returned from his scouting trip. Had a war dance around those potatoes. Believe there is a bushel of them, and like to have killed myself getting them here. After I got into the woods and out of the field, straightened up and got the drawers on my shoulders and picked the way to headquarters. We don't any of us call any such thing as that stealing. It's one of the necessities of our lives that we should have food, and if we have not got it, must do the best we can. Now if we can catch a porker will be fixed all right for some days to come. Think it is about the time of year for butchering. We don't expect to be here more than two or three days at fartherest, although I shall hate to leave this beautiful spot, our nice house and all. Listen all the time for the expected battle at the bridge, and at any unusual sound of commotion in that direction we are all excitement. LATER.—Dave has returned. He went to the main road and saw a negro. Was lucky enough to get a Savannah paper three days old in which there was nothing we did not know in regard to Sherman's coming. The negro said Yankee scouts had been seen just across the river near the bridge, and the main army is expected every day. The rebels will fall back across the river and contest the crossing. Fortifications are built all along clear to Savannah, and it may be reasonably expected that some hard fighting will take place. Savannah is the pride of the South and they will not easily give it up. Dave did not tell the negro that he was a Yankee, but represented himself as a conscript hiding in the woods to keep from fighting in the rebel army. Was glad to see supply of potatoes and says I will do. Has freshly baited his trap for hogs and thinks before night we will have fresh pork to go with the potatoes. LATER. —We went around a drove of hogs and gradually and carefully worked them up to the trap. Pretty soon they began to pick up the corn and one of them went under the figure four, sprung it and down came the logs and such a squealing and scrambling of those not caught. The axe had been left near the trap standing up against a tree, and Dave ran up and grabbed it and struck the animal on the head and cut his throat. How we did laugh and dance around that defunct porker. Exciting sport this trapping for fresh pork. In half an hour Dave and Eli had the pig skinned and dressed. Is not a large one, probably weighs ninety pounds or so, and is fat and nice. Have sliced up enough for about a dozen men and are now cooking it on sticks held up before the fire. Also frying some in a skillet which we are the possessor of. When the hogs run wild and eat acorns, roots and the like, the meat is tough and curly but is sweet and good. We fry out the grease and then slice up the potatoes and cook in it. Thanks to Mr. Kimball we have plenty of salt to season our meat with. The buzzards are after their share which will be small. And now it is most night again and the Astor House larder is full. Seems too bad to go to bed with anything to eat on hand, but must. That is the feeling with men who have been starved so long, cannot rest in peace with food laying around. My two comrades are not so bad about that as I am, having been well fed for a longer period. Have sat up three or four hours after dark, talking over what we will do when we get home, and will now turn in for a sound sleep. It's a clear moonlight night, and we can hear very plain a long distance.

Can also see the light shining from camp fires in many directions, or what we take to be such.

Dec. 22.—As Dan Rice used to say in the circus ring: "Here we are again." Sleep so sound that all the battles in America could not wake me up. Are just going for that fresh pork to-day. Have three kinds of meat—fried pig, roast pork and broiled hog. Good any way you can fix it. Won't last us three days at this rate, and if we stay long enough will eat up all the hogs in these woods. Pretty hoggish on our part, and Dave says for gracious sake not to write down how much we eat, but as this diary is to be a record of what takes place, down it goes how much we eat. Tell him that inasmuch as we have a preacher along with us, we ought to have a sermon occasionally. Says he will preach if I will sing, and I agree to that if Eli will take up a collection. One objection Eli and I have to his prayers is the fact that he wants the rebels saved with the rest, yet don't tell him so. Mutually agree that his prayers are that much too long. Asked him if he thought it stealing to get those potatoes as I did, and he says no, and that he will go next time. We begin to expect the Yankees along. It's about time. Don't know what I shall do when I again see Union soldiers with guns in their hands, and behold the Stars and Stripes. Probably go crazy, or daft, or something. This is a cloudy, chilly day, and we putter around gathering up pine knots for the fire, wash our duds and otherwise busy ourselves. Have saved the hog skin to make moccasins of, if the Union army is whipped and we have to stay here eight or ten years. The hair on our heads is getting long again, and we begin to look like wild men of the woods. One pocket comb does for the entire party; two jack knives and a butcher knife. I have four keys jingling away in my pocket to remind me of olden times. Eli has a testament and Dave has a bible, and the writer hereof has not. Still, I get scripture quoted at all hours, which will, perhaps, make up in a measure. Am at liberty to use either one of their books, and I do read more or less. Considerable travel on the highways, and going both ways as near as we can judge. Dave wants to go out to the road again but we discourage him in it, and he gives it up for to-day at least. Are afraid he will get caught, and then our main stay will be gone. Pitch pine knots make a great smoke which rises among the trees and we are a little afraid of the consequences; still, rebels have plenty to do now without looking us up. Many boats go up and down the river and can hear them talk perhaps fifty rods away. Rebel paper that Dave got spoke of Savannah being the point aimed at by Sherman, also of his repulses; still I notice that keeps coming right along. Also quoted part of a speech by Jefferson Davis, and he is criticised unmercifully. Says nothing about any exchange of prisoners, and our old comrades are no doubt languishing in some prison. LATER.—Considerable firing up in vicinity of the bridge. Can hear volleys of musketry, and an occasional boom of cannon. Hurrah! It is now four o'clock by the sun and the battle is certainly taking place. LATER.—Go it Billy Sherman, we are listening and wishing you the best of success. Come right along and we will be with you. Give 'em another—that was a good one. We couldn't be more excited if we were right in the midst of it. Hurrah! It is now warm for the Johnnies. If we had guns would go out and fight in their rear; surround them, as it were. Troops going by to the front, and are cavalry, should think, also artillery. Can hear teamsters swearing away as they always do. LATER.— It is now long after dark and we have a good fire. Fighting has partially subsided up the river, but of course we don't know whether Yankee troops have crossed the river or not. Great deal of travel on the road, but can hardly tell which way they are going. Occasional firing. No sleep for us to-night. In the morning shall go out to the road and see how things look. Every little while when the battle raged the loudest, all of us three would hurrah as if mad, but we ain't mad a bit; are tickled most to death.

CHAPTER THIRTEEN

Safe and Sound

**Once More See the Old Flag and the Boys
in Blue ✻ Mr. Kimball and
Mrs. Dickinson Recompensed ✻ Find the Ninth
Michigan Cavalry ✻ Interviewed by
Gen'l Kilpatrick ✻ All Right at Last**

DEC. 23.—It is not yet daylight in the morning, and are anxiously awaiting the hour to arrive when we may go out to the road. Slept hardly any during the night. More or less fighting all night, and could hear an army go by toward Savannah, also some shouting directly opposite us. Between the hours of about twelve and three all was quiet, and then again more travel. We conjecture that the rebel army has retreated or been driven back, and that the Yankees are now passing along following them up. Shall go out about nine o'clock. LATER.—Are eating breakfast before starting out to liberty and safety. Must be very careful now and make no mistake. If we run into a rebel squad now, might get shot. We are nervous, and so anxious can hardly eat. Will pick up what we really need and start. Perhaps good bye, little house on the banks of the Ogechee, we shall always remember just how you look, and what a happy time we have had on this little island. Dave says: "Pick up your blanket and that skillet, and come along." NIGHT.—Safe and sound among our own United States Army troops, after an imprisonment of nearly fourteen months. Will not attempt to describe my feelings now. Could not do it. Staying with the 80th Ohio Infantry, and are pretty well tired out from our exertions of the day. At nine o'clock we started out toward the main road. When near it Eli and I stopped, and Dave went ahead to see who was passing. We waited probably fifteen minutes, and then heard Dave yell out: "Come on boys, all right! Hurry up!" Eli and I had a stream to cross on a log. The stream was some fifteen feet wide, and the log about two feet through. I tried to walk that log and fell in my excitement. Verily believe if the water had been a foot deeper I would have drowned. Was up to my arms, and I was so excited that I liked never to have got out. Lost the axe, which Dave had handed to me, and the old stand-by coverlid which had saved my life time and again floated off down the stream, and I went off without securing it—the more shame to me for it. Dave ran out of the woods swinging his arms and yelling like mad, and pretty soon Eli and myself appeared, whooping and yelling. The 80th Ohio was just going by, or a portion of it, however, and when they saw first one and then another and then the third coming toward them in rebel dress, with clubs which they mistook for guns, they wheeled into line, thinking, perhaps, that a whole regiment would appear next. Dave finally explained by signs, and we approached and satisfied them of our genuineness. Said we were hard looking soldiers, but when we came to tell them where we had been and all the particulars, they did not wonder. Went right along with them, and at noon had plenty to eat. Are the guests of Co. I, 80th Ohio. At three the 80th had a skirmish, we staying back a mile with some wagons, and this afternoon rode in a wagon. Only came about three or four miles to-day, and are near Kimball's, whom we shall call and see the first opportunity. The soldiers all look well and feel well, and say the whole Confederacy is about cleaned out. Rebels fall back without much fighting. Said there was not enough to call it a fight at the bridge. Where we thought it a battle, they thought it nothing worth speaking of. Believe ten or so were killed, and some wounded. Hear that some Michigan cavalry is with Kilpatrick off on another road, but they do not know whether it is the 9th Mich. Cav., or not. Say they see the cavalry every day nearly, and I must keep watch for my regiment. Soldiers forage on the plantations, and have the best of food; chickens, ducks, sweet potatoes, etc. The supply wagons carry nothing but hard-tack, coffee, sugar and such things. Tell you, coffee is a luxury, and makes one feel almost drunk. Officers come to interview us every five minutes, and we have talked ourselves most to death to-day. They say we probably will not be called upon to do any fighting during this war, as the thing is about settled. They have heard of Andersonville, and from the accounts of the place did not suppose that any lived at all. New York papers had pictures in, of the scenes there, and if such was the case it seems funny that measures were not taken to get us away from there. Many rebels are captured now, and we look at them from a different stand point than a short time since.

Dec. 24.—This diary must soon come to an end. Will fill the few remaining pages and then stop. Co. "I" boys are very kind. They have reduced soldiering to a science. All divided up into messes of from three to five each. Any mess is glad to have us in with them, and we pay them with accounts of our prison life. Know they think half we tell them is lies. I regret the most of anything, the loss of my blanket that stood by me so well. It's a singular fact that the first day of my imprisonment it came into my possession, and the very last day it took its departure, floating off away from me after having performed its mission. Should like to have taken it North to exhibit to my friends. The infantry move only a few miles each day, and I believe we stay here all day. Went and saw Mr. Kimball. The officers commanding knew him for a Union man, and none of his belongings were troubled. In fact, he has anything he wants now. Announces his intention of going with the army until the war closes. Our good old friend Mrs. Dickinson did not fare so well. The soldiers took everything she had on the place fit to eat; all her cattle, pork, potatoes, chickens, and left them entirely destitute. We went and saw them, and will go to headquarters to see what can be done. LATER.—We went to Gen. Smith, commanding 3d Brigade, 2d Division, and told him the particulars. He sent out foraging wagons, and now she has potatoes, corn, bacon, cattle, mules, and everything she wants. Also received pay for burned fences and other damages. Now they are smiling and happy and declare the Yankees to be as good as she thought them bad this morning. The men being under little restraint on this raid were often destructive. Nearly every citizen declared their loyalty, so no distinction is made. Gen. Smith is a very kind man, and asked us a great many questions. Says the 9th Michigan Cavalry is near us and we may see them any hour. Gen. Haun also takes quite an interest in us, and was equally instrumental with Gen. Smith in seeing justice done to our friends the Kimballs and Dickinsons. They declare now that one of us must marry the daughter of Mrs. Dickinson, the chaplain performing the ceremony. Well, she is a good girl, and I should judge would make a good wife, but presume she would have something to say herself and will not pop the question to her. They are very grateful, and only afraid that after we all go away the rebel citizens and soldiers will retaliate on them. Many officers have read portions of my diary, and say such scenes as we have passed through seem incredible. Many inquire if we saw so and so of their friends who went to Andersonville, but of course there were so many there that we cannot remember them. This has been comparatively a day of rest for this portion of the Union army, after having successfully crossed the river. We hear the cavalry is doing some fighting on the right, in the direction of Fort McAllister. EVENING.— We marched about two or three miles and are again encamped for the night, with pickets out for miles around. Many refugees join the army prepared to go along with them, among whom are a great many negroes.

Dec. 25.—Christmas day and didn't hang up my stocking. No matter, it wouldn't have held anything. Last Christmas we spent on Belle Island, little thinking long imprisonment awaiting us. Us escaped men are to ride in a forage wagon. The army is getting ready to move. Are now twenty-four miles from Savannah and rebels falling back as we press ahead. NIGHT.—At about nine o'clock this morning as we sat in the forage wagon top of some corn riding in state, I saw some cavalry coming from the front. Soon recognized Col. Acker at the head of the 9th Michigan Cavalry. Jumped out of the wagon and began dancing and yelling in the middle of the road and in front of the troop. Col. Acker said: "Get out of the road you——lunatic!" Soon made myself known and was like one arisen from the dead. Major Brockway said: "Ransom, you want to start for home. We don't know you, you are dead. No such man as Ransom on the rolls for ten months." All remember me and are rejoiced to see me back again. Lieut. Col. Way, Surgeon, Adjutant, Sergeant-Major, all shake hands with me. My company "A" was in the rear of the column, and I stood by the road as they moved along, hailing those I recognized. In every case had to tell them who I was and then would go up and shake hands with them at the risk of getting stepped on by the horses. Pretty soon Co. "A" appeared, and wasn't they surprised to see me. The whole company were raised in Jackson, Mich., my home, and I had been regarded as dead for nearly a year. Could hardly believe it was myself that appeared to them. Every one trying to tell me the news at home all at the same time—how I was reported as having died in Richmond and funeral sermon preached. How so and so had been shot and killed, &c., &c. And then I had to tell them of who of our regiment had died in Andersonville—Dr. Lewis, Tom McGill and others. Although Jimmy Devers did not belong to our regiment, many in our company knew him, and I told them of his death. Should have said that as soon as I got to the company, was given Capt. Johnson's lead horse to ride, without saddle or bridle and nothing but a halter to hang on with. Not being used to riding, in rebel dress—two or three pails hanging to me—I made a spectacle for them all to laugh at. It was a time of rejoicing. The Buck boys did not get out of the wagon with me and so we became separated without even a good bye. Before I had been with the company half an hour Gen. Kilpatrick and staff came riding by from the rear, and says to Capt. Johnson: "Captain, I hear one of your company has just joined you after escaping from the enemy." Capt. Johnson said, "Yes, sir," and pointed to me as a Sergeant in his company. General Kilpatrick told me to follow him and started ahead at a break neck pace. Inasmuch as the highway was filled with troops, Gen. Kilpatrick and staff rode at the side, through the fields, and any way they could get over the ground. The horse I was on is a pacer and a very hard riding animal and it was all I could do to hang on. Horse would jump over logs and come down on all fours ker-chug, and I kept hoping the General would stop pretty soon; but he didn't. Having no saddle or anything to guide the brute, it was a terrible hard ride for me, and time and again if I had thought I could fall off without breaking my neck should have done so. The soldiers all along the line laughed and hooted at the spectacle and the staff had great sport, which was anything but sport for me. After a while and after riding five or six miles, Kilpatrick drew up in a grove by the side of the road and motioning me to him, asked me when I escaped, etc. Soon saw I was too tired and out of breath. After resting a few minutes I proceeded to tell him what I knew of Savannah, the line of forts around the city, and of other fortifications between us and the city, the location of the rivers, force of rebels, etc. Asked a great many questions and took down notes, or rather the Chief of Staff, Estes by name, did. After an extended conversation a dispatch was made up and sent to Gen. Sherman who was a few miles away, with the endorsement that an escaped prisoner had given the information and it was reliable. General Kilpatrick told me I would probably not be called upon to do any more duty as I had done good service as a prisoner of war. Said he would sign a furlough and recommended that I go home as soon as communication was opened. Thanked me for information and dismissed me with congratulations on my escape. Then I waited until our company, "A," came up and joined them, and here I am encamped with the boys, who are engaged in getting supper. We are only twelve or fourteen miles from

Savannah and the report in camp is to the effect that the city
has been evacuated with no fight at all. Fort McAllister was
taken to-day, which being the key to Savannah, leaves that
city unprotected, hence the evacuation. Communication will
now be opened with the gunboats on the coast and I will be
sent home to Michigan. I mess with Capt. Johnson and there
is peace and plenty among us. I go around from mess to mess
this pleasant night talking with the boys, learning and telling
the news. O. B. Driscoll, Al. Williams, Sergt. Smith, Mell
Strickland, Sergt. Fletcher, Teddy Fox, Lieut. Ingraham and
all the rest think of something new every few minutes, and I
am full. Poor Robt. Strickland, a boy whom I enlisted, was
shot since starting out on this march to the sea. Others too,
whom I left well are now no more. The boys have had a
long and tedious march, yet are all in good health and have
enjoyed the trip. They never tire of telling about their fights
and skirmishes, and anecdotes concerning Kilpatrick, who is
well liked by all the soldiers. Am invited to eat with every
mess in the company, also at regimental headquarters, in fact,
anywhere I am a mind to, can fill. And now this Diary is
finished and is full. Shall not write any more, though I hardly
know how I shall get along, without a self-imposed task of
some kind.

END OF DIARY

CHAPTER FOURTEEN

What Became of the Boys

**A Brief Description of What Became of
the Boys * Refused Permission to go Home *
A Reference to Capt. Wirtz *
Return Home at the End of the War**

IT MAY INTEREST some one to know more of many who have been mentioned at different times in this book, and I will proceed to enlighten them.

George W. Hendryx came to the regiment in March, 1865, when we were near Goldsboro, N. C. He says that after running away from Andersonville at the time of the discovery of a break in which all intended to get away in the summer of 1864, he traveled over one hundred and fifty miles and was finally retaken by bushwhackers. He represented himself as an officer of the 17th Michigan Infantry, escaped from Columbia, S. C., and was sent to that place and put with officers in the prison there, changing his name so as not to be found out as having escaped from Andersonville. In due time he was exchanged with a batch of other officers and went home North. After a short time he joined his regiment and company for duty. He was both delighted and surprised to see me, as he supposed of course I had died in Andersonville, it having been so reported to him at the North. He did valiant service until the war was over, which soon happened. He went home with the regiment and was mustered out of service, since when I have never seen or heard of him for a certainty. Think that he went to California.

Sergt. Wm. B. Rowe was exchanged in March, 1865, but never joined the regiment. His health was ruined to a certain extent from his long confinement. Is still alive, however, and resides at Dansville, Mich.

Sergt. Bullock was also exchanged at the same time, but never did service thereafter. He is now an inmate of a Michigan insane asylum, and has been for some years, whether from the effects of prison life I know not, but should presume it is due to his sufferings there. His was a particularly sad case. He was taken sick in the early days of Andersonville and was sick all the time while in that place, a mere walking and talking skeleton. There is no doubt in my mind that his insanity resulted from his long imprisonment.

E. P. Sanders arrived home in Michigan in April, 1865, and made me a visit at Jackson that Summer. He was the only one of all my comrades in prison that I came in contact with, who fully regained health, or apparently was in good health. He was a particularly strong and healthy man, and is now engaged in farming near Lansing, Michigan.

Lieut. Wm. H. Robinson, who was removed from Belle Isle, from our mess, it having been discovered that he was an officer instead of an orderly sergeant, was exchanged early in 1864, from Richmond, and immediately joined his regiment, doing duty all the time thereafter. Soon after my escape and while with company "A," a note was handed me from Capt. Robinson, my old friend, he having been promoted to a captaincy. The note informed me that he was only a few miles away, and asked me to come and see him that day. You may rest assured I was soon on the road, and that day had the pleasure of taking my dinner with him. He was on his general's staff, and I dined at head-quarters, much to my discomfiture, not being up with such distinguished company. We had a good visit, I remember, and I went to camp at night well satisfied with my ride. Told me that a pipe which I engraved and presented to him on Belle Isle was still in his possession, and always should be. Was a favorite with every one, and a fine looking officer. He is now a resident of Sterling, Whiteside Co., Ill. Is a banker, hardware dealer, one of the City Fathers, and withal a prominent citizen. It was lucky he was an officer and taken away from us on Belle Isle, for he would undoubtedly have died at Andersonville, being of rather a delicate frame and constitution.

My good old friend Battese, I regret to say, I have never seen or heard of since he last visited me in the Marine Hospital at Savannah. Have written many letters and made many inquiries, but to no effect. He was so reticent while with us in the prison, that we did not learn enough of him to make inquiries since then effective. Although for many months I was in his immediate presence, he said nothing of where he lived, his circumstances, or anything else. I only know that his name was Battese, that he belonged to a Minnesota regiment and was a noble fellow. I don't know of a man in the world I would rather see today than him, and I hope some day when I have got rich out of this book (if that time should ever come,) to go to Minnesota and look him up. There are many Andersonville survivors who must remember the tall Indian, and certainly I shall, as long as life shall last.

Michael Hoare tells his own story farther along, in answer to a letter written him for information regarding his escape from the Savannah hospital. Mike, at the close of the war, re-enlisted in the regular army and went to the extreme West to fight Indians, and when his term of service expired again re-enlisted and remained in the service. In 1878 he was discharged on account of disability, and is now an inmate of the Disabled Soldiers' Home, at Dayton, Ohio. From his letters to me he seems the same jolly, good natured hero as of old.

I hope to see him before many months, for the first time since he shook me by the hand and passed in and out of his tunnel from the Marine Hospital and to freedom.

The two cousins Buck, David and Eli S., I last saw top of some corn in an army wagon I jumped from when I first encountered the 9th Mich. Cavalry. Little thought that would be the last time I should see them. Their command belonged to the Eastern Army in the region of the Potomac, and when communication was open at Savannah they were sent there on transports. I afterward received letters from both of them, and David's picture; also his wife's whom he had just married. David's picture is reproduced in this book and I must say hardly does him justice as he was a good looking and active fellow. Presume Eli is a farmer if alive, and Dave probably preaching.

"Limber Jim," who was instrumental in putting down the raiders at Andersonville, was until recently a resident of Joliet, Illinois. He died last winter, in 1880, and it is said his health was always poor after his terrible summer of 1864. He was a hero in every sense of the word, and if our government did not amply repay him for valiant service done while a prisoner of war, then it is at fault.

Sergt. Winn of the 100th Ohio, who befriended me at Savannah, is, I think, a citizen of Cincinnati, Ohio, and a prosperous man. Any way, he was in 1870 or thereabouts. Was an upright man and good fellow.

Every one knows the fate of Capt. Wirtz, our prison commander at Andersonville, who was hung at Washington, D. C., in 1866, for his treatment of us Union prisoners of war. It was a righteous judgment, still I think there are others who deserved hanging fully as much. He was but the willing tool of those higher in command. Those who put him there knew his brutal disposition, and should have suffered the same disposition made of him. Although I believe at this late day those who were in command and authority over Capt. Wirtz have successfully thrown the blame on his shoulders, it does not excuse them in the least so far as I am concerned. They are just as much to blame that thirteen thousand men died in a few months at that worst place the world has ever seen, as Capt. Wirtz, and should have suffered accordingly. I don't blame any of them for being rebels if they thought it right, but I do their inhuman treatment of prisoners of war.

Hub Dakin is now a resident of Dansville, Mich., the same village in which lives Wm. B. Rowe. He has been more or less disabled since the war, and I believe is now trying to get a pension from the government for disability contracted while in prison. It is very difficult for ex-prisoners of war to get pensions, owing to the almost impossibility of getting sufficient evidence. The existing pension laws require that an officer of the service shall have knowledge of the origin of disease, or else two comrades who may be enlisted men. At this late day it is impossible to remember with accuracy sufficient to come up to the requirements of the law. There is no doubt that all were more or less disabled, and the mere fact of their having spent the summer in Andersonville, should be evidence enough to procure assistance from the government.

And now a closing chapter in regard to myself. As soon as Savannah was occupied by our troops and communications opened with the North, a furlough was made out by Capt. Johnson, of our company, and signed by Assistant Surgeon Young, and then by Col. Acker. I then took the furlough to Gen. Kilpatrick, which he signed, and also endorsed on the back to the effect that he hoped Gen. Sherman would also sign and send me North. From Gen. Kilpatrick's head quarters I went to see Gen. Sherman at Savannah and was ushered into his presence. The Gen. looked the paper over and then said no men were being sent home now and no furloughs granted for any cause. If I was permanently disabled I could be sent to Northern hospitals, or if I had been an exchanged prisoner of war, could be sent North, but there was no provision made for escaped prisoners of war. Encouraged me with the hope, however, that the war was nearly over and it could not be long before we would all go home. Gave me a paper releasing me from all duty until such time as I saw fit to do duty, and said the first furlough granted should be mine, and he would retain it and send to me as soon as possible. Cannot say that I was very sadly disappointed, as I was having a good time with the company, and regaining my health and getting better every day, with the exception of my leg, which still troubled me. Stayed with the company until Lee surrendered, Lincoln assassinated and all the fighting over and then leaving Chapel Hill, North Carolina, in April, went to my home in Michigan. In a few weeks was followed by the regiment, when we were all mustered out of the service. As had been reported to me at the regiment, I had been regarded as dead, and funeral sermon preached.

It was my sad duty to call upon the relatives of quite a number who died in Andersonville, among whom were those

JOHN L. RANSOM, *from a photograph
taken three months after escape.*

of Dr. Lewis, John McGuire and Jimmy Devers. The relics which had been entrusted to my keeping were all lost with two exceptions, and through no fault of mine. At the time of my severe sickness when first taken to Savannah, and when I was helpless as a child, the things drifted away from me some way, and were lost. But for the fact that Battese had two of my diary books and Sergt. Winn the other, they also would have been lost.

I hope that this Diary may prove successful in its mission of truly portraying the scenes at Andersonville and elsewhere during the time of my imprisonment, and if so, the object of its author shall have been accomplished.

Yours Very Respectfully,

John L. Ransom,

Late 1st Sergt. Co. A, 9th Mich. Cav.

ADDENDA

**Michael Hoare's Escape ✳
Rebel Testimony ✳ Summary ✳
What Became of John Ransom**

MICHAEL HOARE'S ESCAPE

Comrade John L. Ransom——

Dear Friend: · · · · The night I left the stockade, going within twelve feet of a guard, I went down to the city. Had never been there before and did not know where to go, but wandered about the streets, dressed in an old suit of rebel clothes, until 12 o'clock that night. It was Oct. 18th, 1864, and I had been captured March 5th, in Col. Dahlgreen's raid, the object of which was to release the officers confined in Libby prison and the privates confined on Belle Island and Pemberton prisons. · · · · My whole uniform was disposed of · · · and I had to wear dirty rebel rags. They marched us to Stevensville. We remained there but a short time when we were marched about two miles and into the heart of a swamp. We did not know what the matter was but found out that Kilpatrick had turned back to look for us, the "forlorn hope," as we were called. If he had been one hour sooner, he would have released us; but fate would have it the other way. From the swamp we were marched to Richmond, surrounded by the mounted mob. They would not let us step out of the ranks even to quench our thirst, and we had to drink the muddy water from the middle of the road. Every little town we came to the rebels would assemble and yell at us, the women the worst. · · · · When we reached the headquarters of rebeldom the whole rebel city was out to meet us · · · · and the self-styled rebel ladies were the worst in their vim and foul language. They made a rush for us, but the guard kept them off until we were safely put in the third story of the Pemberton building, where we were searched and stripped of everything we were not already robbed of. · · · · The next morning the Richmond people cried out for Jeff Davis to hang us, saying we were nothing but outlaws and robbers, on an errand of plunder and rapine. The press tried to excite hostility against us, and succeeded, in a measure. We were kept by ourselves and not allowed to mix with the other prisoners. A special guard was kept over us, and we were allowed but two-thirds the small rations issued to the other men. The windows were all out of the room we were in, and a cold March wind blowing and cutting through our starving, naked bodies. · · · · In July we were going to get hanged in Castle Thunder. We were told the same story every day, and it was getting stale, so we paid no attention to it; but sure enough, we were called out one morning and thought our time had come. They marched us up Casey street toward Castle Thunder, and as we approached it some fairly shivered at their promised doom; but instead of stopping at that celebrated hotel, we were taken across the river and put in cattle cars. Where we were going none knew; but we started and the next day reached Dansville. We were removed from the cars and put into a tobacco warehouse and were kept there until the next morning, when we were put aboard the cars and started south again until we came to the world-renowned hell-hole, Andersonville. When we arrived several men were dead in the cars, and the rebels would not let us remove them. The cars were packed like herring boxes, so you may imagine our situation. · · · · From there I was transferred to Savannah, and from the latter place I made my escape, as previously mentioned.

As I have said, I wandered about until 12 o'clock, and was then in a worn out condition. Not knowing where to turn or lay my head, I sat down under a tree to rest myself, and as I sat there, who should come along but a watchman. "Hello!" says he, "What are you doing here at this hour of the night?" I answered that I was one of the guards guarding the Yankees at the stockade, and that I had been down to Bryan street to see my sister. "All right," said he, "You fellows have a hard time guarding them d—d Yankees. Why don't you shoot more of 'em and get 'em out o' the way?" I passed on until I came to a place with a high board fence. I crawled over and looked around and found a small shed divided by a board partition. In one end they kept a cow and in the other some fodder. I went in where the fodder was and threw myself down and went to sleep, intending to be up before day; but what was my surprise when it proved to be broad daylight before I awoke. I lay there thinking what to do, when I heard the gate of the fence open. I jumped up and looked through a crack in the boards and saw an old man enter with a pail in his hand. Presently he came where I was in the fodder to get some for the cow. As he opened the door he started back with fright, saying, "Who are you and what brings you here?" I saw by his face and voice that he was an Irishman, and I made up my mind to tell him the truth. · · · · He told me to remain where I was and he would try and get me something to eat. He went away and presently returned with a tin pan full of sweet potatoes and bacon. · · · · He told me the only way to get away was by the Isle of Hope, ten miles from the city on the Skidaway shell road. There was a picket post of twelve men right on the road, but

255

I started off, and when I reached the picket put on a bold face and told them I belonged to Maxwell's battery, stationed at the Isle of Hope, and they let me pass. · · · · I passed officers and soldiers on the road, but they never took any notice of me further than to return my kindly greeting. I finally reached the outpost on the road, about a mile from freedom. I had known, even before starting, that to pass that post I should have to have a pass signed by the commanding officer at Savannah; but there were swamps on both sides the road, and I thought I could swim in the marsh and flank the post. I took off my jacket and made the attempt, but had to return to the road. · · · · I saw there was no use trying to escape by the Isle of Hope. I could not pass the outpost, and besides, there was great danger that I should be hung as a spy. So I put back to Savannah that night. I had to wade the marsh to get by the post I first passed. I got safely back to my cowshed and laid there till woke up the next morning by my friend Gleason. When I told him where I had been he would hardly believe me. · · · · He brought me something to eat and went away, but returned at night with two other men. Their names were Wall and Skelley and they belonged to the 3d Georgia artillery. They said they were Northern men, but were in Savannah when the war broke out and had to join the rebel army. I told them the history of my adventure by the Isle of Hope and they were astonished. They said the only way was by the river to Fort Pulaski, fourteen miles from Savannah. The question was, where to get a boat. They were known in Savannah and their movements would be watched. They said they knew where there was a boat, but it was a government boat. I said that made it better, and if they would show me where the boat was, I would do the headwork. So they showed me and left me the management. I went when everything was ready, and muffled the oars and oarlocks, with a sentinel within twenty feet of me. The boat lay in the river, near the gashouse and a government storehouse, and the river was guarded by gunboats and the floating battery, and paved with torpedoes; but there is what is called "the back river," which flows into the Savannah above Smith Island. The mouth of this stream was guarded by a picket crew, sent from the battery every night; so when we left we had to lay in a rice sluice, where we ran the boat in about an eighth of a mile, and raised the grass as the boat passed along to conceal our tracks. We heard them searching the next morning, after the boat had been missed, but the search was at last given up. About this time Skelley began talking about being recaptured, as the shore was picketed all the way. He said there would be nothing done with me, if I was recaptured but to put me back in the stockade, while he and Wall would be shot as deserters. He proposed returning to Savannah at once. · · · · He began to win the other fellow over and I saw the game was up with me. Skelley was the only one of us who was armed and he had a Colt's revolver. · · · · I told him that his plan was the best and that I didn't want to be the means of getting him into trouble. I gained his confidence, but the thought of returning to Savannah never entered my head. I watched my chance, and at a favorable opportunity, snatched his pistol. · · · · I rose to my feet with the pistol at full cock, pointed it at his breast and told him that one move towards returning to Savannah would end his career by a bullet from his own revolver. He turned all colors, but said nothing. I kept my distance, and at four o'clock in the afternoon told them to get into the boat. I then sat down in the stern and told them to pull out, which they did with a vim. Just as we passed the mouth, we heard the click of oars on the picket boat; but they were too late, and all the danger we had to encounter was the pickets on the shore which we had to hug on account of torpedoes in the channel. I don't know how we ever passed safely over the torpedoes and by the pickets, which latter were within forty yards of us all the way along until we reached Pulaski. All that saved us was that the pickets had fires lighted and were looking at them, and our oars and oar-locks being muffled, they did not hear or see us. It was very dark when we struck the mouth of the Savannah, and where-abouts Fort Pulaski lay we knew not; but we kept pulling until halted by a soldier of the 144th N. Y. Infantry, who was guarding the place at that time. We were ordered to pull in, which we did, and were taken up to the commanding officer and questioned. He said it was the most daring escape ever made, up to that time, considering the obstacles we had to en-counter. We were kept in the guard house until my statement was confirmed by the war department, when I was released and sent to Washington, where I reported to the Adjutant-General who gave me a furlough and sent me to the hospital. I remained there until spring, when I rejoined my regiment and was mustered out at the close of the war. · · · · ·

    I remain,

Your true friend,

Michael Hoare

REBEL TESTIMONY

We cannot do better than copy into this book a very complete description of Andersonville Prison, by Joseph Jones, Surgeon P. A. C. S., Professor of Medical Chemistry in the Medical College of Georgia, at Augusta, Ga., as given at the Wirtz trial at Washington, D. C., he being a witness for the prosecution:

"Hearing of the unusual mortality among the prisoners confined at Andersonville, in the month of August, 1864, during a visit to Richmond, I expressed to the Surgeon General, S. P. Moore, Confederate States of America, a desire to visit Camp Sumpter, with the design of instituting a series of inquiries upon the nature and causes of the prevailing diseases. Small-pox had appeared among the prisoners, and I believed that this would prove an admirable field for the study of its characteristic lesions. The condition of Peyer's glands in this disease was considered as worthy a minute investigation. It was believed that a large portion of the men from the Northern portion of the United States, suddenly transported to a Southern climate, and confined upon a small portion of land, would furnish an excellent field for the investigation of the relations of typhus, typhoid, and malarial fevers.

The Surgeon General of the Confederate States of America furnished me with letters of introduction to the surgeon in charge of the Confederate States Military prison at Andersonville, Ga., and the following is my description of that place:

259

The Confederate Military Prison at Andersonville, Ga., consists of a strong stockade, twenty feet in height, enclosing twenty-seven acres. The stockade is formed of strong pine logs, firmly planted in the ground. The main stockade is surrounded by two other similar rows of pine logs, the middle stockade being sixteen feet high, and the outer one twelve feet. These are intended for offense and defense. If the inner stockade should at any time be forced by the prisoners, the second forms another line of defense; while in case of an attempt to deliver the prisoners by a force operating upon the exterior, the outer line forms an admirable protection to the Confederate troops, and a most formidable obstacle to cavalry or infantry. The four angles of the outer line are strengthened by earthworks upon commanding eminences, from which the cannon, in case of an outbreak among the prisoners, may sweep the entire enclosure; and it was designed to connect these works by a line of rifle pits running zig-zag around the outer stockade; those rifle pits have never been completed. The ground enclosed by the innermost stockade lies in the form of a parallelogram, the larger diameter running almost due north and south. This space includes the northern and southern opposing sides of two hills, between which a stream of water runs from west to east. The surface soil of these two hills is composed chiefly of sand with varying mixtures of clay and oxide of iron. The clay is sufficiently tenacious to give a considerable degree of consistency to the soil. The internal structure of the hills, as revealed by the deep wells, is similar to that already described. The alternate layers of clay and sand, as well as the oxide of iron, which forms in its various combinations a cement to the sand, allows of extensive tunneling. The prisoners not only constructed numerous dirt houses with balls of clay and sand, taken from the wells which they had excavated all over these hills, but they have also, in some cases, tunneled extensively from these wells. The lower portion of these hills, bordering on the stream, are wet and boggy from the constant oozing of water. The stockade was built originally to accommodate ten thousand prisoners, and included at first seventeen acres. Near the close of the month of June the area was enlarged by the addition of ten acres. The ground added was situated on the northern slope of the largest hill.

Within the circumscribed area of the stockade the Federal prisoners were compelled to perform all the functions of life, cooking, washing, the calls of nature, exercise, and sleeping. During the month of March the prison was less crowded than at any subsequent time, and then the average space of ground to each prisoner was only 98.7 feet or less than eleven square yards. The Federal prisoners were gathered from all parts of the Confederate States east of the Mississippi, and crowded into the confined space, until, in the month of June the average number of square feet of ground to each prisoner was only 32.3 or less than four square yards. These figures represent the stockade in a better light even than it really was; for a considerable breadth of land along the stream flowing from west to east between the hills was low and boggy, and was covered with the excrements of the men and thus rendered wholly uninhabitable, and in fact useless for every purpose except that of defecation. The pines and other small trees and shrubs, which originally were scattered sparsely over these hills were in a short time cut down by the prisoners for firewood, and no shade tree was left in the entire enclosure of the stockade. With their characteristic industry and ingenuity, the Federals constructed for themselves small huts and caves, and attempted to shield themselves from the rain and sun, and night damps and dew. But few tents were distributed to the prisoners, and those were in most cases torn and rotten. In the location and arrangement of these huts no order appears to have been followed; in fact, regular streets appear to be out of the question on so crowded an area; especially, too, as large bodies of prisoners were from time to time added suddenly and without any preparations. The irregular arrangement of the huts and imperfect shelters was very unfavorable for the maintenance of a proper system of police.

The police and internal economy of the prison was left almost entirely in the hands of the prisoners themselves; the duties of the Confederate soldiers acting as guards being limited to the occupation of the boxes or lookouts ranged around the stockade at regular intervals, and to the manning of the batteries at the angles of the prison. Even judicial matters pertaining to the prisoners themselves, as the detection and punishment of such crimes as theft and murder appear to have been in a great measure abandoned to the prisoners.

The large number of men confined within the stockade soon, under a defective system of police, and with imperfect arrangements, covered the surface of the low ground with excrements. The sinks over the lower portions of the stream were imperfect in their plan and structure, and the excrements were in large measure deposited so near the borders of the stream as not to be washed away, or else accumulated upon the low boggy ground. The volume of water was not sufficient to wash away the feces, and they accumulated in such quantities as to form a mass of liquid excrement. Heavy rains caused the water of the stream to rise and as the arrangements for the passage of the increased amount of water out of the stockade were insufficient, the liquid feces overflowed the low grounds and covered them several inches after the subsidence of the waters. The action of the sun upon this putrefying mass of excrements and fragments of bread and meat and bones excited most rapid fermentation and developed a horrible stench. Improvements were projected for the removal of the filth and for the prevention of its accumulation, but they were only partially and imperfectly carried out. As the forces of the prisoners were reduced by confinement, want of exercise, improper diet, and by scurvy, diarrhea, and dysentery, they were unable to evacuate their bowels within the stream or along its banks; and the excrements were deposited at the very doors of their tents. The vast majority appeared to lose all repulsion of filth, and both sick and well disregarded all the laws of hygiene and personal cleanliness. The accommodations for the sick were imperfect and insufficient. From the organization of the prison, February 24, 1864, to May 22, the sick were treated within the stockade. In the crowded condition of the stockade, and with the tents and huts clustered thickly around the hospital, it was impossible to secure proper ventilation or to maintain the necessary police. The Federal prisoners also made frequent forays upon the hospital stores and carried off the food and clothing of the sick. The hospital was, on the 22d of May, removed to its present site without the stockade, and five acres of ground covered with oaks and pines appropriated to the use of the sick.

The supply of medical officers has been insufficient from the foundation of the prison. The nurses and attendants upon the sick have been most generally Federal prisoners, who in too many cases appear to have been devoid of moral principle, and who not only neglected their duties, but were also engaged in extensive robberies of the sick.

From want of proper police and hygienic regulations alone it is not wonderful that from February 24 to September 21, 1864, nine thousand four hundred and seventy-nine deaths, nearly one-third of the entire number of prisoners have been recorded.

At the time of my visit to Andersonville a large number of Federal prisoners had been removed to Millen, Savannah, Charleston, and other parts of the Confederacy, in anticipation of an advance of General Sherman's forces from Atlanta, with the design of liberating their captive bretheren; however, about fifteen thousand prisoners remained confined within the limits of the stockade and prison hospital.

In the stockade, with the exception of the damp lowlands bordering the small stream, the surface was covered with huts, and small ragged tents and parts of blankets and fragments of oil-cloth, coats, and blankets stretched upon sticks. The tents and huts were not arranged according to any order, and there was in most parts of the enclosure scarcely room for two men to walk abreast between the tents and huts.

If one might judge from the large pieces of corn bread scattered about in very direction on the ground the prisoners were either very lavishly supplied with this article of diet, or else this kind of food was not relished by them.

Each day the dead from the stockade were carried out by their fellow prisoners and deposited upon the ground under a bush arbor, just outside of the southwestern gate. From thence they were carried on carts to the burying ground, one-quarter of a mile northwest of the prison. The dead were buried without coffins, side by side, in trenches four feet deep.

The low grounds bordering the stream were covered with human excrements and filth of all kinds, which in many places seemed to be alive with working maggots. An indescribable sickening stench arose from these fermenting masses of human filth.

There were near five thousand seriously ill Federals in the stockade and the Confederate States Military Prison Hospital, and the deaths exceeded one hundred per day, and large numbers of the prisoners who were walking about, and who had not been entered upon the sick reports, were suffering incurable diarrhea, dysentery, and scurvy. The sick were attended almost entirely by their fellow prisoners, appointed as nurses, and as they received but little attention, they were compelled to exert themselves at all times to attend the calls of nature, and hence they retain the power of moving about to within a comparatively short period of the close of life. Owing to the slow progress of the diseases most prevalent, diarrhea and chronic dysentery, the corpses were as a general rule emaciated.

I visited two thousand sick within the stockade, laying under some long sheds which had been built at the northern portion for themselves. At this time only one medical officer was in attendance, whereas at least twenty medical officers should have been employed.

Scurvy, diarrhea, dysentery, and hospital gangrene were the prevailing diseases. I was surprised to find but few cases of malarial fever, and no well-marked cases either of typhus or typhoid fever. The absence of the different forms of malarial fever may be accounted for in the supposition that the artificial atmosphere of the stockade, crowded densely with human beings and loaded with animal exhalations, was unfavorable to the existence and action of the malarial poison. The absence of typhoid and typhus fevers amongst all the causes which are known to generate these diseases, appeared to be due to the fact that the great majority of these prisoners had been in captivity in Virginia, at Belle Isle, and in other parts of the Confederacy for months, and even as long as two years, and during this time they had been subjected to the same bad influences, and those who had not had these fevers before either had them during their confinement in Confederate prisons or else their systems, from long exposure, were proof against their action.

The effects of scurvy were manifest on every hand, and in all its various stages, from the muddy pale complexion, pale gums, feeble, languid muscular motions, lowness of spirits, and fetid breath, to the dusky, dirty, leaden complexion, swollen features, spongy, purple, livid, fungoid, bleeding gums, loose teeth, œdematous limbs, covered with livid vibices, and petechiæ spasmodically flexed, painful and hardened extremities, spontaneous hemorrhages from mucous canals, and large, ill-conditioned, spreading ulcers covered with a dark purplish fungus growth. I observed that in some of the cases of scurvy the parotid glands were greatly swollen, and in some instances to such an extent as to preclude entirely the power to articulate. In several cases of dropsy the abdomen and lower extremities supervening upon scurvy, the patients affirmed that previously to the appearance of the dropsy they had suffered with profuse and obstinate diarrhea, and that when this was checked by a change of diet, from Indian corn-bread baked with the husk, to boiled rice, the dropsy disappeared. The severe pains and livid patches were frequently associated with swellings in various parts, and especially in the lower extremities, accompanied with stiffness and contractions of the knee joints and ankles, and often with a brawny feel of those parts, as if lymph had been effused between the integuments and apeneuroses, preventing the motion of the skin over the swollen parts. Many of the prisoners believed that scurvy was contagious, and I saw men guarding their wells and springs, fearing lest some man suffering with scurvy might use the water and thus poison them. I observed also numerous cases of hospital gangrene, and of spreading scorbutic ulcers, which had supervened upon slight injuries. The scorbutic ulcers presented a dark, purple fungoid, elevated surface, with livid swollen edges, and exuded a thin, fetid, sanious fluid, instead of pus. Many ulcers which originated from the scorbutic condition of the system appeared to become truly gangrenous, assuming all the characteristics of hospital gangrene. From the crowded condition, filthy habits, bad diet, and dejected, depressed condition of the prisoners, their systems had become so disordered that the smallest abration of the skin, from the rubbing of a shoe, or from the effects of the sun, or from the prick of a splinter, or from scratching, or a mosquito bite, in some cases, took on a rapid and frightful ulceration and gangrene. The long use of salt meat, oft-times imperfectly cured, as well as the most total deprivation of vegetables and fruit, appeared to be the chief causes of the scurvy. I carefully examined the bakery and the bread furnished the prisoners, and found that they were supplied almost entirely with corn-bread from which the husk had not been separated. This husk acted as an irritant to the alimentary canal, without adding any nutriment to the brain. As far as my examination extended no fault could be found with the mode in which the bread was baked; the difficulty lay in the failure to separate the husk from the corn-meal. I strongly urged the preparation of large quantities of soup from the cow and calves' heads, with the brains and tongues, to which a liberal supply of sweet potatoes and vegetables might have been advantageously added. The material existed in abundance for the preparation of such soup in large quantities with but little additional expense. Such ailment would have been not only highly nutricious, but it would also have acted as an efficient remedial agent for the removal of the scorbutic condition. The sick within the stockade lay under several long sheds which were originally built for barracks. These sheds covered two floors which were open on all sides. The sick lay upon the bare boards, or upon such ragged blankets as they possessed, without, as far as I observed, any bedding or even straw.

The haggard, distressed countenances of these miserable, complaining, dejected, living skeletons, crying for medical aid and food, and cursing their government for its refusal to exchange prisoners, and the ghastly corpses, with their glazed eye balls staring up into vacant space, with the flies swarming down their open and grinning mouths and over their ragged clothes, infested with lice, as they lay amongst the sick and dying, formed a picture of helpless, hopeless misery which it would be impossible to portray by words or by the brush. A feeling of disappointment and even resentment on account of the United States Government upon the subject of the exchange of prisoners, appeared to be widespread, and the apparent hopeless nature of the negotiations for some general exchange of prisoners appeared to be a cause of universal regret and injurious despondency. I heard some of the prisoners go so far as to exonerate the Confederate Government from any charge of intentionally subjecting them to a protracted confinement, with its necessary and unavoidable sufferings, in a country cut off from all intercourse with foreign nations, and sorely pressed on all sides, whilst on the other hand they changed their prolonged captivity upon their own government, which was attempting to make the negro equal to the white man. Some hundred or more of the prisoners had been released from confinement in the stockade on parole, and filled various offices as druggists, clerks, carpenters, etc., in the various departments. These men were well clothed, and presented a stout and healthy appearance, and as a general rule they presented a more robust and healthy appearance than the Confederate troops guarding the prisoners.

The entire grounds are surrounded by a frail board fence, and are strictly guarded by Confederate soldiers, and no prisoner except the paroled attendants is allowed to leave the grounds except by a special permit from the commandant of the interior of the prison.

The patients and attendants, near two thousand in number, are crowded into this confined space and are but poorly supplied with old and ragged tents. Large numbers of them were without any bunks in their tents, and lay upon the ground, ofttimes without even a blanket. No beds or straw appeared to have been furnished. The tents extend to within a few yards of the small stream, the eastern portion of which, as we have before said, is used as a privy and is loaded with excrements; and I observed a large pile of corn-bread, bones, and filth of all kinds, thirty feet in diameter and several feet high, swarming with myriads of flies, in a vacant space near the pots used for cooking. Millions of flies swarmed over everything, and covered the faces of the sleeping patients, and crawled down their open mouths, and deposited their maggots in the gangrenous wounds of the living, and in the mouths of the dead. Mosquitos in great numbers also infest the tents, and many of the patients were so stung by these pestiferous insects, that they resembled those suffering from a slight attack of the measles.

The police hygiene of the hospital were defective in the extreme; the attendants, who appeared in almost every instance to have been selected from the prisoners, seemed to have in many cases but little interest in the welfare of their fellow-captives. The accusation was made that the nurses in many cases robbed the sick of their clothing, money, and rations, and carried on a clandestine trade with the paroled prisoners and Confederate guards without the hospital enclosure, in the clothing, effects of the sick, dying, and dead Federals. They certainly appeared to neglect the comfort and cleanliness of the sick entrusted to their care in a most shameful manner, even after making due allowances for the difficulties of the situation. Many of the sick were literally encrusted with dirt and filth and covered with vermin. When a gangrenous wound needed washing, the limb was thrust out a little from the blanket, or board, or rags upon which the patient was lying, and water poured over it, and all the putrescent matter allowed to soak into the ground floor of the tent. The supply of rags for dressing wounds was said to be very scant, and I saw the most filthy rags which had been applied several times and imperfectly washed, used in dressing wounds. Where hospital gangrene was prevailing, it was impossible for any wound to escape contagion under these circumstances. The results of the treatment of wounds in the hospital were of the most unsatisfactory character, from this neglect of cleanliness, in the dressings and wounds themselves, as well as from various other causes which will be more fully considered. I saw several gangrenous wounds filled with maggots. I have frequently seen neglected wounds amongst the Confederate soldiers similarly affected; and as far as my experience extends, these worms destroy only the dead tissues and do not injure specially the well parts. I have even heard surgeons affirm that a gangrenous wound which had been thoroughly cleansed by maggots, healed more rapidly than if it had been left to itself. This want of cleanliness on the part of the nurses appeared to be the result of carelessness and inattention, rather than of malignant design, and the whole trouble can be traced to the want of the proper police and sanitary regulations, and to the absence of intelligent organization and division of labor. The abuses were in a large measure due to the almost total absence of system, government, and rigid, but wholesome sanitary regulations. In extenuation of these abuses it was alleged by the medical officers that the Confederate troops were barely sufficient to guard the prisoners, and that it was impossible to obtain any number of experienced nurses from the Confederate forces. In fact, the guard appeared to be too small, even for the regulation of the internal hygiene and police of the hospital.

The manner of disposing of the dead was also calculated to depress the already desponding spirits of these men, many of whom have been confined for months, and even for two years in Richmond and other places, and whose strength had been wasted by bad air, bad food, and neglect of personal cleanliness. The dead-house is merely a frame covered with old tent cloth and a few bushes, situated in the southwestern corner of the hospital grounds. When a patient dies, he is simply laid in the narrow street in front of his tent, until he is removed by Federal negroes detailed to carry off the dead; if a patient dies during the night, he lies there until the morning, and during the day even the dead were frequently allowed to remain for hours in these walks. In the dead-house the corpses lie upon the bare ground, and were in most cases covered with filth and vermin.

The cooking arrangements are of the most defective character. Five large iron pots similar to those used for boiling sugar cane, appeared to be the only cooking utensils furnished the hospital for the cooking of two thousand men; and the patients were dependent in a great measure upon their own miserable utensils. They were allowed to cook in the tent doors and in the lanes, and this was another source of filth, and another favorable condition for the generation and multiplication of flies and other vermin.

The air of the tents was foul and disagreeable in the extreme, and in fact the entire grounds emitted a most nauseous and disgusting smell. I entered nearly all the tents and carefully examined the cases of interest, and especially the cases of gangrene, upon numerous occasions, during the prosecution of my pathological inquiries at Andersonville, and therefore enjoyed every opportunity to judge correctly of the hygiene and police of the hospital.

There appeared to be almost absolute indifference and neglect of the part of the patient, of personal cleanliness; their persons and clothing in most instances, and especially those suffering with gangrene and scorbutic ulcers, were filthy in the extreme and covered with vermin. It was too often the case that the patients were received from the stockade in a most deplorable condition. I have seen men brought in from the stockade in a dying condition, begrimed from head to foot with their own excrements, and so black from smoke and filth that they resembled negroes rather than white men. That this description of the stockade has not been overdrawn, will appear from the reports of the surgeon in charge.

We will first examine the consolidated report of the sick and wounded Federal prisoners. During six months, from the 1st of March to the 31st of August, forty-two thousand six hundred and eighty-six cases of sickness and wounds were reported. No classified record of the sick in the stockade was kept after the establishment of the hospital without the prison. This fact, in conjunction with those already presented relating to the insufficiency of medical officers and the extreme illness and even death of many prisoners in the tents in the stockade, without any medical attention or record beyond the bare number of the dead, demonstrates that these figures, large as they seem to be, are far below the truth.

As the number of prisoners varied greatly at different periods, the relations between those reported sick and well, as far as those statistics extend, can best be determined by a comparison of the statistics of each month.

During this period of six months no less than five hundred and sixty-five deaths are recorded under the head of *morbi vanie*. In other words, those men died without having received sufficient medical attention for the determination of even the name of the disease causing death.

During the month of August fifty-three cases and fifty-three deaths are recorded as due to marasmus. Surely this large number of deaths must have been due to some other morbid state than slow wasting. If they were due to improper and insufficient food, they should have been classed accordingly, and if to diarrhea or dysentery or scurvy, the classification in like manner should have been explicit.

We observe a progressive increase of the rate of mortality, from 3.11 per cent in March to 9.09 per cent of mean strength, sick and well, in August. The ratio of mortality continued to increase during September, for notwithstanding the removal of one-half the entire number of prisoners during the early portion of the month, one thousand seven hundred and sixty-seven (1,767) deaths are registered from September 1 to 21, and the largest number of deaths upon any one day occurred during this month, on the 16th, viz: one hundred and nineteen.

The entire number of Federal prisoners confined at Andersonville was about forty thousand six hundred and eleven; and during the period of near seven months, from February 24 to September 21, nine thousand four hundred and seventy-nine (9,479) deaths were recorded; that is, during this period near one-fourth, or more, exactly one in 4.2, or 23.3 per cent terminated fatally. This increase of mortality was due in great measure to the accumulation of the sources of disease, as the increase of excrements and filth of all kinds, and the concentration of noxious effluvia, and also to the progressive effects of salt diet, crowding, and the hot climate.

CONCLUSIONS

1st. The great mortality among the Federal prisoners confined in the military prison at Andersonville was not referable to climatic causes, or to the nature of the soil and waters.

2d. The chief causes of death were scurvy and its results and bowel affections—chronic and acute diarrhea and dysentery. The bowel affections appear to have been due to the diet, and the habits of the patients, the depressed, dejected state of the nervous system and moral and intellectual powers, and to the effluvia arising from the decomposing animal and vegetable filth. The effects of salt meat, and the unvarying diet of corn-meal, with but few vegetables, and imperfect supplies of vinegar and sirup, were manifested in the great prevalence of scurvy. This disease, without doubt, was also influenced to an important extent in its origin and course by the foul animal emanations.

3d. From the sameness of the food and form, the action

of the poisonous gases in the densely crowded and filthy stockade and hospital, the blood was altered in its constitution, even before the manifestation of actual disease. In both the well and the sick the red corpuscles were diminished; and in all diseases uncomplicated with inflammation, the fibrous element was deficient. In cases of ulceration of the mucous membrane of the intestinal canal, the fibrous element of the blood was increased; while in simple diarrhea, uncomplicated with ulceration, it was either diminished or else remained stationary. Heart clots were very common, if not universally present in cases of ulceration of the intestinal mucous membrane, while in the uncomplicated cases of diarrhea and scurvy, the blood was fluid and did not coagulate readily, and the heart clots and fibrous concretions were almost universally absent. From the watery condition of the blood, there resulted various serious effusions into the pericardium, ventricles of the brain, and into the abdomen. In almost all the cases which I examined after death, even the most emaciated, there were more or less serous effusions into the abdominal cavity. In case of hospital gangrene of the extremities, and in case of gangrene of the intestines, heart clots and fibrous coagula were universally present. The presence of these clots in the cases of hospital gangrene, while they were absent in the cases in which there were no inflammatory symptoms, sustains the conclusion that hospital gangrene is a species of inflammation, imperfect and irregular though it may be in its progress, in which the fibrous element and coagulation of the blood are increased, even in those who are suffering from such a condition of the blood, and from such diseases as are naturally accompanied with a disease in the fibrous constituent.

4th. The fact that hospital gangrene appeared in the stockade first, and originated spontaneously without any previous contagion, and occurred sporadically all over the stockade and prison hospital, was proof positive that this disease will arise whenever the conditions of crowding, filth, foul air, and bad diet are present. The exhalations of the hospital and stockade appeared to exert their effects to a considerable distance outside of these localities. The origin of hospital gangrene among the prisoners appeared clearly to depend in great measure to the state of the general system induced by diet, and various external noxious influences. The rapidity of the appearance and action of the gangrene depended upon the powers and state of the constitution, as well as upon the intensity of the poison in the atmosphere, or upon the direct application of poisonous matter to the wounded surface. This was further illustrated by the important fact that hospital gangrene, or a disease resembling it in all essential respects, attacked the intestinal canal of patients laboring under ulceration of the bowels, although there were no local manifestations of gangrene upon the surface of the body. This mode of termination in case of dysentery was quite common in the foul atmosphere of the Confederate States Military Hospital, in the depressed, depraved condition of the system of these Federal prisoners.

5th. A scorbutic condition of the system appeared to favor the origin of foul ulcers, which frequently took on true hospital gangrene. Scurvy and hospital gangrene frequently existed in the same individual. In such cases vegetable diet, with vegetable acids would remove the scorbutic condition without curing the hospital gangrene. From the results of the existing war for the establishment of the independence of the Confederate States, as well as from the published observations of Dr. Trotter, Sir Gilbert Blane, and others of the English navy and army, it is evident that the scorbutic condition of the system, especially in crowded ships and camps, is most favorable to the origin and spread of foul ulcers and hospital gangrene. As in the present case of Andersonville, so also in past times when medical hygiene was almost entirely neglected, those two diseases were almost universally associated in crowded ships. In many cases it was very difficult to decide at first whether the ulcer was a simple result of scurvy or the action of the prison or hospital gangrene, for there was great similarity in the appearance of the ulcers in the two diseases. So commonly have those two diseases been confined to their origin and action, that the description of scorbutic ulcers, by many authors, evidently includes also many of the prominent characteristics of hospital gangrene. This will be rendered evident by an examination of the observations of Dr. Lind and Sir Gilbert Blane upon scorbutic ulcers.

6th. Gangrenous spots followed by rapid destruction of the tissue appeared in some cases where there has been no known wound. Without such well established facts, it might be assumed that the disease was propagated from one patient to another. In such a filthy and crowded hospital as that of the Confederate States Military Prison at Andersonville, it was impossible to isolate the wounded from the sources of actual contact with gangrenous matter. The flies swarmed over the wounds and over filth of every kind, the filthy, imperfectly washed and scanty supplies of rags, and the limited supply of washing utensils, the same wash-bowl serving for scores of patients were sources of such constant circulation of the gangrenous matter that the disease might rapidly spread from a single gangrenous wound. The fact already stated, that a form of moist gangrene, resembling hospital gangrene, was quite common in this foul atmosphere, in cases of dysentery, both with and without the existance of the entire service, not only demonstrates the dependence of the disease upon the state of the constitution, but proves in the clearest manner that neither the contact of the poisonous matter of gangrene, nor the direst action of the poisonous atmosphere upon the ulcerated surface are necessary to the development of the disease.

7th. In this foul atmosphere amputation did not arrest hospital gangrene; the disease almost universally returned. Almost every amputation was followed finally by death, either from the effects of gangrene or from the prevailing diarrhea and dysentery. Nitric acid and escharoties generally in this crowded atmosphere, loaded with noxious effluvia, exerted only temporary effects; after their application to the diseased surfaces, the gangrene would frequently return with redoubled energy; and even after the gangrene had been completely removed by local and constitutional treatment, it would frequently return and destroy the patient. As far as my observation extended, very few of the cases of amputation for gangrene recovered. The progress of these cases was frequently very deceptive. I have observed after death the most extensive disorganization of the stump, when during life there was but little swelling of the part, and the patient was apparently doing well. I endeavored to impress upon the medical officers the view that on this disease treatment was almost useless, without an abundance of pure, fresh air, nutricious food, and tonics and stimulants. Such changes, however, as would allow of the isolation of the cases of hospital gangrene appeared to be out of the power of the medical officers.

8th. The gangrenous mass was without true puss, and consisted chiefly of broken-down, disorganized structures. The reaction of the gangrenous matter in certain stages was alkaline.

9th. The best, and in truth the only, means of protecting large armies and navies, as well as prisoners, from the ravages of hospital gangrene is to furnish liberal supplies of well-cured meat, together with fresh beef and vegetables, and to enforce a rigid system of hygiene.

10th. Finally, this gigantic mass of human misery calls loudly for relief, not only for the sake of suffering humanity, but also on account of our own brave soldiers now captive in the hands of the Federal Government. Strict justice to the gallant men of the Confederate armies, who have been or who may be, so unfortunate as to be compelled to surrender in battle, demands that the Confederate Government should adopt that course which will best secure their health and comfort in captivity; or at least leave their enemies without a shadow of an excuse for any violation of the rules of civilized warfare in the treatment of prisoners."

(END OF WITNESS'S TESTIMONY.)

SUMMARY

The variation—from month to month—of the proportion of deaths to the whole number of living is singular and interesting. It supports the theory I have advanced above, as the following facts taken from the official report, will show:

In April one in every sixteen died.
In May one in every twenty-six died.
In June one in every twenty-two died.
In July one in every eighteen died.
In August one in eleven died.
In September one in every three died.
In October one in every two died.
In November one in every three died.

Does the reader fully understand that in September one-third of those in the pen died, that in October one-half of the remainder perished, and in November one-third of those who still survived, died? Let him pause for a moment and read this over carefully again, because its startling magnitude will hardly dawn upon him at first reading. It is true that the fearful disproportionate mortality of those months was largely due to the fact that it was mostly the sick that remained behind, but even this diminishes but little the frightfulness of the showing. Did anyone ever hear of an epidemic so fatal that one-third of those attacked by it in one month died; one-half of the remnant the next month, and one-third of the feeble remainder the next month? If he did his reading has been much more extensive than mine.

John Ransom

PUBLISHER'S NOTE

After the war, John Ransom returned to his home in Jackson, Michigan, where he regained his health. He went back to work in the composing room of the Jackson *Citizen*, married, moved later to Clearwater, Michigan, where he continued to follow the printer's trade. Eventually, he moved to Chicago and worked for the Merganthaler Linotype Company. He died in 1919 at the age of 76. His only child, a daughter, died in California many years ago.

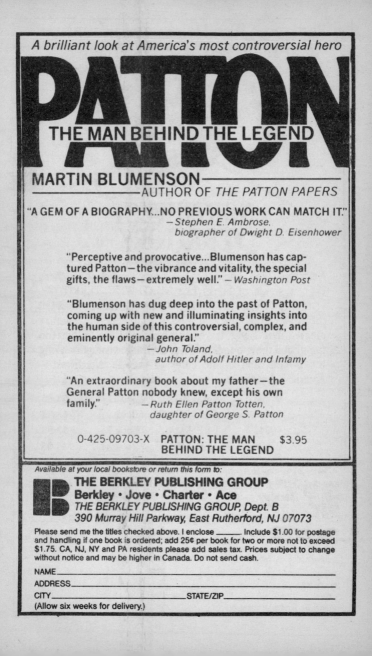